"Kimberley has done it yet again. Wha[...] knuckle-biting thrill of a ride. I highly re[...] you [...] this one up and make arrangements to read it in one sitting!"

LYNETTE EASON, award-winning, best-selling author of the Extreme Measures series

"Do not pick up *8 Down* unless you are ready to be taken on a roller-coaster ride of adrenaline. Filled with the twists of a demented mind and the race to catch him before more harm happens, this book is one I couldn't put down! There's also a sweet layer of romantic tension woven in. I loved every page."

CARA PUTMAN, award-winning author of *Lethal Intent* and *The Vanished*

"Kimberley Woodhouse delivers another spine-tingling novel sure to send chills down readers' backs—and not just because it's set in Alaska! The suspense builds as a devious serial killer sends crossword puzzle clues to investigators who are intent on stopping him before anyone else dies. Clever, beautifully crafted, and completely addictive! I highly recommend *8 Down*!"

NANCY MEHL, author of the Ryland and St. Clair series

"Another page-turner of action, adventure, and thriller intrigue with a touch of romance thrown in on the side. Kimberley Woodhouse has created an amazing series that you'll want to read. With crossword puzzle clues, the Alaska Bureau of Investigation finds themselves up against a race to solve the mystery before it's too late. Kim has long been a favorite author of mine in historical romance, but she's proven herself a hard-to-beat author of contemporary romantic suspense."

TRACIE PETERSON, award-winning and best-selling author of the Pictures of the Heart series

"Put on your parkas as we head into a cold world of cybercrime, and hang on for the ride! Kimberley Woodhouse once again takes us on a nail-biter of a ride, and you won't want to quit until you've read the last page!"

JAIME JO WRIGHT, author of *The Lost Boys of Barlowe Theater* and Carol Award finalist *The Souls of Lost Lake*

"Bone-chilling! Kimberley Woodhouse nails it in this riveting story and its unique, thrilling concept! *8 Down* is a ripped-from-the-headlines story that will make you think twice about using today's tech!"

RONIE KENDIG, best-selling, award-winning author of The Tox Files

"What's an eight-letter word for *8 Down* by Kimberley Woodhouse? If you said *riveting* or *chilling* or *shocking*, you would be right! I could hardly tear myself away from this story, fully absorbed in the characters and their race against a madman's whims. Woodhouse weaves suspense, romance, and faith into an engaging narrative that will keep you reading late into the night. If you thought the killer was ruthless in *26 Below*, just wait until you see what he's up to now! I'll never look at an 8 DOWN crossword clue the same way again!"

CARRIE SCHMIDT, ReadingIsMySuperPower.org

ALASKAN CYBER HUNTERS

26 Below
8 Down
70 North

ALASKAN CYBER HUNTERS | BOOK TWO

DOWN

KIMBERLEY WOODHOUSE

KREGEL
PUBLICATIONS

8 Down
© 2024 by Kimberley Woodhouse

Published by Kregel Publications, a division of Kregel Inc., 2450 Oak Industrial Dr. NE, Grand Rapids, MI 49505. www.kregel.com.

All rights reserved. No part of this book may be reproduced, stored in a retrieval system, or transmitted in any form or by any means—for example, electronic, mechanical, photocopy, recording, or otherwise—without the publisher's prior written permission or by license agreement. The only exception is brief quotations in printed reviews.

Kimberley Woodhouse is represented by and *8 Down* is published in association with The Steve Laube Agency, LLC, www.stevelaube.com.

The persons and events portrayed in this work are the creations of the author, and any resemblance to persons living or dead is purely coincidental. The main character's name has been used by permission of Carrie Kintz.

The profiling steps quoted on page 91 are from David Webb, *Criminal Profiling: An Introductory Guide* (self-pub., CreateSpace, 2013).

Scriptures taken from the Holy Bible, New International Version®, NIV®. Copyright © 1973, 1978, 1984, 2011 by Biblica, Inc.™ Used by permission of Zondervan. All rights reserved worldwide. www.zondervan.com. The "NIV" and "New International Version" are trademarks registered in the United States Patent and Trademark Office by Biblica, Inc.™

Library of Congress Cataloging-in-Publication Data
Names: Woodhouse, Kimberley, 1973– author.
Title: 8 down / Kimberley Woodhouse.
Other titles: Eight down
Description: Grand Rapids, MI: Kregel Publications, a division of Kregel Inc., 2024. | Series: Alaskan cyber hunters; book 2
Identifiers: LCCN 2023035193 (print) | LCCN 2023035194 (ebook)
Subjects: LCGFT: Christian fiction. | Thrillers (Fiction) | Novels.
Classification: LCC PS3623.O665 A612 2024 (print) | LCC PS3623.O665 (ebook) | DDC 813/.6—dc23/eng/20230824
LC record available at https://lccn.loc.gov/2023035193
LC ebook record available at https://lccn.loc.gov/2023035194

ISBN 978-0-8254-4773-0, print
ISBN 978-0-8254-7016-5, epub
ISBN 978-0-8254-7234-3, Kindle

Printed in the United States of America
24 25 26 27 28 29 30 31 32 33 / 5 4 3 2 1

This book is dedicated to
CARRIE KINTZ
*For seventeen-plus years, you have been
one of my dearest and most trusted friends.
I love how much you love Jesus.
I love how much you love story.
And I love how you love to laugh, brainstorm,
talk theology, and do a million other things
with this crazy friend of yours.
You amaze me. You cheer me on. You challenge me.
You are brilliant.
Thank you for almost two decades of friendship
and the love of books.
Here's to the next two decades,
and the next two after that . . .
(And FYI, it's First, Second, and Third John. Just sayin'.)*

PREFACE

Dear Reader,

It is an awesome privilege to bring you the second book in the Alaskan Cyber Hunters series, *8 Down*.

For this book, I had some fun researching the Federal Bureau of Investigation (FBI) and the Alaska Bureau of Investigation (ABI). The ABI is a division of the Alaska State Troopers. I've used the FBI in a couple of my books before and had a wonderful source there, but this is the first time for me to include the ABI.

Let me tell you, I have the utmost respect for the troopers in Alaska. What they do in the conditions they do it in—wow. It is both humbling and mind-blowing.

The policies and procedures of the Anchorage Police Department (APD), the Alaska State Troopers, the ABI, and the FBI are unique to each organization. Jurisdiction and duties likewise are distinctive. I am thankful for the work each one of them does. Out of respect for all these law enforcement agencies, I have intentionally fictionalized many aspects in this story for protection purposes. While the location of the ABI in Anchorage is actual, many details—again—were changed for artistic license and protection of the people who put their lives on the line for citizens daily.

The study into the human mind and behaviors is intense. I had the incredible opportunity to speak with a forensic psychologist about the subject and, after reading all the recommended resources, I have to admit it was challenging to bring the behavior of a serial killer onto the page. It was with the help of this psychologist that I was able to hopefully portray that character for you.

Many of us might have a difficult time understanding how someone can do the evil things that they do. But as a child of God, I know that sin is the culprit. We live in a fallen world. And while we are here, there will be trouble. Just like Scripture states. But we do not need to fear. Fear is not from the Lord. We can rest in Him and the hope we have in Him.

Once again, I'm more than a bit amazed by technology. Having a son-in-law who is a literal cyber expert is wonderful for me as an author—and I must admit quite entertaining as we brainstorm—but there's also the side of me that often wants to run away and live off the grid after he has enlightened me on the happenings taking place in the ever-changing technology-cyber-security-crazy-computer world we live in.

Thanks to Steven, the cyber world in this book has come alive.

Now that we have survived the deep freeze of *26 Below*, are you ready for *8 Down*?

Can you figure out the clues?

Enjoy the journey,
Kimberley Woodhouse

PROLOGUE

DOWN

8. Six letters. Number 6 on the periodic table.

November 25—9:57 a.m.
Fairbanks, Alaska

NOTHING COULD HAVE PREPARED HER for the dead body at the crime scene. None of her training, classes, or visits to the morgue could have accomplished that feat. The impeccably dressed woman before her had been dead for several days.

Walking a 360-degree perimeter around the deceased, Carrie Kintz took in every detail. Because she was a brand-new major crimes investigator for the Alaska Bureau of Investigation, the need to prove her mettle pushed everything else aside. She used the voice memo function on her phone to record her observations but kept to herself her opinion of the horrible stench that almost made her lose her breakfast.

No blood. No signs of a struggle. No bullet holes, knife wounds, scratches. Nothing.

Was there a chance this woman had simply died of natural causes and the only reason they'd called in the ABI was because of who she was?

"Hey, there's the rookie." Kevin, her supervisor and head of the division, pointed his pen at her with a wink. "So . . . have you figured it out yet?"

The veteran investigator had welcomed her like family and answered every one of her questions. Too bad he was retiring soon. She'd felt a camaraderie with him right away and would learn from him for as long as she could. "You mean, how she died?"

"Don't you mean, who killed her?" He tapped the pen to his chin. Okay. So he was certain it was murder. Even before an autopsy. Huh. What did he see that she didn't? "Sure."

"Bet you weren't anticipating your first case with us to be the murder of the mayor of Fairbanks."

"There's been a lot I didn't anticipate." She let out a breath. One entire day on the job and she'd already driven from Anchorage to Fairbanks. The Parks Highway was everything she'd read about and more. She'd seen Denali. She'd seen moose. She'd even seen a mama bear and two cubs feasting on what must have been a last meal before hibernation.

And right now, she'd gladly take the threat of being trampled by a moose or eaten by a bear in the nose-hair-freezing weather outside over the stench in this remote cabin.

With the entire Fairbanks office of the Bureau working the aftermath of the cyberattack that could have killed thousands of people, her boss in Anchorage had sent her north with a team to handle this delicate case. Said there was no time like the present for her to get her feet wet.

Funny how things worked out. Here she was, part of the ABI with the Alaska State Troopers. A year ago, she'd been a police officer back home in North Dakota, just dreaming of becoming part of the FBI. Then an old mentor with connections mentioned that the Alaska State Troopers were looking for investigators, and she'd jumped at the opportunity to leave her small town behind. Her fascination with profilers and investigators and the work they did drove her to pursue the physical training required.

The training was intense—probably a hundred times more grueling than anything she'd ever done at home. But she didn't give up, and she'd passed every test with flying colors. Then her assessments must have caught someone's attention because she ended up with a recommendation for the ABI. It was something she'd aspired to but hadn't expected so soon in her career.

It was an incredible opportunity, and she was determined to soak up every bit of knowledge and experience she could. After all, her hope of being part of the FBI still floated in front of her.

Maybe one day. A girl could dream.

"Why didn't the Fairbanks police move the body?" She faked a nose scratch, just to give her an excuse to breathe behind her hand for a second.

"They didn't find her until this morning and called us first thing. Boss asked them not to move her or touch the crime scene until we arrived. Just in case." Kevin studied her then clasped one hand over his other wrist and narrowed his eyes. "The medical examiner is waiting on us to release the body, so we need to be thorough."

Alan—the third member of her ABI team from Anchorage—snapped hundreds of pictures around the body, the room, and then went outside to photograph the exterior of the cabin.

"All right, Kevin." Carrie knelt in front of the woman who'd been powerful and alive a week ago. "What do you see? Teach me."

"My gut is telling me this was no accident. It didn't happen because the power was off. She's not layered in blankets. There's a top-of-the-line generator out there that runs on natural gas. It's capable of running the entire cabin, but it never kicked on. So we can rule out the power outage and temperature.

"The mayor disappeared on the twentieth in the middle of the crisis. Her security team looked for her, but all other hands were needed elsewhere. This cabin has been in her family for over a decade, but *why* did she come out here? Especially when she was needed. *How* did she get out here? There's no vehicle.

"The cabin has the highest security features available. She's sitting on her couch like she was comfortable. No sign of alarm or fear.

We're not aware of any health problems. So, based on all that . . . I'm thinking carbon monoxide poisoning."

Carrie shook her head. "But there are two carbon monoxide detectors in plain sight right here. Wouldn't she have an alarm for that with the advanced status of her system?"

Kevin smiled. "Smart girl. Yep."

"Then why would you still think it's carbon monoxide?" If only she could get inside his brain and learn to see the way he did. The man was a legend.

"Because, as we unfortunately all know, cyberterrorism is on the rise. I'm betting someone hacked the system. And"—he stepped to the side and pointed to the window behind him—"that's open."

Only a couple of inches, but enough to feel the frigid temps of the outdoors. "I'm not following you. I figured someone opened it because of the smell."

"Nope. Her security detail sent a file to the office. The mayor hated open windows. Some weird pet peeve of hers." He waved her closer and showed her the file on his iPad. "Look, right here. As soon as they noticed the open window, things changed."

"Hm. So . . . what? The killer somehow bypassed the alarm system and CO alarms, then opened the window to let the place air out? Why?" But as soon as she asked it, she didn't need him to answer. "Ah . . . they needed time to search for something and didn't want to breathe in the poison themselves."

"Look at this place." Kevin stuck out a hand and made a circle. "It's immaculate. Pristine."

The pieces fell into place—she could picture it, almost like a movie. "This was cold. Calculated. Well planned. The victim is untouched. Not only did the killer take their time with the murder, they took even more time searching for whatever they were looking for, and then they cleaned it all up."

Alan entered through the back door and picked up the conversation without missing a beat. "Yep. Not a single print found on the premises." He poked his thumb over his shoulder. "I can ask them to check again. Just in case?"

"No." Kevin crossed his arms over his chest and stared at the scene. "They're thorough. It's just as I suspected anyway."

Alan's phone rang, interrupting his next question. He tapped his earbud. "Yep. Whatcha got?"

Carrie held her breath and waited.

With a nod, Alan disconnected. "There are some files at the mayor's office that we need to see. Looks like she might have been one of the planners behind the cyberattack."

"What?" Carrie frowned. "That's hard to believe, at least from my research of her."

Kevin shrugged as he knelt in front of the dead woman. "People are capable of crazy things."

"I know. But it doesn't seem congruent with her public persona." She couldn't put her finger on it, but something wasn't right. Carrie ran all the information they had so far through her mind. "No. To me, it doesn't add up."

"These things rarely do." Kevin stood again and wrote on his iPad.

"What if she was framed?" Alan stuck a piece of gum into his mouth, a sure sign his mind was working in overdrive.

"If she was, then this case just got a lot more interesting."

Kevin strode to a space heater in the middle of the room and narrowed his eyes to examine the box.

Carrie tilted her head to one side. "He's taunting us."

A smile lifted Kevin's lips. "Good observation. What do you see?"

"This old, decrepit space heater." The excitement of the chase was in full force now. "Why would the mayor even have it when everything else in here is top-of-the-line? Besides, what's the point of it when there's a giant fireplace directly in front of you and a generator fully capable of running everything?"

"Exactly."

"So, my theory is that the killer left it here. Specifically for us to find. But why? To pin the cause of death on it? Isn't that a bit . . . elementary?" She studied the heater. In the exact center of the room.

"That's it. Your instinct is right on, Carrie. Whoever did this? I think they're insinuating we're not smart enough to figure it out. It's brash. The person we're looking for isn't going to be easy to find. The only thing they left behind is this heater—obviously intentional." He knelt beside the heater and let out a long sigh. "We're being challenged, dared almost, to get in on the chase and find them."

CHAPTER ONE

DOWN

8. Five letters. Related to metrical stress.

Two months later
January 21—10:03 p.m.
Anchorage, Alaska

THE MEDIA WAS STUPID.

He flipped to another channel. Stupid.

He flipped to another. Ignorant.

Then another. Completely incompetent.

Why weren't they talking about his brilliant attack anymore? It should still be the top story. The Emergency Operations Center might have brought the power back on, but they hadn't stopped him. Not by a long shot.

They hadn't even caught him.

Imbeciles. They had no idea who they were dealing with or what he was capable of. Not even the Members—his fellow partners in the cause—knew. Nobody did.

Because he was smarter than everyone else.

After all these years of planning, waiting, prepping . . . it was time for the world to understand his power.

The small taste he'd gotten of unchecked power during the blackout only made him hungry for more.

Much more. And he wanted it. Craved it. *Needed* it.

Popping a pill into his mouth, Griz did his best to settle the aggravation that threatened to explode out of him.

He'd blown up his boss's plan and executed an even better one. Gotten rid of all the excess baggage. Shocked the authorities and news outlets alike. They hadn't seen it coming. Not even with that crazy woman spouting that the end was near.

He'd pulled off the greatest cyberterrorism plan in history.

Because he was smarter than everyone else.

Hadn't he already proven that with everything he'd accomplished up in Fairbanks? Griz scanned the room. Monitors displayed all the news stations. A few months ago, they'd been filled with his brilliance. The world—not just Alaska—had panicked watching what he'd done. Knocking out power and communications and emergency services. He'd blindsided the government, cut them off at the knees. And their response proved how useless they were.

He'd had everyone's attention. The citizens had doubted the authorities and protested in the streets when it was twenty—even thirty—below zero.

And for weeks after, protests had erupted around the world. Everyone was afraid it would happen to them next.

But now? People were right back to their stupidity and their ordinary lives. Not even hesitating to trust the authorities again and every device they owned. They'd forgotten it all.

And politicians were taking credit for restoration when they hadn't done a single thing.

It was an absolute waste of his time and talent.

He popped another pill. Then scribbled in his notebook. Too many pills today. But he needed them. They kept him focused. He itched to take another. No. He could wait. For a little bit. He was sharp.

After his triumph, he'd been ready for the next phase of his plan. The most brilliant power grab of all time.

He could do it too. Down to the last detail.

But those stupid media outlets weren't playing nice. He'd show them. Society would completely change. The world would change. All because of him.

Fire raced up his chest, and the rage inside him began to boil.

His followers were loyal, but they wouldn't expect this either. So what if he'd altered the plan a bit? It was a better plan. A scarier plan.

In the end, they all wanted the same thing. He would accomplish it, and no one would come close to stopping him.

People would pay attention again. Which was exactly what the Members wanted. And what he needed.

This time no one would forget.

◻ ◻ ◻

DOWN
8. Nine letters. Creates a multitude of rubberneckers.

January 25—11:13 a.m.
Department of Public Safety, Anchorage

"You just saved my backside for real, dude. Thanks for your help."

Scott Patteson shook the hand of his college roommate and grinned at the guy his basketball team had dubbed *Tiny.* No matter the size of the man now, he definitely hadn't grown out of his fraternity gaming vocabulary. "Not a problem. Glad I could help."

"Me too. I was afraid we'd have to wait several weeks, and the boss wasn't going to be happy about that."

Stuffing his laptop into his messenger bag, Scott lifted his eyebrows. "Yeah, that would have been a problem. Ever since Jason left to start the Cyber Solutions office up in Fairbanks, we've been stretched thin. Good thing you called me, otherwise—"

"Otherwise, I'd have been toast." Tiny shook his head. "You'd think after what happened up in Fairbanks, the bigwigs would want to throw a bit of money that direction. But this *is* the government we're talking about."

Scott scratched the side of his jaw, biting his tongue against what he wanted to say. Three years of working in the governor's office had given him too many opinions. When would people wake up to the cyber threat? Every Wi-Fi, cell-data enabled, Bluetooth-connected device had the potential of being hacked. Which meant practically every person in the United States was at risk.

"Well, that's why we're here," he said. "Just make sure you keep that new malware-prevention software up-to-date. Especially in this office. I'd hate for something to get on the network and hinder the good work you guys do here." There. That wasn't too negative.

"I know you, Scott. You're holding back on what you really want to say." Tiny grinned and glanced at his door. "And I appreciate that."

"You're welcome." He winked and slid into his coat, then grabbed his bag. "I'd better get to my next appointment."

"See ya at the reunion?" Tiny called after him.

Scott shrugged. "Maybe. Depends on the workload." He waved a hand and picked up his pace down the hall. Ugh. He hated reunions. Too many people. Too much talk about the good ol' days. To him, they were pointless. Either people wanted to revel in the past, or they wanted to show off and brag about what they were up to now. Neither appealed to him.

Yeah. Definitely count him out. Walking down memory lane wasn't his idea of a good time, and, well, there wasn't a lot to brag about. Other than the fact that he worked too much.

He headed toward the stairs. The buzzing of his phone made him slow down and pull it out.

Jason. He stopped to read the message.

> Got some intel on M. Will send
> meeting link. 3 p.m. if available.

> 3 p.m. Got it.

His stomach plummeted. He'd been waiting for this for years, but he knew the news wouldn't be good. Might as well accept that now.

"Excuse us." A blond woman with a tall, dark-haired man behind her raised her eyebrows. A trying-to-be-polite-but-about-to-be-annoyed look filled her face.

What? For a millisecond, he frowned and stared into her brown eyes, but then glanced away and realized he was blocking the staircase by standing right in the middle of the landing. "My apologies." Good job, Patteson. Moving to the side, he stuffed his phone into his coat pocket and hugged the railing in case they needed to get out quick. These were the troopers' offices after all. Even though they weren't in uniform, that didn't mean they weren't on urgent business. The duo sent him a quick nod.

"Thanks." She glanced at his visitor badge as she passed.

"Yep." Not a very congenial response, especially since he'd been the one blocking their exit, but it was all he could muster. He made his way down the stairs, his pace more sedate than the officers ahead of him, his mind still on Jason's text.

Once again he'd allowed the past to turn him inside out.

All with one little mention of her.

Warmth rose within him and filled his cheeks. Would he ever learn?

The two in front of him reached the bottom, and the guy's shoulders dropped as he patted his pockets. "Great. I've got to run next door for the extra camera battery. This one's almost dead."

Without missing a beat, she headed out the double doors. "I'll get the car. Meet me there."

Scott followed the woman out of the building. Her steps were determined and quick as she made her way toward the building on their left. Which was the ABI.

Huh. No wonder they weren't in trooper uniforms.

He zipped up his coat and shoved his hands into his pockets as he made his way to his car. He'd almost applied to the Alaska State Troopers himself once. But the cyber world had beckoned, and he dove in headfirst.

The crisp five-degree temperature made his eyes water. Pushing the remote start for his SUV, he cringed. Should've done that sooner. Now it wouldn't have much time to warm up. Oh well, he hadn't been inside helping Tiny too long. Of course, if he hadn't gotten all worked up about Jason's text, things would be different.

He shook it off and forced himself to refocus. Inside his vehicle, he clicked the seat warmer to high, buckled up, and then texted his boss.

Done at AST. On to Littleton's.

He set the maps app for his next appointment and pulled out of the parking space.

Following a silver truck out of the parking lot toward Tudor Road, he focused on the next job. It was a big one. Finding cyber guys with the right training had been difficult, so his office was making do . . . not something you wanted to say when it was cybersecurity on the line. But this was his reality right now. The long hours should keep him occupied.

Jason's text replayed in his brain. Scott glanced down at the clock on his dash. The thought of having to wait another couple of hours before finding out what the cryptic message meant didn't sit well.

The silver truck pulled out to turn right, and Scott inched forward.

A red Subaru darted past him, swerving a split second before it smashed into the back of the truck. For a moment, Scott stared and blinked. What in the world was that? The collision wasn't a bad one, but it jolted him. He had to get out of his head!

He put his SUV in Park and unbuckled. Hopefully everyone was all right. At least it didn't look like a lot of damage.

The blond woman who'd been inside the Department of Public Safety exited the silver pickup as he got out of his SUV. She held up a badge, then did a double take in his direction. "We're fine here. Are you all right, sir?"

With a duck of his chin, he cleared his throat. "I'm fine. No collision on my part."

"Good. Let's check on the other vehicle. We need to get out to an investigation. Did you witness the whole thing?" A large man exited the silver truck—the guy who'd gone after the battery—and passed by them. His brow furrowed as he stepped toward the intersection of Tudor and Boniface. Scott followed his gaze.

The traffic lights were blinking green. Odd.

"Sir?" The woman grabbed his attention.

"What? Oh. Yes, I did. I saw the whole thing." Scott followed her to the little red Subaru. A woman was crying in the front seat. His adrenaline kicked up a notch. There was more than one person crying. "Are you all right?" He tapped on the driver's window.

The woman in the car nodded, unbuckled, and opened her door. "I'm so sorry." She put a hand to her chest and went to the back door of her vehicle. "Honey, are you okay?" Wails came from the back seat.

A child! Every protective impulse in him surged to the forefront. He pulled out his phone to call 911.

The officer touched his arm. "We've got someone on the way already." Her voice was softer now.

The mother from the red Subaru reached in for her toddler. The impact hadn't done a tremendous amount of damage. No broken glass. But the child was crying and shaking. She hugged her little boy close. "I think we're okay."

"It's still best to get checked out. An emergency crew is on its way." The blond patted the other woman's shoulder. A trooper vehicle pulled up behind them. Two men stepped out of the vehicle. The big man went over to them and said a few words. They nodded and spoke into their radios.

The woman continued to soothe the mother and child with soft tones. Whatever she was saying had a calming effect on both. The mother visibly relaxed and nodded eagerly as the agent spoke. The boy's wails were now whimpers. Scott didn't have much experience with state troopers or agents, but he was impressed with her kindness. At that moment, she didn't seem to be talking as an officer of the law. Compassion and warmth flowed with the words.

The large man approached and whispered something in her ear. She nodded and smiled at the mother, even though the new crease in her forehead was hard to miss. "Here's my number. Don't worry, it's all right. We're fine. Just take care of yourself and your son, okay?" She gave the young mother her card. "If you need anything, give me a call."

One of the troopers approached Scott, interrupting his observation. The other went to the woman and her child. "We need your statement, Mr. . . . ?"

He snapped his attention back to the man in front of him. "Patteson. Scott Patteson."

"Patterson?" The furrowed brow of the man writing the report wasn't unusual for Scott to see. Rarely did anyone ever spell his name correctly.

"No. Without the r. P-a-t-t-e-s-o-n." He glanced at his watch. Not exactly how he'd hoped his morning would go, but at least everyone appeared unscathed.

The blond woman caught his gaze over the trooper's shoulder and nodded at him. "Thank you."

He dipped his chin and waited for the investigator's next question.

His phone buzzed again. Slipping it out of his pocket, he glanced at the screen. Jason.

> Got free early. Now a good
> time?

"Sir?"

Scott shoved his phone back in his pocket. "I'm sorry. Will this take long? I need to get to a meeting."

"Let's get through the questions. It shouldn't take more than fifteen minutes."

A quarter of an hour. He'd been waiting for years. What was another fifteen minutes?

CHAPTER TWO

DOWN
8. Six letters. A different way to get where you're going.

January 25—11:40 a.m.
Anchorage

CARRIE CLIMBED BACK INTO THE truck and slammed the door. Thank God no one was hurt. At least there was a witness and it had happened right in front of the Department of Public Safety. The damage was minimal, but it still made her heart ache. Leaving the scene with that woman and her small child had just about broken her.

"Sure you're okay?" Alan's voice tore through her thoughts. In the few months they'd been working together, he'd become like a big brother. Something she didn't mind one bit since she was so far from home.

"Yeah." She started the engine. "Kevin will probably think twice next time he puts me in charge." Her attempt to laugh it off didn't work as she pulled out into traffic and raced toward their assignment.

"It's not your fault. The woman stated she glanced away and had been trying to hand her son his juice. Besides, Kevin rotates who he assigns cases to—and you came up for the draw. It's how we all work as a team. And stay humble." He tapped the dash. "If you haven't noticed, rookie or not, the boss has faith in you. I do too. Now let's get this investigation underway."

It was true. The head of their division had been tough on her as he challenged her in her training but had never treated her like a rookie. The team in the office might tease her with the nickname now and then, but Kevin continued to push her to be a better investigator. Hadn't hesitated to bring her into the middle of things. It had encouraged her and boosted her spirits. Probably why she hated to think of letting anyone down.

Alan had more years under his belt, but he'd just finished up another tough investigation, so Kevin had called Carrie to the lead. She wasn't sure she was prepared for that, but it was her job. She'd do it to the best of her ability.

At the intersection of Northern Lights Boulevard and Boniface Parkway, she parked the truck at the gas station and surveyed the scene. "Whoa. No wonder he sent us out here. What on earth could have caused this?"

Nine cars sat smashed and mangled in the middle of the intersection.

Alan released a low whistle as he pulled on his gloves and opened his door. "We'd better find out. They've got traffic blocked in all directions. Which isn't good, but they've been waiting for us."

Carrie geared up, then slammed her door and darted as fast as she dared over the ice and snow to the crash scene. Alan's quick footsteps sounded beside her.

Trooper Campbell—one of the tallest men she'd ever seen—met them in the middle of the icy intersection. "This one is a mess. One DOA, but we're looking at three potential casualties. The other two are critical, and it doesn't look good. Seven other major injuries. Six, minor. Every person we've taken statements from has said the same thing—their light was green."

Without missing a beat, Alan took pictures of the scene.

Carrie turned to Trooper Campbell. "I was wondering why they sent us to a traffic accident."

"This was no accident. We've got twenty witnesses from all different sides who all swear the lights were green."

Alan stood and looked at Carrie, arms folded. "The intersection of the fender bender we were in . . . those lights were all green too."

She inhaled sharply, her mind racing. What on earth was happening? Could it be a glitch? No. Optimistic thinking in this scenario didn't work.

Trooper Miller approached them, speaking into the radio on his shoulder. He released the radio and nodded at Carrie. "HQ called the signals operations team. They were hacked. That's why you're here." He pointed to the four- and five-lane roads on either side of them. "Both roads are detoured for now, but we need to get this cleared before the lunch hour if at all possible."

They were lucky the fender bender on Tudor hadn't been worse. But wait. That happened after this accident. So . . . a distraction? On purpose, to slow her down? She dismissed the thought. It made no sense for this to be personal.

Carrie eyed the scene again. She'd learned early—long before winter was upon them in full force—that it was a common practice for Anchorage drivers to wait after a light turned green. No responsible driver gunned it in the wintertime. Intersections often became like skating rinks as cars moved through. Snow and ice accumulated during winter weather. Sitting cars warmed the snow and ice and melted it again. Then it would refreeze. More accumulation packed down, the waiting cars would melt it, it froze again in the frigid temps, and the cycle went round and round. It basically became like glacial layers over the course of the winter. It was neither illegal nor unusual for someone who was attempting to stop to slide right through the red light, and that meant people were cautious at intersections.

She peered up at the traffic lights. "These vehicles didn't just start up and all go at the same time. There was speed behind them. What was the estimated speed at impact?"

Trooper Campbell whistled and waved at another trooper. "Billings!"

The man came over and Campbell repeated the question.

"Best guesstimate is between thirty and thirty-five miles per hour on impact."

She narrowed her eyes. "Which means none of them were stopped or trying to stop."

"No, ma'am." Trooper Billings pointed to the car at the center of the pileup. "That driver was going the fastest—reached the intersection first, possibly going forty to forty-five. He's our DOA. Hit on each side by another vehicle. Compounded by the other crashes."

Carrie made mental notes even as she wrote it all down. Alan finished his circle of the area and strode up to her. "I've documented every possible angle."

They walked the scene three times, hashing out everything they saw from the crash site. When she had a question, Alan checked the photos on the camera to ensure they had the visual reminders for later. He also took notes on his tablet while she recorded voice memos on her phone. She glanced at her watch.

Campbell approached. "We'll gather all the evidence and bring the vehicles in."

"Good." She nodded and studied the intersection one more time.

"Do you need anything else from us?"

"Not right now. But thanks." Squatting down, she eyed the whole scene from another angle. They'd been thorough, but it was always good to get another perspective.

Alan stepped close and squatted down as well. "Good thinking. See anything else?"

"No. Which is good. We need to get to the traffic signal maintenance department." She stood back up to her full height and searched on her phone. "It's at the city's Planning and Development Center." Of course, Alan probably knew that since he'd lived here forever. With a final nod to the troopers, she thanked them and returned to her vehicle.

When they were both back in and buckled up, she shared a look with Alan. "This wasn't just a hack to see what could be done with the lights."

"Nope." He shook his head, jaw clenched.

"Whoever did this *wanted* to cause injuries. Possibly even death." What was their world coming to? The longer she spent as an investigator, the more she grappled with the question. Downright evil seemed to be invading every area of their lives. *God, help us.* "Could someone have been the target? Or was it random?"

Alan's head wagged from one side to the other, and he blew out a long breath. "That's the question of the hour. I think it's safe to say this was premeditated."

Her stomach soured. "And once it hits the media, fear will run rampant. We've got to find whoever was behind this, and fast."

◻ ◻ ◻

DOWN
8. Eleven letters. Lawsuit due to negligence.

January 25—1:22 p.m.
Alaska Bureau of Investigation, Anchorage

For the second time that day, Scott found himself parking in front of the Department of Public Safety. The two buildings here housed the State Troopers and the ABI. He had just gotten situated at the other job, when Tim—his interim boss at Cyber Solutions—called and told him to postpone and pack up. The owner of Littleton hadn't been pleased, but when he found out it was an urgent call from the state troopers about a deadly accident, he'd backed off.

As Scott drove back to the offices on Tudor Road, Tim briefed him on what he knew of the new situation. Traffic lights had been hacked. It had caused at least one death. As soon as he hung up with Tim, Scott dialed Jason in Fairbanks. This was all too similar to what had happened a few months ago.

"Hey, Jase—it's me, Scott, again." It hadn't been more than forty-five minutes since they spoke. Scott was doing his best to push *that* conversation to the back of his mind. His personal life wasn't relevant right now. There were other lives on the line.

"Hey, look, I know this isn't easy—"

"A man was killed this morning." Scott threw the words out. Easier to change the subject and get to business. "I need you to fill me in on a few details about the cyberattack up there a few months ago. Didn't someone try to kill you and Darcie by hacking traffic lights?"

"Yep. I can still feel the bruises. Had to have surgery on my shoulder twice." Jason's voice changed and met the gravity of the situation. "Whatcha need to know?"

"Cyber Solutions has been called in to help the ABI down here with a similar incident. I'm on my way there now, so I don't have all the details, but they know that someone hacked into the signal operations and caused a massive accident."

"How many vehicles?"

"Multiple, but I'm not sure."

"Targeted?"

"Maybe? It's hard to believe they would call us if it wasn't beyond their scope."

"Well, what I do know is that our accident was targeted. Our vehicle. After that, everything went back to normal."

"Huh. Did the hacker leave any breadcrumbs?"

Jason filled him in on the details.

"Okay. This should get me started. I'll call you when I know more."

"I don't envy you. I'm praying, man."

"Thanks." Scott ended the call and stared out the windshield. In the past few months, his team at Cyber Solutions had endured more than their fair share of trauma and grief. What had started as a small team in Anchorage had grown into two flourishing offices.

Mac would be so proud. *Mac.* Just the thought of his boss made his jaw clench. What would it be like to lose a wife and child? Scott couldn't even fathom it.

He hated having to bug Jason with this, but this was the future their world faced.

Cyberterrorism. There really wasn't any other way to word it. People had always hurt people. But now, in addition to guns and bombs, they could shut down the power and communication systems, or in this case, traffic lights.

Who would do something like that?

That's what he didn't want to wrap his brain around. The cyber part was easy, at least in his mind. He had a master's degree in computer science. Computers always made sense to him. Code. Programming. Hardware. Software.

But put an evil presence behind it, and all that technology could be used to harm innocent citizens.

If someone was planning another cyberattack, his team and law enforcement needed to be ready. Anchorage was much larger than Fairbanks. A lot more lives were on the line.

But hadn't they caught the perpetrators behind the attack in Fairbanks? This couldn't be a rogue sympathizer, could it? Maybe a copycat?

Getting out of his SUV, Scott lifted his messenger bag over his shoulder and headed to the building for the Alaska Bureau of Investigation. It wasn't his job to speculate. It was his job to help them figure it out and fix it.

Once he was buzzed in, given a new visitor badge, and made it through the metal detector, he went to the front desk. "I'm supposed to report to a"—he looked down at his notes—"Ms. Kintz?"

The blond woman he'd seen twice that morning rounded a corner and took swift steps toward him. Her no-nonsense manner didn't dispel her natural good looks. Her hair was pulled back into a ponytail, but it was her big, brown eyes that drew him in. As she came closer, the same double take she'd done earlier crossed her features. "I'm Carrie Kintz." She studied him. "I assume you're from Cyber Solutions?"

"Yes, ma'am." He stuck out a hand for greeting. "Scott Patteson."

She shook his hand. "Thank you for coming. If you'll follow me." She turned on her heel and led him down the hall to a conference room. "You're the man who witnessed the accident this morning, aren't you?"

"Yes, ma'am."

"What were you doing at the DPS?" Her tone sounded slightly accusatory.

But even though they'd run into each other three times in one day, it wasn't exactly surprising. Anchorage was the largest city in Alaska, but it often felt like a small town. He ran into the same people a lot, but that might be just because he was a regular at his favorite places.

"I was assisting with a cyber issue." He wasn't sure how much to say.

She entered the room and turned her gaze back to him with a relieved smile. "Oh, you're Tiny's friend. Yes, we've heard a lot about you."

"Really?" He followed her in and spotted the man who had been with her that morning. Papers were strewn across the table in front of him, but the man seemed to know where every piece of the puzzle was as he shifted his hands from one pile to the next.

"Yep. Tiny's a talker."

"All good, I hope."

She nodded, but the smile disappeared as she went to the head of the table where a file sat. Back to business.

The gravity of the reason for his presence hit him once again.

The other guy half stood and reached out a hand in greeting. "Alan Sanderson. Nice to meet you. Sorry about the circumstances."

"Scott Patteson. Good to meet you too."

"Any relation to Leah Patteson?"

At the mention of her name, Scott smiled. "My sister."

"She was my niece's favorite teacher. I remember because she was adamant about everyone pronouncing and spelling her last name correctly." After the shared connection and a quick handshake, Alan reclaimed his seat and shifted a couple of pages toward Scott. His demeanor shifted to all business.

"We've got quite a case. Not sure what you'll need, but here's a summary of what we know so far. I'll be the first to say I'm really glad you're here. This is unnerving."

"I'll do everything I can." Matching the somber tone of the room, Scott pulled out his laptop, found an outlet to plug it into, then took a seat. "What can I do to help, Ms. Kintz?"

"Call me Carrie. We don't have time for formality." She walked to the map of Anchorage on the wall. "We called your office because there was a nine-car collision that occurred at 11:21 a.m. at the intersection of Northern Lights Boulevard and Boniface Parkway."

"Whoa." Scott typed in the notes. "Not your usual fender bender."

"Not usual at all. It was planned. One fatality so far. Two still in critical." She planted her hands on her hips. "It ticks me off the longer I think about it." The rigid set of her body reinforced her words.

Scott stood and walked to the map to study it with her. "My boss told me the lights were changed on purpose."

"Someone hacked into the municipality and manipulated the traffic lights."

"Could this have been a distraction from what the criminals were really up to?" Maybe he watched too many crime and police procedural shows on TV, but it seemed logical. "That's what happened in Fairbanks, right?" Not that he wanted to be a pessimist, but these days—

Her stare stopped him short, and he stepped back.

"Sorry. You guys have probably already thought of that."

"I thought that at first too . . . until we saw the scene and talked it through. And nothing else happened at the time of the incident, as far as we know." She checked her watch. "It's been too long for this to be a distraction."

He studied her face. Those eyes. Piercing. They seemed to be assessing his motivation, his authenticity, him.

She blinked and turned her attention to the map once again. "All the vehicles involved were driving around or above the speed limit. No one was stopped from any direction or at any side of the intersection." She tapped a finger at each of the surrounding intersections.

"That's odd." Scott examined the outlying crossroads, then looked between Carrie and Alan. Then back at the map. "Yeah, this was calculated." He grunted and stomped back to his seat. Taking a few deep breaths, he clenched his jaw. What made people do such things?

He dared another glance in her direction. Her lips were pinched. If he had to guess, he'd say this ticked her off even more than it did him. Heaven help whoever had done this, especially if they underestimated her. One look at the expression on her face was enough to know he didn't want to get on her bad side.

She handed him a paper. "You've been given access to the municipality's site for the next twenty-four hours. See if you can figure out how they did this and why."

"The who would be helpful too." Alan lifted his eyebrows in a quasi challenge.

The more Scott studied the map, the more his heart dropped. "To cause an accident like that, he had to have been watching." Scott logged in to the municipality's site. "It would take a lot of work unless someone was on the inside."

"So the person we're looking for works for the city?" Disgust dripped from Carrie's voice. Not that Scott could blame her.

Alan scratched his chin. "Hm. That or someone who works for the city was blackmailed, coerced. Any number of things."

Scott studied the history from that morning, then pointed to the map. "Can you mark on the map for me? Red and green."

"Sure." Carrie grabbed a couple dry-erase markers to use on the plastic overlay.

"They were very specific." He scrolled through the code. "The lights at Baxter and Northern Lights, north–south traffic, were green while east–west was red. For several minutes. That backed up the traffic there."

The marker squeaked on the map.

"The lights at Wesleyan and Northern Lights, same thing."

She circled that intersection as well. "I don't like where this is going."

He gritted his teeth. "Me neither. The lights at Twenty-Fourth and Boniface, east–west traffic, were green while north–south was red. Lights at Thirty-Fourth, Emmanuel, and Boniface, same thing. East–west traffic was green while north–south was red. They were all manipulated prior to the crash at Northern Lights and Boniface. People got impatient. Traffic piled up. Then everything that had been red was surged green at the same time. And all the signals—north, south, east, and west—at Northern Lights and Boniface were green while all the vehicles from the outside intersections headed toward them."

They stared at the map in front of them. Every intersection around the crash site had been manipulated.

Alan slammed a hand down on the table. "What kind of demented person does something like this?"

Scott hated it when a hacker used his skills to hurt people. The longer he thought about it, the greater the anger inside him grew. "Every vehicle was barreling ahead because they'd all been waiting. All they saw was a green light."

"Until they collided." Carrie's shoulders dropped as she released a huff. "There are days I don't like this job." She rubbed her forehead. "But this is where we need your expertise. Can you track how they were able to get in?"

Scott scanned the code. "That's going to take some time. Again, I think whoever did this has someone on the inside. I hate to say it, but—"

"Okay." She turned to Alan. "Check the backgrounds of every employee who has access."

"On it." The look they shared seemed to hold more meaning than someone following an order. Was there something between them?

Scott hated that his mind even went there. What had gotten into him?

Carrie walked over and took the chair next to Scott. "My biggest objective for you is to make sure it can't happen again. That they're not planning more. Yeah, I want to catch whoever did this, but let's not miss the fact that someone could be aiming for something bigger. I don't want to be blindsided. The last thing Alaska needs is more negative coverage."

"Got it." Scott picked up his cell. "Let me text my boss and let him know this might take more than one day." He wasn't as familiar with municipality systems as he would be corporate, but hackers were hackers. Once he went down the rabbit hole, he knew he'd better be prepared.

"Thanks." She stood and crossed her arms over her chest. "I don't need to tell you what kind of chaos we'll be dealing with if people find out what actually happened here."

"Understood."

She placed her palms on the table, leaning close. "One more thing"—her words were agitated, clipped—"Alan noticed all the lights were flashing green after our little fender bender earlier. Could you check into that for me too?"

"Will do." He watched her walk away, a large knot forming in his throat. As soon as he'd seen those lights this morning, he'd had a bad feeling. To think of that young mom and her child . . .

No. He couldn't go there. Best to focus on tracing the hacker.

Easier said than done. His stomach churned as his brain spun through all the possibilities. What kind of maniac were they dealing with?

CHAPTER THREE

DOWN
8. Nine letters. A metronome for your ticker.

January 27—4:21 p.m.
Palmer, Alaska

"Why don't you take a break and let me handle things for the rest of the day?" Her voice, calm and soothing, was too distracting.

Griz shook his head. "I'm the one giving orders. Not the other way around."

Palms up, she clamped her mouth shut. Squaring her shoulders, she reached for her designer handbag. She'd bragged the fur-covered monstrosity had cost her five thousand dollars. She flaunted it whenever she could. "I'm going to let that slide. This time. I was just offering to help. You look like you could sleep for a month and still not be rested." Shoving the bag under her arm, she sashayed her way out of the room, her heels clicking in a staccato rhythm.

It wasn't true. That's how druggies appeared. Not him. Even so, maybe he would take a sleeping pill and knock himself out tonight. A full night couldn't hurt.

He straightened his tie and didn't bother to say anything as she left. He wouldn't give her any control in his plan.

Control. That's what was lacking. Griz paced the floor, his mind pinging between five different ideas. It was incredible what his intellect could conjure up, how much he could accomplish.

It wouldn't be long now before everyone else saw his genius. They wanted a real leader? He was that leader. Not the government. Not the country. Not any authority in place.

Him.

He lifted his chin.

In Fairbanks, he'd shown them all. He had the power. Complete control after he eliminated the dead weight. The plan had been beautiful. It made him smile.

Yeah, but you didn't get everything you wanted. In the end, you failed. The snide voice echoed through his mind.

He walked over and slammed his palm against the wall. No! He hadn't failed. His plan was still in motion. Nothing could stop him.

But they did stop you.

No, they didn't. Only momentarily.

He paced the room, willing the voice away. Nothing was going to get in his way.

He shook his head and cleared his throat. The feelings he was having right now weren't normal. No way would he let depression take hold. The pathetic lack of confidence wasn't him. That's who he *used* to be. A long time ago. Before he learned to control the drugs instead of them controlling him.

Yes. He was in control. He simply needed . . . more.

He was getting it back. Just wait. He'd show them all.

The urge to pop another pill was strong, but movement in the corner reminded him he had an audience.

"This is everything you wanted for the setup." The new guy was a mess. Greasy hair. Bloodshot eyes. But he was hungry and willing to do whatever it took. Besides, he was expendable, which was exactly what Griz needed. After eliminating the team from Fairbanks, he'd built a new one around him. Loyal to a fault. Ready to do whatever he asked. A few of them just needed a bit of polishing.

"Let me check the list." He eyed all the equipment, his list, and the equipment again. "You've got the exact same setup at the loft?"

"Yep." Too bad the kid was another casualty of addiction. He could've done so much more with his skills in this life.

"Good." Griz lifted his chin. "Why don't you go take a shower and put on some clean clothes. The next job is a bit more . . . upscale. Are you up for playing with the big guns?" He held out an envelope of cash.

A smile stretched across the kid's face. "Of course. Anything for the cause."

"Perfect." He strode over to the massive computer setup. No need to get his hands dirty. Not when there were so many dedicated to the ultimate cause. The Members expected results, especially with the amounts of money they'd invested. Over the years, they had refined into the most clandestine vested-interest powerhouse on the planet.

The ten-year plan was almost to fruition. Of course, he'd changed things along the way. A tweak in personnel a few years go, which enabled them to get into the governor's office three years earlier than planned. He'd edited some of the code in the 26 Below attack too. Sometimes they were too risk avoidant. Their vision was a bit narrow, but he would correct that over time. Perhaps it was a good moment to call up the rest of his troops.

That would definitely boost his spirits. Cause a little more chaos. Give him time to explore all the possibilities.

The voice attempted to take over again. He paced the room with rapid steps, forcing it into the back of his mind where it belonged.

Where was he? Oh, that's right. The plan. *His* plan. The Members. Calling up troops.

No. Not yet. Once the media got hold of it, he might give them a hint.

No one needed to know what he was doing behind the scenes. Once he was done, they would all cheer.

◻ ◻ ◻

DOWN
8. Eleven letters. What claustrophobia can inspire.

January 28—8:56 a.m.
Alaska Bureau of Investigation

Carrie knocked on Kevin's door.

"Come in." The head of their division smiled as she entered.

Her eyes widened at the sight of crutches by his desk. "What happened to you?"

"That's why I called you in here." He swiped a hand down his face. "Broke my leg skiing Alyeska last weekend."

"Ouch." That wasn't good. She attempted to keep her face neutral, but six from their office had been called out to help with remote locations yesterday. Nine others from the scheduled day shift were already out on other cases. Which left her, Alan, and Kevin. Didn't look like Kevin would be going anywhere for a while. She sat in the chair across from him. "How long will you be in a cast?"

"The next ten weeks, at least. It's not a pretty break." He shuffled some papers on his desk. "Alan flew out this morning for a fraud case down in Juneau."

That she *didn't* know. Oh boy. Make that her and Kevin. Or really . . . just her.

"I wanted you to be prepared; you'll have to handle anything else that comes in. I'm chained to the office, but I'll help with anything you need. We can always call next door for extra hands."

She blew her hair off her forehead. At least it was quiet right now. "Okay. I can do that. I'm just finishing up the paperwork from the other day."

Even though the accident was devastating and two people had died, they'd wrapped up the case pretty quickly. Scott had found the man on the inside through his digital footprints, and their team had gone in and raided the home with the hacker's IP address. The only person there was a gamer in the basement who insisted he knew nothing about it. They'd arrested him anyway, along with his cohort at the municipality. Neither had turned on the other yet, but she was confident it would happen. It was in the hands of the DA now.

"I can see those wheels of yours turning. Whatcha thinking?" Kevin fidgeted with his pen.

She narrowed her eyes. "I can't stop thinking about the motive. Why'd they do it? Why cause an accident so horrific that it kills people? And then not do anything else?"

Kevin rubbed his chin. "To be honest, I think it's a precursor for something bigger. Someone was testing it out, maybe planning an attack like Fairbanks." He shook his head. "Not something any of us want to deal with right now. The ABI team in Fairbanks is still reeling."

"I can't even imagine. I've read their reports to try to stay on top of everything, but it just twists my brain in knots."

"Yeah, it'll do that. At least they got it stopped. I hope we have too." He leaned back and tapped his pen on the desk. "I'm not trying to be a pessimist, I promise. I'm glad we caught the guys here before they hurt anyone else."

"Me too." But somehow that didn't make her insides feel any better. "I appreciate you giving me the opportunity to lead an investigation."

"Don't think I was doing you any favors, Kintz." His tone wasn't harsh, but the glint in his eyes brooked no argument. "Everyone here has to carry their weight and understand every single aspect of the investigative process. When you're assigned a role, you make sure you do it to the best of your ability. If you're lacking in any area, we'll make sure you get up to speed. If one part of the team is deficient— the whole team is deficient.

"It was your turn to take the lead. Plain and simple. Senior or rookie, each member is equal and valuable. It also keeps a better sense of camaraderie and family. Everyone pulls their own weight."

With a nod, she held his gaze.

His lips lifted into a grin, and he pointed to his leg. "And now, you're going to have to help pull mine. At least until more of the team returns."

"You got it."

"You've done a great job these past few months, Carrie. I'm proud of you."

Once again, she wished he wouldn't retire so soon. She couldn't have asked for a better mentor. "Thank you, that means a great deal. You've taught me so much. Are you sure you want to give all this up? I mean, there's so much . . . glamour. And coffee."

His laugh filled the room. "I'm getting too old for this. Besides, you guys are much better at the techie stuff than I am. I'm tired of trying to keep up."

"Whatever." She stood from her chair. "We're normally the ones trying to keep up with *you*."

"Nice try, Kintz." He waved her off. Always pushing attention off himself. "I'll let you get back to the paperwork. Just wanted you to be aware that you are on call."

"Yes, sir." She winked at him. He hated being called *sir*.

"You'd better leave before I come up with something tedious for you to do."

She scooted out the door and went back to her desk. The phone was ringing as she reached her chair. "ABI, Carrie Kintz."

"Hi, Carrie. This is Scott Patteson from Cyber Solutions." The warmth in his voice was calming. Friendly.

"Hey, Scott. How can I help you?" The man was brilliant, meticulous, and obviously good at his job. But even with all the ways he impressed her during the investigation, the biggest thing that she'd noticed was how he cared about people. It hadn't been black-and-white with stats on paper for him. It had been real lives on the line. That made an impression on her.

He cleared his throat. "Actually, I was wondering if you'd like to grab a cup of coffee this afternoon?"

Well, *that* wasn't what she was expecting. She tried to cover her surprise. "Do you need to talk more about the case?"

"Nope." He cleared his throat. "It was my feeble attempt to ask you out."

"Oh." Her mind went blank for a moment.

"My apologies. If this was inappropriate—"

"I'd love to have coffee." She couldn't allow him to think he had crossed a line. "It depends on what the day holds. I'm on call for any local cases that come in."

"I could always bring the coffee to you." The line muffled for a moment. "I'm between jobs right now and could swing by for a few minutes."

Blinking faster than usual, she thought that one through. The office was quiet, so it shouldn't be a problem. "Sure. Sounds good."

"What would you like?"

"A mocha. Extra sweet. Extra chocolate." Might as well let him get to know the real Carrie right from the start.

"I'll be there in about fifteen minutes."

That was the great thing about Anchorage. Small, drive-through coffee huts abounded, even more populous per capita than coffee shops in Seattle. Which was saying a lot since Seattle was the birthplace of Starbucks.

And the coffee in Alaska's tiny coffee huts was amazing. An extra-sweet mocha was exactly what she needed to face whatever might land on her desk today.

Finishing the paperwork she needed to get to Kevin, she allowed her thoughts to go back to Scott. How interesting that he had called out of the blue like that. They'd worked well together on the case, and of course, she'd noticed his chocolate-brown eyes that held a hint of a secret.

But other than that, she hadn't expected to see Scott Patteson again.

She hadn't dated in years. In part because most guys she met weren't interested in a woman in law enforcement. On the other hand, she was so busy with the job that she rarely made time for anything other than church. Which was hard enough to coordinate. Getting up from her desk, she shook away the thoughts and took the folder to Kevin's office. She was getting ahead of herself. Scott had simply asked her out for coffee—correction, was *bringing* her coffee. It didn't have to mean she was ready to date the guy. Although the thought was a pleasant one.

She tidied up her desk and checked her computer for email. All was quiet for the moment. Which was nice. But she always hated just sitting still.

Her phone buzzed. "Mr. Patteson is coming through to see you."

"Thank you, Molly." Carrie stood back up and walked over to meet him.

His bright smile lit up his face. His dark hair was short and a bit tousled—probably from wearing a hat out in the cold.

"Hi." He held up two coffees. "As promised."

Since no one else was in the normally loud and busy squad room, she led him over to her desk. She took the offered cup and removed the Alaska-shaped sticker over the hole in the lid so she could sip it. "Thank you." The rich, dark blend melded with chocolaty sweetness hit her tongue and made the world feel right again, if just for a moment. "Mm, perfect."

Her coffee addiction wasn't worse than anyone else in law enforcement, except her dad liked to tease her about only drinking it doctored up. In his mind, she couldn't be a real cop until she drank it black. Yuck.

"Glad you like it. I know I'm pretty picky about how I drink my coffee. Wish I was one of those guys who could just chug it black, but I can't."

Funny. That was almost like he knew what she'd been thinking. She hid her grin behind the cup as she took another sip.

He waited for her to sit, then settled across from her and propped his ankle up on his knee. "You're probably wondering why I called out of the blue."

She shrugged. "I was a bit surprised." What was she supposed to say?

He sighed, and his foot started pumping up and down.

Was he nervous?

"Look, I'll be honest. When we were working on the case the other day, I noticed the Bible app on your phone. It's the same one I use."

Her heart picked up its pace. "Oh yeah?" Her words came out breathier than she intended.

"I took a chance. We worked well together. Outside of church, I don't have the opportunity to meet many smart, attractive women who might have the same faith." He licked his lips, set his coffee cup on her desk, and leaned forward. "I'm making a complete mess out of this. Help?"

Feeling every bit of embarrassment in the moment, she grimaced. "I doubt I'll be any help. Most men shy away from me when they find out what I do."

His shoulders relaxed a bit. "Probably because it intimidates them. I just bore people to death."

After another sip, she glanced at Scott. "Bore people? You weren't boring the other day. You helped us solve the case. We would have been lost without your skills."

"I'm a bit of an information junkie." His soft chuckle made his eyes light up. "My mom tells me that I should have been a professional student. Yes, I'm good for fixing her computers, but if she asks me a question and it takes more than three sentences for me to explain, I get the look."

"My mom has one of those looks as well. But for me, it's because she doesn't want to hear anything graphic. Anything rated PG is too intense for her." They shared a laugh, but Carrie couldn't get over the awkward feeling. Why were relationships so difficult for her?

"What church do you go to?"

His question made her wince. "That's the thing. I've been trying out different churches every few weeks. Haven't landed on one that fits yet. And with my job, well, I only get to go to church every other week."

"You're new to the area?" He looked surprised. "I would have never guessed that."

"Moved from North Dakota to go through the Alaska Law Enforcement Training program. Once I was done and hired on by the ABI, I started looking for a good home church."

His phone buzzed, and he pulled it out of his pocket. "Excuse me." He grinned at her and took another sip before he answered. "Hey, Tim." He listened for a moment. "All right, send me the specs and I'll get right on it."

"Work?"

"Yep. I'm sorry." He stood, a lopsided grin on his face. "Look, I'm not any good at this, but . . . would you like to have dinner together? I promise to do better."

What did she have to lose? He was a decent enough guy. Cute. Smart. "Sure."

"Maybe tonight? If you're free?" He looked hopeful.

"Okay."

"What time do you get off work?"

"Since I'm on call, not until seven, when the night shift is fully staffed. Is that too late for you?"

"Not at all. I'll call you." His grin stretched, and her stomach did a little flip. He definitely had an effect on her.

Her desk phone buzzed, and she jumped. "Sorry. Let me get this."

"That's okay. I'll head out." He waved and turned to walk away as she picked up the receiver.

She couldn't help but smile as she watched his back. A genuine, good-looking guy had just asked her out. All because of a Bible app on her phone. That didn't happen every day. "ABI, Carrie Kintz."

"People are dying. And they will keep dying." The female voice was mechanical and warbled.

Her stomach plummeted. She hit Record and held her breath. Would the person keep talking?

"I've left you clues. Why haven't you figured it out? One might think you don't care about the citizens of Alaska. Such a shame." The voice went silent, and then the line went dead.

CHAPTER FOUR

DOWN
8. Four letters. Penicillin source.

January 28—11:24 a.m.
Alaska Regional Hospital, Anchorage

"How are you doing this morning, Jenny?" the nurse asked as she rolled in her portable computer station.

Her arm was killing her, but she wasn't about to say that. "I've been better. But I can't complain. Is it time for meds?" *Please, God, let it be time for meds.*

The nurse—Angie?—nodded and swiped her badge on the computer. "We've got meds, and I'll start your new bag of antibiotics. It's important to keep any infection at bay."

"Sounds good." Jenny shifted in the bed and held out her wrist.

After she'd confirmed her full name and date of birth, Angie turned the white hospital band to find the barcode and scanned it. With the ease that came from experience, she twisted the new vial into the IV and pressed the plunger. Whatever concoction of meds it contained rushed through Jenny's veins.

"There. Hopefully those pain meds'll help you feel better soon. They'll be in to draw blood in a few hours." Angie typed something, then pushed the computer cart back. "Do you need anything else?"

"No, I'm good." Jenny closed her eyes. She was feeling woozy. Medication always made her feel that way though.

"Okay. Ring if you need anything." Angie headed out the door, turning off the light behind her.

Jenny shifted a pillow behind her head and frowned. Her throat felt tight. She grabbed her water cup and sipped slowly. She sputtered, coughing the liquid all over her blankets.

Panic rippled through her and sweat broke out on her forehead and back. She tried to take a deep breath, but her chest was so tight. Her heart pounded against her rib cage.

The room started to whirl. The call button for her nurse was on her tray. She pushed forward and tried to pick it up, but it clattered to the floor.

Determined to reach it, she lunged for it with every ounce of strength, but it was just out of reach.

She stretched and her fingers grabbed at the air.

Jenny wheezed again. Black spots clouded her vision. And then there was nothing.

◻ ◻ ◻

DOWN
8. Seven letters. Sweet sugar high for your body.

January 28—2:19 p.m.
Alaska Bureau of Investigation

Carrie sat across from Kevin, listening to the recorded message for the hundredth time. "I've left you clues. Why haven't you figured it out? One might think you don't care about the citizens of Alaska. Such a shame."

Her mentor's eyes were narrow, his brow furrowed. "What did it say before you hit Record?"

"That people were dying. And would keep dying." It sent a chill up her spine.

Kevin leaned back in his chair. "I don't get it. How are people dying? And where are all these dead people?"

She straightened a bit in her chair. "Should I go back and check recent deaths? Missing persons?"

"Maybe." Leaning forward, he scribbled on the paper in front of him. "The part that really has my hackles raised is the fact that it says, I've left you clues."

"Yeah, me too." Carrie studied him as he tapped the pen on the desktop. "You thinking about the murder of the mayor up in Fairbanks?" It was still unsolved and had created quite a stir in the media since accusations had been made about the mayor's involvement in the blackout.

He raised one eyebrow. "Great minds. That is where my mind went. It's the only obvious clue I can think of. I hate cases without resolution. But I could be off base. This might have nothing to do with it. Besides, whoever it was, they called this office. Not Fairbanks. Did you have them trace the call?"

She dipped her chin. "Yep. A burner."

"Of course."

Silence reigned in the office for several moments. Carrie waited, her thoughts bouncing all over the place. The call had come to her desk because she was the one on call. But it could have gone to anyone in the ABI. The caller hadn't asked for her specifically. Funny, though, the call came in as a female who'd asked to speak to an investigator. She must have hit the voice changer as soon as she heard Carrie's voice.

"Sarah at dispatch said the woman sounded quiet and hesitant but refused to say anything else until an investigator got on the line." She clasped and unclasped her hands in her lap. "What do you want me to do?"

"A female, huh? Was she coerced into making the call, or is she the one behind it?" He swiped a hand down his face as he sighed. "I hate for you to get buried in busy work if this is just a prank, but you're going to have to follow the lead. Check missing persons. Check any recent deaths, at least the past couple weeks." He turned, shifting how he had his leg propped up. "But if something else comes in, you'll have to set this aside."

"And what if they call back?"

"Let's hope that doesn't happen."

"Right."

Three hours later, she'd combed through so many files, she wasn't sure she could keep them all straight. But none of the deaths were out of the ordinary, and none of them seemed related in any way. The missing persons files didn't give her anything to go on either. Leaning back in her chair, she rolled her shoulders and prayed the knots would ease.

But that wouldn't happen. Not after that phone call.

Best case scenario would be that someone was pranking the ABI. Yeah, it was a lot of wasted time. Frustrating, definitely. But at least, if that were true, people weren't dying.

Worst case scenario? The phone call—the threat—was real.

Did they have a psycho on the loose who wanted to cause mass destruction? Someone who wanted notoriety? Hated a people group? Angry at loss in their own life?

Or a serial killer?

That last thought was more than she wanted to think about. She wished the office was buzzing with her ABI team members. Then she wouldn't have to carry this burden on her own. She was too new for this. Inadequate. Ill-equipped.

"Any progress?" Kevin's voice behind her made her shoot up out of her chair.

"Not a thing." She placed her hands on her hips and willed her heart to calm down.

He leaned on his crutches. "I was afraid you'd say that." He sifted through the files on her desk. "This has got you on edge."

That was an understatement. "Yeah. Sorry." Might as well lay it all out. "I would love for this to be a prank. But my gut is telling me that it's not an idle threat. I think it's a lot worse than we realize."

Kevin grimaced. "I wish I had a different feeling, but I think you're correct. Something is telling me to be prepared. But for what? I don't know."

While the validation of her instincts should make her proud, in this instance, she'd wish to be wrong.

◻ ◻ ◻

DOWN
8. Seven letters. It cuts like a knife.

January 28—7:25 p.m.
Glacier Brewhouse, downtown Anchorage

Scott paced the tiled entry hall at the downtown eatery, his still-damp hiking boots squeaking on the floor. The hall from the double-door entry on Fifth Avenue opened up to an Alaskan art gallery and several quaint shops on the right, while the brewhouse was on the left. It gave him plenty of room to take long strides and steadying breaths and try to walk off the nerves. It had been a long time since he'd asked anyone out on a date.

When he'd touched base with Carrie about dinner an hour ago, he'd already made the reservation, hoping she'd still be available. Her voice had held a strain, but she apologized because of a new investigation that had her buried in research.

At least she hadn't backed out. That was encouraging. Especially after their coffee encounter earlier. Of course, he was probably remembering it worse than what had actually happened. He was good at that.

No matter what, his little sister would have teased him incessantly had she witnessed his first attempt at a date with Ms. Kintz.

Just the thought of Becca made him relax. Her treatments in the lower forty-eight were finally done and she'd come back home to Anchorage last month. Just in time for Christmas. It had been the best present ever. For the entire family.

It was like they were all able to take a full breath for the first time in several years. Life could finally move forward. In fact, Becca was the one who made him promise that he would date again. They'd had enough loss to last a lifetime.

He couldn't allow his thoughts to stay in the past. It was time to live in the present again. He'd taken a huge step by asking Carrie out. Glacier Brewhouse was one of his all-time favorite places to eat. It had great atmosphere and yet wasn't over-the-top fancy for a first date. Everyone could feel comfortable in the environment. Truly the Alaskan way.

With a glance down at his phone, he watched the time change to 7:30. Perfect. She should be here any minute. Maybe it would look better if he stopped pacing the hall and appeared like a normal human being waiting on a date. Casual. Laid-back. Relaxed. Yeah, sure.

"Scott?" Her voice made him turn toward the double-door entry.

"Hi." Several other people walked past as he waited for her at the bottom of the stairs to the brewhouse. The rigid set of her shoulders and the small frown on her face weren't encouraging. "You look like it's been quite a day."

They headed up the steps together to the host station as she spoke. "Yeah, my brain hurts from all the research I've had to do." She turned to him and offered a smile. Her shoulders relaxed a bit, but her brown eyes couldn't hide her weariness. "I am looking forward to dinner. I really need this. I appreciate your invitation. Let's just hope it doesn't get interrupted by a crisis."

He shrugged. "If it does, I'm flexible. I can always get everything to go and bring it to you later."

"That's awfully sweet of you, but I wouldn't want you to go to any trouble."

It was their turn at the host station, and they stepped forward. He turned his attention to the hostess. "Two. For Patteson."

As they were led to their table, the fire in the fireplace at the center of the room crackled and the warmth greeted them.

Beautiful exposed beams and an open view of the kitchen added to the restaurant's charm. He held out a chair for Carrie and she took it.

"Thank you." Her voice was soft in the din of the busy dining room.

"You're welcome." He walked over to the chair across from hers and took his seat. "I love this place. Hope you're hungry."

The hostess handed them menus. "Enjoy your dinner."

Carrie glanced down at the menu and her eyes widened a bit. "Wow. This looks incredible."

Their brief conversation earlier had filled him in that she hadn't eaten here yet. A fact that made him smile. It would be fun to see what she thought of the place. "Hopefully it will be a favorite for you as well."

"Anything in particular that you recommend?" She hadn't looked up from the menu yet.

"Everything." He set down his own menu and leaned his elbows on the table. "Seriously. I've had everything they offer."

When she glanced up at him, their eyes connected, and she tilted her head. "Everything? I'm impressed." Slowly, a grin tipped the corners of her mouth and the hard edges around her eyes eased. Then her shoulders visibly relaxed. With a deep breath, she set her menu down. "Thanks, Scott. I really needed this."

"I can tell." He'd been the one to do that. It was all the encouragement he needed. His stomach relaxed. This was the right step for him.

Their server appeared. "May I start you off with one of our craft beers?"

"I'd love one of your house-brewed cream sodas." Scott pitched in his choice.

Her eyes widened. "Oh, that sounds good. How's the root beer? Is it house-brewed too?"

"Yes, and it is excellent." Scott sent her a smile, leaned back, and watched her.

She looked up at their server. "Then I'll have a root beer." Her blond hair was pulled back in a ponytail, which seemed to be her hairstyle of choice for work. It accentuated her neck and jawline. Her profile was just as lovely.

"Any appetizers?" The seasoned waiter didn't write anything down.

Carrie looked to Scott. "There are so many choices. What's your recommendation?"

For a second, he missed what she'd said as he'd been studying her, then his brain caught him up to the conversation. "How about we split a skillet jalapeño cornbread and then each get a bowl of the seafood chowder?" He licked his lips. He could practically taste it.

"Let's do it." Her eyes crinkled at the corners.

"Perfect choice." Their server smiled. "I'll be back momentarily with your drinks. Take your time with the menu."

It was only a couple minutes before he returned with their drinks.

Carrie took a sip immediately. "Oh, yum. I think that's the best I've ever had."

Scott ordered the shrimp and grits, and she ordered the Alaska alder-grilled salmon. A basket arrived with slices of homemade spent-grain bread, and his mouth began to water. "Do you mind if I pray?"

"I'd love that. Thank you." Placing her napkin in her lap, she bowed her head.

He offered up a quick prayer of thanks and then offered her a slice of bread. "Fun fact, this bread is made by a nearby bakery. They use the leftover spent grain from here."

Her eyebrows rose. "That's pretty cool."

"Yeah, then the rest of the leftover grain is sent to the reindeer farm." He shut his mouth before he started spouting too much information.

"I've been wanting to get out to Palmer and see the farm. I hear it's quite the sight." She buttered her slice of bread, then tore it in half.

Placing her elbows on the table, she said, "So, tell me about living in Alaska. Have you lived here long?"

Slathering butter on his own slice, he wiggled his eyebrows. "Yep. My whole life. Alaska grown, as they say." He took a bite and then swallowed. "What would you like to know? If I don't know the answer, I bet I know someone who does." His attempt to tone it down probably wasn't working. But she did ask.

"I've seen the sweatshirts with Alaska Grown on them." She grinned, then took a bite of her bread. "Mm. I have to say, Alaskans are some of the coolest people I've ever met. I love how everyone pitches in in a crisis. And they seem so down-to-earth."

"I couldn't put it better myself." Encouraged by her assessment of Alaskans, he leaned back in his chair. Their soup and cornbread arrived, giving him a nice pause. "The maple butter puts it over the top. Do you mind?" He held up the butter to spread it over the whole skillet.

"Go for it." She gave him a wide grin. "I do love butter."

Conversation flowed with ease and comfort as they enjoyed their chowder and cornbread. A stark difference to the afternoon's coffee. The more the tension in her visibly eased, the more Scott relaxed and enjoyed the simple time being with her.

As she opened up, he learned a lot. One of six kids, she'd made a name for herself in her small town in law enforcement but had always wanted to do something bigger. Like the FBI.

Her family cheered her on, and when she said she was moving to Alaska, no one had doubted her or thought she was nuts. Which was refreshing. It was obvious she was ambitious, but there was a natural air about her—what you see is what you get.

"Well, I for one am glad you followed the call to come to the last frontier." Hopefully he wasn't coming on too strong. He didn't know how else to act other than just be honest and be himself. Dorky tech geek and all.

"Thank you. I'm glad I came as well. I've been here awhile now, but I've spent so much time in training that I really haven't explored as much of Alaska as I would like. I love winter, so that's good. But I can't wait for—oh, what do they call it? The time when all the snow melts?"

He loved the eagerness on her face. "Breakup."

"That's it! Breakup. I hear it can be fast and furious and people wash their cars every day, but spring roars in and tourist season will be right around the corner."

"That pretty much sums it up. Normally, breakup lasts about a week or so. You know, there's a lot to do here year-round. Do you snowshoe, ski, or ride a snowmachine?"

She released a light laugh behind her napkin. "We call them snowmobiles back home. For some reason, that makes me giggle every time I hear it. Although, I must admit, I like *snowmachine* better." After another sip from her glass, she leaned forward with a conspiratorial gaze. "I would love to snowshoe sometime. Or take snowmachines out. As long as you know where you're going."

Sounded like she was up for a second date. "Let me know when your schedule allows for it, and I'll see if I can line up a day off."

"It's a date." With a grin, she lifted a spoonful from her bowl to her mouth. "Mm, this is the best chowder I've ever eaten."

"Wonderful to hear." Their server had returned and filled in the next few seconds with his presentation of their dinner.

It gave Scott a moment to savor the fact that he had another outing with Carrie to look forward to in the near future. It had definitely been too long since he'd done this, because he felt like a gawky teenager on his first date. It was an odd sensation to have at thirty years old.

Their server left, and the dining room buzzed with conversation while the scents of fire-roasted pizzas and meats filled the air.

"This has been perfect, thank you." Carrie dabbed at her mouth with her napkin.

"Thanks for agreeing to come along." He forked a bite of creamy grits into his mouth. The smoky flavor of the cheese came through perfectly.

"I've talked so much about myself, it seems a little one-sided. Tell me about you. I know you were born and raised here—what about your family?"

"Mom and Dad are still here. Loving every minute of retirement in Alaska. My sister Leah is a second-grade teacher. My younger sister, Becca . . . she recently returned after"—he paused and searched for the right word that wouldn't violate Becca's privacy—"battling an addiction."

It was obvious Carrie had picked up on the need for discretion. "Well, I pray that she's doing better."

"Yes, she is. Thank you." He rolled his thoughts around in his mind, needing to change the subject and hoping to say the right thing. "Even though the circumstances of our first few meetings weren't good, I have to say, I'm really glad we met. I'm enjoying getting to know you." Once the words were out, he wanted to scold himself for being so stiff.

"Me too." Her smile put him at ease.

He definitely didn't want to wait for a day when they could schedule an all-day outing. "Would you like to have dinner again later this week?"

Her phone buzzed on the table. "I'd like that."

"Tomorrow?" Did he sound too eager?

"Sounds great." She lifted her phone and glanced at the screen. "Sorry, I've got to take this."

"Not a problem." He turned his attention to his food.

But then her voice changed. As he caught her gaze, her face paled, her eyes wide. She laid her phone down. "I've got to go. There's been a murder."

CHAPTER FIVE

DOWN
8. Seven letters. A pilot's home away from home.

January 29—6:03 a.m.
Alaska Bureau of Investigation

ALL THE COFFEE IN THE world couldn't make up for the fact that she hadn't gotten a lick of sleep last night.

Carrie chugged another sugared-up cup of the black stuff and prayed for the energy and brain power to make it through.

The call last night had jolted her out of a relaxing evening into the world of mayhem where she was now entrenched. Hearing that there was a murder case for her to investigate was one thing. But hearing the rest . . . well, it had made her stomach drop down into her feet.

The cause of death wasn't known right away. It wouldn't even have been labeled a murder except for the fact that Anchorage Police found a sticky note on the forehead of the deceased. That's why the ABI had been called.

The bright green Post-it read: CLUE. 8 DOWN.

What did it mean? She'd called Kevin immediately, and he'd headed back to the office to help her. So far, they had nothing.

The victim's home hadn't given up a single fingerprint, hair, or the slightest bit of DNA evidence. The perpetrator had been thorough.

She and Kevin returned to every file that she'd combed through yesterday. Every outstanding missing person's report, every death. The problem was, they didn't know what they were looking for.

There wasn't time for sleep. She was determined to figure out this puzzle.

But how?

Kevin had given in and taken a nap on the couch in his office at four in the morning. He'd told her to go home. But she didn't. Couldn't. As much as her body needed the rest, her mind wouldn't stop spinning.

"I've left you clues."

The taunt repeated itself over and over in her mind.

Clues.

What clues?

Other than the heater at the mayor's cabin outside of Fairbanks and the sticky note last night, she couldn't find any other evidence or any other sign of a clue. Not of any sort. It was infuriating.

"You didn't go home, I take it?" The thump of Kevin's crutches accompanied the step of his good foot.

"No. This is driving me crazy." She placed her palms on the sides of her forehead and zigzagged her gaze over the mess of her own making. Papers were strewn across not only her desk but the desk she'd dragged across the floor to give her more space to spread out. The cart that usually made its way around the office delivering mail, coffee, and donuts was there, too, loaded with paper.

Sadly, none of it had helped.

"Any news from the medical examiner?" He propped himself next to her.

Carrie checked her watch. "No. Not yet. But she said she'd do the autopsy as soon as she finished the one she was working on."

"Should be any time then. That's good." He hobbled around her desk and sat on the other side. "Why don't you take a break from spinning your wheels and walk me through everything that we've got so far."

"Okay." She let out a long breath. "But I don't really think I have—" Her desk phone rang and she reached for it. "ABI, Carrie Kintz."

"This is Dr. Blanchard. I've finished my examination of the body."

"Thank you. I'm sure it was a long night." She put the call on speaker so Kevin could hear. What a relief. Maybe they'd finally have some answers.

"It's our job, isn't it, Ms. Kintz?" The woman cleared her throat. "Cause of death was heart failure."

"Heart failure?" Carrie looked at the file in front of her. "Wasn't the victim only thirty-six years old?"

"That is correct. The victim's pacemaker forced his heart to beat too fast. Over the course of about twelve hours, it seemed the victim was in distress, heart beating faster and faster. Ultimately, it caused his death."

Carrie could feel her brow scrunching low. "Why did he have a pacemaker?"

"A car accident several years ago did damage to his heart and lungs. The pacemaker was inserted"—a pause and shuffling of papers sounded over the phone—"two years ago. The patient was in great health after the surgery and responded well. There's been no evidence of any issues. The device had been doing its job."

"What would cause a pacemaker to speed up like that?" Carrie hoped that Dr. Blanchard would forgive her ignorance in medical matters. "Was it some sort of malfunction?"

"Most definitely not." The doctor's response was firm. "The data we gathered from it shows the details. We're sending it to your forensic people. Someone did this intentionally. The device was hacked."

Her breath caught in her throat, and Kevin asked the doctor several questions. By the time he was done and they'd disconnected the call, Carrie was ready to bolt out of her chair and go scream outside.

Kevin's face was grim as he stood.

She locked eyes with him. "The pacemaker was hacked. The traffic lights were hacked. The mayor's cabin up in Fairbanks was hacked. These can't all be coincidence." Her jaw clenched.

"Yeah. I'm not a big believer in coincidences. At this point, I think we have to assume they're connected." He picked up the evidence bag with the sticky note.

"Whoever is behind this wants us to feel stupid. Like he had to give us a hint."

"Well, let's be honest. He *did* give us a hint. Otherwise we wouldn't have been called in." He rapped a knuckle on Carrie's desk. "I don't like it any more than you do, but this is where we're at."

"But what—" She wasn't even sure which questions to ask. "Eight down. Does it mean they've already killed eight? So there are five more bodies out there that we haven't found? Or haven't connected to the case?" Her next thought was one she didn't want to utter. But she had to. "Or does it mean something totally different? What am I missing?"

"No matter what it means . . ." Kevin shook his head and blew out a long breath.

She finished the thought. "We have a serial killer. Don't we?"

"I hate to say it, but I think that's how we have to look at it."

Silence filled the massive room as she digested the news.

Her phone rang again, and she jumped. She took a deep breath before answering it. "ABI, Carrie Kintz."

"This is Rebecca Wilson from channel two, KTUU-TV. I was wondering if I could get a statement from you about a story we're covering today."

"A statement? About what?"

"The news services were all sent an anonymous tip about a serial killer leaving clues. You're named as the head of the investigation."

◻ ◻ ◻

DOWN
8. Six letters. Snowed under.

January 29—9:00 a.m.
Big Lake, Alaska

Griz scanned the room.

Eager faces greeted him. The most trusted of his loyal followers.

Fifty men and women handpicked, groomed, and willing to do whatever it took to make their vision a reality.

"Good morning." He liked punctuality, and everyone was either in the room or on the big screen via his end-to-end encrypted video platform. "Thank you for answering the call and supporting the most important cause of our lifetimes."

Affirming nods and applause filled the air.

These people were sold out for a change in the government. Just like him.

Perfect.

He held up a hand for quiet. "In the past year, we've accomplished more than anyone thought possible. In time, the world will see that we are independent and more powerful than the America that is becoming more divided every day. No one will be able to stop us." The passion from each of the Members made the air practically sizzle.

He paused for effect. "Our goal is still the same. To see Alaska secede from the United States and become its own country. We can't allow the stupidity in Washington to continue. Career politicians are so corrupt; they have no business making decisions for us. They try to tell us what to do. Try to control our resources. Try to control our land and people. Yet none of them have any inkling or concern about what is best for us."

Several of the Members pounded on the tables in front of them. The drumming grew louder until it drowned out any other sound.

With a smile, Griz continued. "They have put a stranglehold on our resources. Resources that don't belong to them. Resources they don't deserve."

More drumming.

He shouted over the noise, his fist held high. "They want to pretend like our voice doesn't matter."

The pounding increased in speed.

"They want to control every aspect of our lives and keep us reliant upon the government like prisoners in our own land."

For several seconds, he allowed the rhythm to build.

Bowing his head, he held up a hand once again.

Silence blanketed the room.

With a slow lift of his chin, he pinned each person with his gaze. One at a time, he stared every one of them down. "But they will pay attention and listen."

Just like each Member waited with bated breath for him to speak.

He had no intention of letting them know his plan. He wasn't that stupid. The plans for the group would move forward. Raising money. Gathering loyalists. Planting seeds of power in every branch and sector of government, each cog in the wheel of society's infrastructure, every aspect and segment of their culture. By the time he was done with his little sideshow, they would all know his power and bow to him alone.

He would be in control. Of everything.

And as they rose to the New World power, no one would stand in his way. No one.

◻ ◻ ◻

DOWN

8. Eleven letters. Irregular heartbeat.

January 29—3:30 p.m.
Cyber Solutions Office, Anchorage

Scott lifted his phone to his ear and listened to the other line ring. After the third ring, it connected.

"Hey." Carrie's voice was breathless and tired.

"Hey yourself. You doing okay? We still on for dinner?" He kept his tone upbeat.

She sighed. "I don't know. It's been quite a day. I don't know when I'll be able to leave."

A male voice in the background said something Scott couldn't understand.

"That was Kevin. Did you hear what he said?"

"No, sorry."

"He asked if it was you. Said he put in a call to your boss earlier. Seems like we need you again on this case."

Scott scanned the office. "I just got back here myself. Let me go track Tim down. Want me to call you right back?"

"Sure." She yawned. "Sorry. Call me back. Which reminds me, sorry that I had to leave abruptly last night. It was the best evening I've had in, well, a long time."

"It's not a problem. I had a great time too. Talk to you in a few minutes." With a smile, he went in search of the interim boss.

Tim rounded the corner and pointed at him. "I was just looking for you."

"Yeah, I just talked to the ABI."

"I cleared it with Mac. We're shorthanded, but he's got some feelers out for new hires. I told them they could have you for as long as needed. Not every day we get asked to help with a serial killer case." Tim's eyes widened as he gripped Scott's shoulder. "Better you than me. I don't do well with the thought of dead people."

"Can't say I've ever been around dead people, but I'll do my best."

After a quick briefing with Tim over the other projects he'd been assigned, Scott tugged on his coat, threw his messenger bag over his shoulder, and headed out to his SUV. He dialed Carrie's cell, and the call connected to his vehicle.

She answered on the first ring. "Hey again."

"Looks like I'm headed your way. Is it all right if I take the time to pick up some food for us? I have a feeling once we get started, there won't be a lot of breaks."

"Oh, that would be terrific. I'm starved. Kevin and I haven't even had lunch, and Alan just got back." Her voice sounded a bit lighter than a few seconds ago.

He would do whatever he could to ease the burden. "How many need food? Are there more in the office?"

"No. Just four of us. You, Alan, Kevin, and me. It was just Kevin

and me, but Alan wrapped up his investigation sooner than antici-
pated. He just flew in. Good thing, too, because everyone else is out
on cases, and I'm in way over my head."

"It's going to be a long evening, isn't it?" He winced as he said it,
but better to be prepared.

"Let's just say I haven't left since yesterday."

Oh boy. This case must be worse than he expected. "You know
what, if I call Moose's Tooth right now and get some pizzas ordered,
by the time I get there, they should be ready. I'll be at your offices in
about forty-five minutes. Tell me what everyone wants."

"Let me ask the guys what they want, and I'll look at a menu."

He waited several minutes while conversation happened on the
other end.

With a clearing of her throat, she was back. "Okay, one Call of
the Wild, one Lu-Wow, one Backpacker, and one Elf on the Shelf,
please."

He tapped the order into a note on his phone. "Got it. I'll be there
as soon as I can."

"Thanks."

They hung up and he called Moose's Tooth to get the order in.
Thank goodness it was the middle of the afternoon. Off-peak hours
meant the place wouldn't be quite as slammed as normal. They said
they should have it ready in record time.

Half an hour later, the scent of dough, cheeses, and meats filled
his vehicle. As he drove to the ABI office, he shot up a quick prayer.
"God, I have no idea what I'm heading into, but it sounds intense.
I need Your guidance. Give me whatever wisdom I need to face the
situation and help however I can." He cranked up the radio and made
his way through town.

Bitter cold greeted him after he parked and opened his door. Ugh.
It was five below zero. He grabbed the food and his bag and ran toward the door.

Alan greeted him at the entry. "Glad you're here. We've just had
another development." His face was grim.

"What happened?"

"It's hit the papers. And it's not pretty. Carrie is named as the investigator, and whoever's behind all this just called her out. They're taunting her."

CHAPTER SIX

DOWN
8. Four letters. It's breath taking.

January 29—4:23 p.m.
Alaska Bureau of Investigation

EVEN THE AROMA OF PIZZA—her favorite food on the planet—couldn't help right now.

Scott had obviously arrived along with the food, but she couldn't look up. Not yet. With her head buried in her arms on her desk, Carrie took steadying breaths. As soon as she'd read the highlighted news feature, she thought she might be sick. It had been bad enough that the TV station wanted her statement. Kevin had advised against it until they had more information because the tip was so cryptic. *"People are dying."*

There was a serial killer on the loose.

They've left clues but think the police aren't smart enough to figure it out.

This? It had taken it to another level. With *her* under the magnifying glass.

The guys had been kind enough to stay silent and give her some space, but she couldn't hide from this.

The phones had been ringing nonstop for the past twenty minutes. Kevin told the front desk to handle everything related to the news coverage. No calls from the media or press were to be put through.

Lifting her head, she took another long breath. Kevin and Alan watched from chairs around her desk. Another desk filled with pizza boxes was where she spotted Scott. He didn't say anything, but she could sense his unease. "All right." She turned her attention to Kevin. "How should I deal with this?"

The seasoned investigator shook his head and swiped a hand down his face. "*You* don't deal with this. *We* do. It's just like any other case. We take one step at a time, together. As a team." Leaning forward, he pointed to her computer monitor. "Read it again."

Swallowing the lump in her throat, she looked at the screen and prepared herself for the words. "'To the citizens of Anchorage,'" she read, "'I feel it is my duty to inform you of the grave situation in which we find ourselves. People are dying. People will continue to die. And the authorities have no control. They haven't even figured out the deaths that are connected.

"'Because I care about you, it is imperative to keep you aware. You are not safe. You would be wise to remember what happened up in Fairbanks. You cannot stop this. Ms. Carrie Kintz of the ABI cannot stop this. As she is the lead investigator on this case, you would be wise to show the Anchorage Police and Alaska State Troopers that you do not have faith in their efforts any longer.

"'More people will die. I'll be in touch, so watch and learn.'"

Leaning back, she couldn't stop the chill that raced up her spine.

The puzzled look on Scott's face turned to anger. "Who would print such a thing? Why?"

Kevin grimaced. "The *Anchorage Daily News*. The editor is on her way over here now with an explanation."

"How much you wanna bet that she was blackmailed in some way?" Alan looked like he could spit nails. "I know her. There's no way she would allow that to be printed unless there was some kind of major . . . incentive."

"Why would this person name Carrie?" Scott crossed his arms

over his chest and paced. "I don't like it." The fact that he defended her would be sweet in other circumstances. Not now.

Carrie sighed. "I don't exactly like it either, but let's face it. I'm the newbie. Easy to pick on. Especially since I was the one on call for the case last night. It wouldn't have been hard for someone to research and figure out that the"—she made exaggerated finger quotes in the air—"'rookie' was on the case." Although that was the least of her worries, it was still humiliating.

Kevin stood and propped himself up with his crutches. "I know this isn't easy. But we have a lot of work ahead of us. Carrie, I'm almost certain that the mayor's murder was also the work of our UNSUB, but I'm a bit incapacitated. Since you were the lead on the traffic accident, you're the lead on this. I'll help however you need, but your job is to rise above the bait and find this killer."

He waved a hand toward the pizzas. "Scott was kind enough to bring us some food and will be assisting again. I think we should go into the conference room with our laptops and every piece of evidence we have, eat, and then buckle down with what we've got." He turned to Scott. "Thanks for coming in. We're going to need your cyber expertise now more than ever."

"Glad to help."

Everyone shuffled around, gathering what they needed and moving it into the conference room.

Carrie didn't want to admit it, but she was hungry. And that always made her grumpy. So, yeah, she'd been called out in the paper. Her dreams of making it to the FBI were smashed unless she could catch this scumbag. As much as she wanted to keep a positive attitude, the negative thoughts spiraled. She set up a little nest for herself at the conference table and then headed to the ladies' room. Some cold water on her face and neck might help her to focus and calm down.

In the bathroom, she took a long hard look at herself in the mirror. Had she made the right decision coming up here?

Yeah, she loved her job. But if one crazy person could get the public to distrust her, would she ever have a chance to prove otherwise? One thing was certain through all this, she didn't like media attention.

After splashing her face several times with cold water, she couldn't delay the inevitable any longer. Time to get back out there and catch a killer.

Kevin was waiting for her outside the bathroom, along with another man she didn't recognize.

"Agent Mike Hudson, FBI." The stranger showed her his badge. "Could we talk for a minute?"

The FBI? What were they doing here? Even though this case unnerved her, she couldn't bear the thought of it being taken away. That would be even more humiliating than the press coverage.

"Of course." Her tone held a bite to it as she crossed her arms over her chest.

He held up his hands and backed up a step. "Forgive me, I am not here to take the reins. This case still belongs to the ABI."

Relaxing a hair, she replied, "Good to know. Why *are* you here?"

"Our office is still entrenched in the joint investigation with the ABI into the 26 Below attack. But we wanted you to be aware that we are watching this situation with a close eye. There are enough similarities to raise some red flags. For the sake of the population, I hope nothing comes of it. But, if we have to step in, I hope we'll have your full cooperation?"

Carrie shared a glance with her mentor.

He shrugged. "We have no choice. But it won't matter. You'll catch the guy."

"I've always hated the way television crime shows portray the different law enforcement agencies unwilling to work together." She stuck out her hand. "Rest assured, if we need your help, we'll call and if the time comes for you to be involved, we will gladly work with you." Was that diplomatic enough without giving up to this guy?

"All right then. Keep us in the loop." With a last nod toward her, Mike Hudson turned on his heel and walked away.

Carrie narrowed her gaze at Kevin. "Did I handle that adequately?"

"Perfect."

When she entered the conference room, a tall woman with dark brown hair stood there with her hands clasped in front of her. "I'm Gretchen Silva. Managing editor at the *Anchorage Daily News.*"

Carrie nodded at her and took her seat.

"Mrs. Silva was just explaining to us what happened." Alan held out a hand toward the woman. "Would you mind starting back at the beginning?"

The woman's straight hair hung to her shoulders, and her mouth was pinched into a thin line. "I dropped my son off at school this morning like usual. When I arrived at the office, this"—she held out a packet—"was on my desk. A messenger dropped it off prior to my arrival. Inside the envelope is a phone with a video of my son blindfolded, bound, and gagged. The note instructed me to print the enclosed story on the front page if I wanted my son back."

"You didn't call the police?" Alan wrote on a notepad in front of him while Kevin opened the packet.

"No. It said if I did, my son would be dead. But as soon as I made the story public, he would be returned." She took a breath and looked out into the squad room.

Carrie followed her gaze through the window and saw a small boy sitting at a desk with two APD officers beside him.

Mrs. Silva continued. "I confided with a few of my colleagues to make it happen, and within five minutes of the story going live, my son arrived at the office. I called the police immediately after that. We've been with them this whole time, giving our statements. They examined the packet, but there were no fingerprints. The phone is a burner that was purchased two years ago in California. They're trying to track the original buyer, but I doubt they'll find anything. As crazy as this person is, they're smart."

"Does your son remember anything that would help the police?" Carrie's knee bounced up and down under the table.

"No. He was blindfolded the whole time. Most likely left alone because he doesn't remember hearing anything either." The editor's hands shook in front of her. The stiff facade was beginning to crumble.

Kevin turned to Alan. "I'm sure APD is on it, but have a look at any security cameras there and in the area. To return the boy in five minutes is quick."

"On it." Alan left the room and made a call from the squad room.

"I'm very sorry for all this." The woman caught Carrie's eye. "Please accept my apology, Ms. Kintz. I'm not one to allow slander—"

"Let me stop you there. Don't worry about me. I can't imagine what it felt like to be in your shoes and to have to make that decision. I probably would have done the same thing if my child were in danger." Carrie leaned forward and smiled at the woman, hoping to give her some semblance of comfort. "I'd rather have my name run through the mud than see something happen to your son." That was true. As soon as the words were out, her spirits bolstered. This wasn't about her. The maniac behind this just wanted to get under the skin of her team any way they could. Emotions had run too high today. She was going to have to work on that if she was going to be a better investigator.

"There's one more thing—" The tough newswoman's frown deepened. "They promised to leave us alone as long as I print whatever they request in the future."

Kevin crossed his arms over his chest. "Did you agree to this?"

"I had no way to respond."

"Well, we'll cross that bridge when we come to it. You need to let us know if you receive something else. But it's best to cooperate for your safety. For now. I'll talk with the APD and make sure you have security around the clock until we catch whoever is behind this." Her supervisor nodded at the woman and then back to Carrie. He pulled his crutches up under his arms and followed her out to the squad room where the officers waited.

The editor left with her son and the APD a few minutes later. They'd endured a horrible situation today. Carrie didn't envy them the next few days as they recovered. Staring down at the files in front of her, she determined to ignore her personal emotions and simply focus on the case. That's where she needed to be right now.

Scott cleared his throat and broke the weird silence. "I don't know about you guys, but I'm starved. Why don't we eat while you catch me up on this case." He opened a box and pulled out a slice. "It's still *kinda* warm."

She smiled to herself as the guys dug in and she opened the file from last night. Maybe her stomach would settle enough for her to eat in a little bit.

A small piece of paper lay on top of the contents. That hadn't been there before. In all capital letters it read:

TRY TO KEEP UP

◻ ◻ ◻

DOWN
8. Eight letters. Silent killer.

January 29—7:30 p.m.
Alaska Bureau of Investigation

Scanning the code from the victim's pacemaker was a bit more intense than Scott imagined it would be. Sure, there was a printout of the data for the doctors. But his job was to get behind it and analyze the actual code. That's how it would have been hacked. Medical devices weren't easy to get into like the crime shows on TV suggested. There was some sophisticated technology behind them.

He hated to admit it, but whoever hacked the pacemaker had skills. The more he studied the code, the more he thought about the traffic lights . . . and then about Fairbanks. Maybe he should give Jason another call. Maybe this was connected.

He'd asked the team if they thought the events were connected as he ate a piece of leftover pizza, but the general consensus had been that the cyberattack up in Fairbanks had been about showing power. Hatred of the government.

This was—at least what they could deduce from what they knew now—personal, individual. All of which pointed to a serial killer. The two weren't connected.

But what was the killer after? And why? It didn't make sense. Especially with the return of the editor's son. Why kill people and then kidnap a boy, only to return him? Simply to get their weird piece in the news?

His thoughts spun in the other direction. Why put it out there for everyone to see?

Carrie strode back into the room, a pencil behind her ear and an open file in her hands. "Hey, can you guys help me out for a minute?"

"Sure."

"Yeah."

"Of course."

Even though they all answered in the affirmative, it was more than apparent they were bleary-eyed.

She set the file down and went to the whiteboard. "All right. Scott's thoughts about the Fairbanks attack made me pause and rethink things. I started a profile of our killer." A blue marker squeaked along the surface as she wrote. "First, they want attention. Taking lives isn't enough. Thus, the phone call, the newspaper, the notes sent to media. They're killing people for a reason. But what is it?"

She shook her head and looked at them. "That's the part that's stumping me. The motivation. Second, they're smart and want us to *know* that they're smart. Honestly, I think they want to prove that they're smarter than we are. But not just us. The world." She sighed as she stared at what she'd written. "Third, they want a chase." She drew an arrow linking back to number two. "Again, because they need to show us how smart they are. That they have power. Sound familiar?" She stepped back.

"Sounds like you're pretty convinced it's the same person who murdered the mayor up in Fairbanks." Alan leaned back and locked his hands behind his head.

Oh? This was new to Scott. "I don't have that file. Want to fill me in?" He shifted forward.

"Yeah, I'm definitely gravitating toward that theory. But that means . . . I think Scott was right."

Now he was really confused. "Wait. I was right? About what?"

Her gaze connected with his. Intense and foreboding. "That this could all be connected to what the media has dubbed the 26 Below attack. We're pretty sure the mayor was murdered in connection with the cyberattacks. She was implicated in them." She bit her lip. "I know it's far-fetched, but I don't think we should ignore the possibility."

Kevin's jaw clenched and unclenched as his gaze narrowed. "This case keeps getting worse and worse." He leaned toward Scott. "There was pandemonium after the cyberattack on Fairbanks."

Scott nodded, remembering the situation all too well. "My buddy Jason was working on it with the city government up there when it happened." He frowned. "But I didn't hear anything from him about the mayor."

Kevin shifted in his seat, rubbing his good knee. "Not surprising. They didn't connect it publicly. In the middle of getting the city back on the grid, the mayor disappeared. Fairbanks police found her a couple days later, decomposing in her family cabin. But the place was clean. No sign of forced entry. No prints. Just a crusty old space heater and an open window despite a state-of-the-art security system and generator. We suspect the system was hacked, but all hands were on deck for the attack on Fairbanks. I'm not sure if the system was ever looked into."

"What do you think?" Carrie's arms were crossed over her middle.

Scott studied the board and then the notes on his computer. "I'm inclined to agree with you. The entire attack up in Fairbanks was cyber. Sounds like the murder of the mayor was also. Now this?" He pointed to everything she'd written out. "I know I'm not as acquainted with the details as you guys are, but I thought they caught everyone connected to 26 Below. How can our suspect—whoever it is—be a part of this? And why the different pattern? I'm not used to trying to jump into criminal minds, so you're going to have to help me grasp this."

"As far as anyone knew, they caught the men behind the attack." Kevin fidgeted with a crutch. "But there was evidence found in the mayor's office connecting her to the planning. Carrie isn't convinced she was in on it—which would mean it was planted." He shook his head.

"Besides, your guy up in Fairbanks helped the team thwart the bad guys and get the power restored. There wasn't a peep after that. The guys in jail had everyone else killed that worked with them before they were caught. It was quite the body count, all gunshots to the chest."

"Maybe that's what they wanted us to believe." Carrie shuffled through the files on the table. "I think we need everything we can find on what happened up in Fairbanks." She looked at Scott. "Do you think you could talk to your friend and get him to brief us?"

"Sure." He picked up his phone and sent Jason a text, labeling it urgent.

"Thanks. We're going to need all the help we can get on this." Kevin's attention went back to Carrie who was studying the board. "What are you thinking?"

"With my profiler training, there's one question that's really bugging me—and scaring me, if I'm honest—about the person behind this."

Kevin straightened. "What is it?"

Her mouth pressed into a thin, bloodless line. "Is the person we're after a psychopath or sociopath? Neither answer is pleasant. Neither one has empathy. Sociopaths have a bit more of a conscience, but not much. Psychopaths believe their actions are justified. There's absolutely no remorse. One is most likely a talented actor—they know how to act like they care. They're good at mimicking the emotions they see in others. The other does what they want without caring about how anyone else is affected."

Alan's arms crossed over his chest as he nodded and his frown deepened. "No matter which one our UNSUB is, it freaks me out."

Scott understood that feeling. More than he wanted to right now. But still . . . "Why does the question of psychopath or sociopath bug you?" Maybe if he understood all this a bit more, it would help him with the case. "Profiling is way out of my league."

"It bugs me"—Carrie pursed her lips and chewed on the inside of her cheek for a second—"because if we know which one we're dealing with, it could help us stop him."

CHAPTER SEVEN

DOWN
8. Eight letters. Mishap and mayhem.

January 30—1:15 p.m.
Palmer, Alaska

"THANK YOU FOR TAKING THE time to meet me." One of the younger and more arrogant Members clasped his hands behind his back.

"I don't have a lot of time. What's so urgent that we needed to meet out here?" The icy wind tore through Griz's coat, but he wouldn't show this peon the effect it had on him.

A smirk filled the man's face.

What was he up to?

The Member rubbed the corners of his mouth. "There are a few of us who are a bit concerned about the fact that things in Fairbanks didn't go as planned. You failed."

Time to cut the skeptic off before he could cause trouble. "A few of you? Or just you?"

"I'm not the only one with concerns. Many are worried that you are obsessed and spiraling." The words were a threat.

Griz rose to his full height and glared at him. "Let's get one thing straight right now. We didn't fail. We pulled off the most elaborate hack of all time. It fulfilled every aspect of our plan. The Members have no room for an arrogant fool in the midst of us."

"Arrogant fool? Really? Have you looked in the mirror lately? We're still under the thumb of Washington." The naysayer shook his head.

Griz stepped closer. Allowed the fury to rise up within him. "I don't have to tell you what happens to those who disagree with me. This isn't a game."

Fear flashed across the man's face. Then he narrowed his eyes and clenched his jaw. "I'm not here to play games." But the bobbing of his Adam's apple as he swallowed gave him away.

"Then you won't mind the next job I have for you."

Another swallow. "Of course not. As long as it lines up with our manifesto. Secede. Be independent. Become the next world power untainted by career politicians and the ridiculousness that ensues from leaders kowtowing to the noise of the masses. I'm committed to our cause."

"Are you now?" Griz shoved his hands into his pockets and watched the guy squirm for a second. He'd have to find out if there really were more like him among the Members. It didn't matter what the man said, thought, or did. Nothing could save him now.

Griz's next victim had just been identified.

◻ ◻ ◻

DOWN
8. Five letters. Isolated.

January 30—2:15 p.m.
9,000 feet above sea level: Latitude 61.43777° N, Longitude 147.75056° W

Something didn't feel right. He couldn't figure out what it was, but something was off. All the instruments in the small plane were functioning correctly. He'd checked and double-checked.

Preflight check had been perfect. Everything had gone great during takeoff. Everything had been smooth since.

But in the last twenty minutes . . . something in the back of his mind was setting off warning bells. No matter what he did, he couldn't shake it.

Then there were the clouds that he'd flown into a few minutes ago. Thick and swirling.

He couldn't seem to get out of them. Couldn't see a thing. And that unnerved him.

Had he gotten off course? He checked the instruments again and shook his head. He was exactly where he should be.

But when he lifted his gaze, his heart plummeted.

Yanking back on the yoke, he willed the small plane to gain altitude.

But it didn't work. The face of the snow-covered Chugach Mountains sucked the nose of his plane into it.

The brilliant white of the snow was the last thing he saw before he closed his eyes for impact.

◻ ◻ ◻

DOWN
8. Seven letters. Misdemeanor or felony battery.

January 31—10:13 a.m.
Cyber Solutions Office

Scott had filled Tim in on what was going on, and now he felt the urge to get back as soon as possible to help Carrie. Cyber Solutions agreed to assist the ABI with the case, and Scott was on their clock for the foreseeable future. He just needed to grab a few things from his office.

He snagged a box from the supply closet. Actually, he needed quite a bit of equipment, and he didn't want to keep trekking back and forth to his car. One thing was for sure, he needed his most powerful laptops.

Kyle knocked at his door. "Hear you're on a wild case."

"Yeah. I tell you what, I love what we do here, but it's a whole 'nother world in law enforcement. And they really need us. People are getting crazier every year, it seems."

"Ain't that the truth." Kyle stepped closer. "I don't want to stick my nose in, but Tim briefed us yesterday on what he could and told us to keep our eyes and ears open to help you. Anyway . . . ya know how I love crossword puzzles, right?"

"Yeah." The kid was always doing at least one on a computer monitor, had a book of them on his desk with a pencil, and he kept multiple magazines with the crosswords open and in progress. "How many of those puzzle books do you finish in a week?"

Kyle shrugged. "Two, maybe three."

"Impressive."

The kid blushed. "Nah. I just enjoy the puzzles. Gotta keep my mind occupied."

"Ah. Why the books though? Aren't they all digitized now?"

"They are. But I'm a purist. Online, it's too easy to cheat. And sometimes clue websites give you the wrong word. Messes up your whole puzzle. Besides, I'm on computers all day. Sometimes it's nice to hold a book in my hands."

Scott glanced at his watch. This conversation was taking up too much time. "That makes sense. Well, good to catch up, but I've gotta run back to the ABI."

Kyle nodded. "That's why I stopped you. One of my crossword puzzle clues caught my eye." He held out a magazine to Scott. "It's a long shot, but maybe it'll help."

Scott couldn't imagine how a crossword puzzle in a magazine could help them out, but he didn't want to burst the kid's bubble. "Um, yeah. Sure. Put it in the box here, and I'll take it over."

"No, listen. It's highlighted. You know the guy with the pacemaker? The clue is: 'The heart's pacemaker.' The answer was *sinoatrial node*. It came out the same day that the guy died. I just thought that was weird."

What did he say? Sound in the room stopped as Scott's brain rewound and registered Kyle's words. He blinked. The world whirred back to life around him.

Kyle was still talking. "Anyway, I'd wish you guys luck, but I know it's going to take a lot more than that to stop this creep." He sauntered away from Scott's desk. "See ya when you get back."

A moment passed. "Uh, yeah." He found his voice. "Later." There was no way there was a connection—was there? It had to be a coincidence—but he'd still take the magazine. Maybe solving it would be a good brain break later.

Pushing aside Kyle's words, he forced himself to focus on the task at hand. What would be of the most use that the ABI didn't have? Hands on his hips, he scanned his desk, the bookshelves, the corner where he piled up everything that didn't have a place. Nothing else jumped out at him, so he slapped the lid on the box and lifted his bag to his shoulder. With a quick glance at the clock, he figured with traffic he could meet Carrie for coffee right on time. Or, at least, hopefully she wouldn't have to wait too long.

He rushed out the door and climbed into his SUV. It wouldn't take long to warm up since he'd only been in the office about fifteen minutes. This winter was proving to be plenty cold. He rubbed his gloved hands together and put the vehicle into Drive.

As he navigated the streets of Anchorage, he couldn't keep his mind off Carrie.

It had been a long time since any woman had interested him. Not since Maria.

He blinked away the memories. Remembering her was never a wonderful thing. His therapist had worked for years to help him not fixate his thoughts on her. On what he could have done differently.

Meeting Carrie Kintz had been just the jolt he'd needed. God had clearly shown him that it was time to move forward, and Scott was having no trouble not thinking about Maria now.

He'd only known Carrie a few days, but he felt connected to her and wanted that connection to grow. Watching her in action was a marvel. No one had time to put up facades during investigative work like they were doing. She didn't seem like someone who put up false fronts anyway, which was refreshing after the lies he'd endured.

All in all, he had to admit he was enamored with the woman from small-town North Dakota.

It didn't bother him one bit that they were spending so much time together. It didn't even bother him that it was under stressful circumstances. Getting to know her—the real Carrie—was as intricate and enticing as a clean line of complex code. And if this case took a long time, he'd be okay with that too. It would give them a chance to take things slow.

Right now, slow and easy sounded perfect.

◘ ◘ ◘

DOWN
8. Eight letters. A violent, shaking attack; can be brought on by flashing lights.

January 31—10:42 a.m.
Kaladi Brothers Coffee, Anchorage

After sixteen hours of sleep, Carrie still felt like she could sleep for another twelve. But as soon as she'd entered the office, Kevin had shooed her out the door, telling her to meet Scott for coffee and brainstorm their next steps.

"Everyone needs a change of scenery and a pick-me-up. Get going," he'd ordered. The words kept rattling around in her mind, but they didn't make her feel any better.

They hadn't made one bit of progress. Hit one wall after another. And it didn't help that the rest of the ABI was being pulled in five million other directions. They were overtaxed. Exhausted. Overwhelmed.

With a serial killer on the loose.

A serial killer who most likely hadn't just started. Which meant they had so much more ground to cover. Carrie knew they had to find the beginning of the trail. But how to make the connection? It had to do with the "eight down" clue, but for the life of her, she couldn't figure out what.

She stood in line to order her coffee, checking her watch for the umpteenth time. Her edginess wasn't helping. Maybe Kevin was right. She was new at this. But she had to find a way to regroup, recharge, and jump-start her brain. People's lives were at stake.

Not that she needed a reminder. It was on a constant loop in her head. The media and public hadn't left them alone either. Social media channels were full of conspiracy theories. Which made things worse. The full-time hotline team was overwhelmed with calls, texts, and tips. Most of them were bogus. Why couldn't people understand that it was a waste of her team's time to answer questions? Their resources were more valuable when they were actually working on the case!

The rant in her head must have registered on her face because the poor barista who greeted her looked a bit skittish. "Um . . . are you okay? Would you like to order?" The words squeaked out.

Poor kid. She could only imagine how fierce her expression was, and the guy couldn't be more than twenty.

She schooled her features. "Sorry. My mind was on work." Forcing a smile, she scanned the board. "I'll have the Covey Blend, lots of chocolate, lots of sweet."

He smiled back. "You got it. Name and size?"

"The biggest you have." She gestured at the bags she knew were under her eyes. "Carrie's the name." With her right hand, she reached into her pocket for some cash.

"It's on the house." He pointed to her badge that had become visible when she'd moved her coat aside.

"You don't have to do that."

"I want to. Thank you for serving our community." He tipped a finger at her and scurried to make her order.

Carrie dropped a ten-dollar bill in the tip jar. He deserved it. She stepped away so the next person in line could be served. She spotted a table open in the back corner where she could watch the door. Perfect. As she headed toward it, she heard Scott call her name. She turned toward the door and, with a wave, pointed to the table. Then she claimed it before anyone else could. This place was busy.

Taking her seat, she scanned the room. An eclectic crowd. The norm for Alaska. Her eyes landed on a man in the corner. Sitting alone, he was watching her. Then he smirked.

A chill raced up her arms and neck. She looked away, pretending she hadn't noticed. But when her gaze came back around, the man was still looking at her with the same expression on his face. There was no newspaper or laptop in front of him. Simply a coffee cup.

This time, she didn't look away. Instead, she tilted her head and made a mental sketch of him. If he kept it up, she'd have no qualms taking a picture with her phone. If he was going to be unnervingly brazen and stare, she could be brazen right back.

He leaned back in his chair. Crossed one leg over the other. Looked like he had all the time in the world.

Dark hair cropped short. Glasses. Darkish eyes behind thin metal rims. She couldn't ascertain their color from across the room. His skin was olive toned. Square jaw with a cleft in his chin and a long nose. Looked like it had been broken a time or two.

She was about to lift her phone to take that picture when the barista brought her coffee and blocked her line of sight.

"Thank you." She touched his wrist as he handed her the cup. "Act natural. Don't look right now, but I need to know if you recognize the man sitting by himself in the southeast corner by the window. Directly behind you. If you have a name or anything, I'd really appreciate it."

"Sure thing. I'd love to help." He smiled as if nothing were amiss, turned around, and headed back to the counter.

But the man in the corner was gone.

CHAPTER EIGHT

DOWN
8. Eight letters. A breakdown in communication.

January 31—10:57 a.m.
Kaladi Brothers Coffee

SWIRLING THE LAST OF HIS coffee in the bottom of the cup, Scott stared across the table at Carrie.

"That guy got under your skin, didn't he?" He hated how uncomfortable she'd been since he sat down. But what could he do about it? Life in the world of a major crimes investigator was new and foreign to him. Even though he'd been bombarded with a lot of facts the past few days.

"I can't shake the way he stared at me." She'd taken a notepad from her coat pocket and jotted down everything she could remember about him, listing it off verbally to Scott as well. "I wish I was good at sketching people. Better yet, I wish I'd taken a picture of him while I had the chance. Rookie mistake."

The barista hadn't been able to help either.

Scott leaned his elbows on the table. "Could he have followed you here?"

"That's the thing. I don't know. I was standing in line for a good while. I don't remember seeing him when I first came in, but that doesn't mean anything because I didn't scan the whole place when I entered. The line was too long and obstructed my view." Her eyelids dropped to half-mast as she bit her lip. "He already had a cup of coffee, so he had to have gotten here before me. I think."

"Well then, maybe he was just a weird guy checking you out." While the thought wasn't pleasant, it was better than someone stalking her.

Several seconds passed as she stared into her cup. "Maybe you're right." With a swift shake of her head, she connected gazes with him again. "I'm sorry. The whole point of this was for us to have a change of scenery and to refresh our minds. I've wasted all this time worried about some weird guy who smirked at me."

"Nothing to apologize for. You have excellent instincts. I don't think you should discount them."

"I appreciate that." She bit the corner of her lip and jotted down a few more details before capping her pen. "I think I'll talk to Doug, our forensic artist, when we get back. Ask him to do a sketch."

Scott smiled. "Good idea."

Carrie sighed, wrapping her hands around her mug. "Thank you for your encouragement. I appreciate it." She took a long drink of coffee, then set her mug down, her face serious. "Now let's shift our focus back to the case."

"You got it." He swigged down the last drops in his cup. "Maybe I should get us some refills?"

"Nah. We've got plenty of coffee at the station." She gave him a conspiratorial look. "Ever since I came on board, I've bought beans from here so we'd have the good stuff in the office. Everyone loves me for it. But it was costing me a lot—as you can imagine, we go through a lot of coffee—so Kevin makes sure I get reimbursed now. No one wanted to go back to the cheap, generic stuff."

They laughed together, which helped ease some of the tension. "All right . . . so back to the case. There's a lot you've got to teach me, especially when it comes to the profiling. I know you guys have me here for the cyber side of things, but wrapping my brain around that will help me do a better job." He pulled out his iPad to take notes.

"Are you sure you want to dive into the minds of serial killers? It is not a fun road to venture down."

"If it helps to stop them? A resounding yes. Let's just hope I don't get nightmares." He grinned over the top of his tablet, then set it down.

Her shoulders rose as she inhaled, and her eyes widened. "You asked for it." She pulled out her own tablet and opened the browser. "Longtime profilers and homicide detectives have taught seminars and written books on the subject. I did a great deal of studying to be a profiler, but I'm new at it and don't have experience. Only my penchant for reading. Actually, I was chosen for the ABI because my aptitude tests showed strengths for investigative work. A lot of people are thrust into the job within police departments and such, but not everyone has the innate ability for it. I'm told I do. Doesn't mean I'm prepared for this. I've been reading absolutely everything I can find, trying to educate myself." She passed her tablet to him. "This will explain some of it better than I ever could."

First glance at the screen told him he should have braced himself. The gruesome images were enough to make any sane person want to lose their lunch. Then he started reading.

A few minutes passed as he dove into the article. "This 'signature' philosophy—each killer has one?"

"Horrifying and yet fascinating all at the same time, isn't it?" She leaned closer.

He did the same. "It's how the killer expresses him- or herself." The thought rolled around a few times while he grasped it. "But these gruesome killers—whether they're showing their mastery over their victims' bodies or pointing out the victims' vulnerabilities—they're definitely not like our killer."

"Right. Is it a male? Female? We might have a team. It was a woman's voice on the first phone call. But serial killers do tend to be men. Based on the initial profile we've built, I think it's safe to say we're looking for a man."

"Good point." Scott studied her face. He loved watching the way her mind worked, the way she threw herself completely into the investigation. "So how do you profile someone who is into killing people, but completely hands-off?"

Carrie's eyes brightened as she leaned even closer and patted his hand. "You, my dear Watson, are going to make an excellent detective."

"Does that mean I'm not a complete idiot when it comes to this?"

"You bet." She reached for her coat and slipped her arms into the sleeves. "Let's head back to the office, and we'll dive into the world of profiling, which includes about seven different steps and then systematic stages of investigation. Who knows? That brilliant computer brain of yours might pick up on something we haven't."

"Systematic stages? Sounds intriguing."

"Most people find it a bit boring, but it always gets my neurons firing." Her light laugh washed over him.

"It's good to hear you laugh like that."

"Amazing what some sleep and good company can do to boost a girl's spirits."

She lowered her head and stepped past him but not before he saw the pink in her cheeks.

Good company. She said he was good company. It might have boosted her spirits, but it just gave him a shot in the arm that made him feel like he could take on the serial killer all by himself.

◻ ◻ ◻

DOWN
8. Seven letters. Reaction with aversion.

February 1—1:23 p.m.
Alaska Bureau of Investigation

The day had not gone well. Not at all.

Yesterday he'd learned the steps of profiling and then the stages of investigation methodology from David Webb's book, *Criminal Profiling*. He glanced back at his notes. The profiling steps included:

1. Evaluation of the criminal act itself.
2. Comprehensive evaluation of the specifics of the crime scene(s).
3. Comprehensive analysis of the victim.
4. Evaluation of preliminary police reports.
5. Evaluation of the medical examiner's autopsy protocol.
6. Development of profile with critical offender characteristics.
7. Investigative suggestions predicated on construction of the profile.

If that wasn't enough to make his head swim, the stages of criminal profiling and investigation were even more difficult to understand at first—profiling inputs, decision processing, crime assessment, criminal profile, and investigative use.

The terms themselves didn't make a lot of sense, but at least now he understood that stage one involved gathering all the evidence and information they could. Stage two involved the behavioral classifications based on all they'd gathered in stage one. So much of the victim's profile impacted the offender's profile. In stage three, they would piece together the chain of events before, during, and after the crime. They'd also decide whether the crime had the characteristics of an organized or disorganized offender or, in some cases, an odd mix of both. The profile of the criminal wouldn't be made until stage four, and then, in the fifth and final stage, they would put all the pieces together for use in the investigation. The profile was often updated and expanded a good bit during stage five.

It was all fascinating. Overwhelming, but fascinating.

And not an iota of it had helped him accomplish anything. He'd hoped understanding the UNSUB would help him track down the data breaches or the code or give him a structure to start with. But he had nothing. Feeling useless and like a failure wasn't normal for him. More than anything, he wanted to help them catch the bad guy. He just had no idea how to do it.

Today had been a new day, but the longer he worked, the more the hopelessness inside him grew. He'd combed through everything from the mayor's files up in Fairbanks, all the notes Jason had sent him from the attack, the traffic light hack, and the victim with the pacemaker. What was he missing?

"This is so frustrating." Carrie slammed her hands on the conference room table.

He couldn't blame her. He wanted to do the same thing.

She stood up and paced to the whiteboard.

Every bit of pertinent information they had was on that board. With nothing to tie it all together.

She ran her hands through her hair, pulling it back into a ponytail. "What are we missing? Our UNSUB wrote 'eight down.' What does that mean? Our first assumption was eight bodies, but we could only come up with three. Could it mean something else? Was the pacemaker the first attack? Did he give us a clue about a pacemaker?"

His memory sparked. Without saying a word, he raced out of the room and searched through the box he'd packed back at his office. Kyle had put it in here, right?

Scott pulled the *Alaska Magazine* out of the box, flipped to the dog-eared page, and found the highlighted section.

In the puzzle boxes, the only answer highlighted was *sinoatrial node*. It was fourteen letters, filling in . . . 8 DOWN.

Scott scanned the page and found the clue. The clue to the answer at 8 DOWN was listed as "The heart's pacemaker."

A crossword puzzle.

He sucked in a shaky breath as his heart pumped faster. Could this really be what they were missing?

He looked again. This had to be it. Wishing he'd paid more attention to Kyle's suggestion, he ran back to the conference room and shoved the magazine at Carrie. "Look. One of the guys in my office is a crossword junkie and gave this to me when I picked up my equipment."

She didn't hesitate to march it over to Kevin. Alan joined them.

No words were said as everyone digested the information.

Then Kevin set the magazine down and growled. "Get me every issue of the *Alaska Magazine* since September of last year."

Alan nodded. "I'll do it." And he surged out of the room.

Carrie plopped down into her chair. "Eight down meant crossword puzzle clues? Why would he do that? Is he really killing people based on crossword puzzle clues?" Her shoulders slumped.

Kevin studied the page in front of him. "I don't know. But we'd better find out."

She rubbed her forehead. "I think you need to take over this one—"

"Nope. Not a chance." He leveled his gaze on Carrie. "You're the lead on this case. Look at the evidence. Trust your intuition along with the facts. What do you think?"

Her head jerked back and forth. "That this is over my head. You or Alan would be—"

"Don't argue with me on this, Kintz." His jaw was firm, his eyes blazing. "Alan and I will be right by your side. Both of us. But everyone has to have their first big case. This one is yours."

Scott shifted his gaze between the two. While he applauded Kevin for the decision, he completely understood Carrie's hesitation. Would *he* want to take on something of this magnitude? Of course, he was already entrenched, but he didn't have to be the one in charge. Something he was more and more grateful for as the minutes ticked past.

His brain started swirling with ideas. "I've got a hunch." He held up a finger and sat back down in front of his laptops.

"I can use all the help I can get." Carrie strode across the room and watched over his shoulder.

"Look." He pointed to the screen that had come up after his furious search. "Most crossword puzzles for magazines and newspapers are purchased from an outside source."

"All right." She didn't seem impressed. "But how does that help us?"

"That means that our killer, our UNSUB"—he had to get used to the terminology—"must have hacked the puzzle supplier, not the magazine."

"How do we track down the creators of the puzzles?" She took the chair beside him.

He grimaced. "That's going to take a bit of work. I'll start on it right now."

Alan rushed back into the room with his arms full of magazines. "I brought a copy of all the issues for each of us. They had a surplus of them at the state veterinarian's office across the street."

"That was fast." Kevin pointed at Carrie. "This one tried to pawn off her case."

"Nuh uh, no way." Alan plopped into a chair. "I'm not taking it. This one is all you."

Carrie moaned while the two men went back and forth, their teasing getting louder and louder. "Okay, okay!" She shook her head. "Enough. It's my case. But that just means I get to order you two around and make you do all the grunt work."

"Sounds good. Lay it on me, boss." Alan pulled his chair closer to the table and opened a magazine. "I assume we're just looking at the crossword puzzles for anything connected to the deaths that we know about?"

"Yeah, it's like a needle in a haystack." She groaned. "But let's see what we can find. Especially any at eight down."

"One thing you could do as you look at the puzzles is search for the answers online. Kyle, my buddy who gave me the crossword, said the sites can be a bit iffy. There can be multiple answers for one clue, and some of them might be the wrong answers. Still, it might cut out some of the guesswork."

The smile Carrie gave him was wide. It took his breath away. "You really are a genius. I'll go grab my laptop." Scott turned his attention to scouring every online source he could, trying to find out exactly how crossword puzzles were created and sold to publications, all while ignoring the racing of his heart.

Carrie came back in and grabbed her magazine. She sat in the empty seat next to him, not meeting his gaze. But Scott noticed the smile on her lips. He wasn't going to complain if the smartest, prettiest woman he'd met in a long time wanted to sit next to him. Not one bit.

His computer dinged with a news alert. Clicking it open on his other laptop, he scanned the article.

8 DOWN.

I have killed eight people, and I will kill eight more and then eight more and then eight more and so on until my demands are met. Why are you so slow to KEEP UP?

I've given Ms. Carrie Kintz, ABI investigator, an advantage since she's new and doesn't seem to know what she's doing. Let's see if she's smart enough to find it.

After that, my next communication will be my demands. Don't be stupid. Give me what I want or else.

With a huff, he turned the screen around. "You guys need to see this. He's gone public again."

Kevin and Alan came to stand behind him and Carrie. As they read the article, their frustration was palpable.

"What news station was this from?" Kevin asked.

Scott scrolled to find the source. "It's originating with KTUU, but I'll do a quick search and see who else has picked it up."

"I'm sure every news outlet has it," Carrie muttered, rubbing her temples with her forefingers.

Scott didn't respond. She was probably right. Things like this spread across the internet in no time. He opened a new browser tab to do a quick search and frowned. The internet was down? That was odd. "Can anyone else get online?"

The trio of investigators picked up their phones and tapped.

"Nope," Kevin confirmed.

"I can," Alan said. "But my phone is connected to the cell network. Not the office Wi-Fi."

Carrie slid her phone back on the table. "Same." She tapped the trackpad on her laptop. "And my browser won't refresh, saying it's not connected to the internet." She stood and started pacing. "Is this him? Is he messing with us? Now we can't even get online to read his threats."

Someone tapped on the door and a short man stuck his head in, a wary look on his face. "Apologies for interrupting."

"No problem, Jim." Carrie's smile looked thin. "What's up?"

"We just got word that there is an internet outage in our area. Apparently, it's impacting at least a two-mile radius. They said it should be fixed by this evening."

They all groaned.

Jim threw his hands in the air, palms up. "Don't blame the messenger. I'll let you know as soon as I hear anything." He left and shut the door hard behind him, the blinds rattling against the glass.

"Well." Scott exhaled. He picked up his pencil and magazine. "I guess it's back to the old-fashioned way of solving a crossword."

No one responded. It was going to be a long afternoon.

CHAPTER NINE

DOWN
8. Five letters. Breaks. Pounds. Thumps.

February 1—4:57 p.m.
Alaska Bureau of Investigation

Carrie hung up the phone with the news station. Another person had been threatened. Their UNSUB had even taken a picture of their child at school. Thus the story had been aired immediately. *Without* calling the ABI and giving them a heads-up.

It irked her, but given the circumstances, she couldn't blame them.

Of course, if she gave the media the press conference they were hounding her about, she might get them on her side. Get a little sympathy.

She doubted it. They were going to do what got them ratings. Not what helped her catch a serial killer.

None of the puzzles they'd gone through in the *Alaska Magazine* issues had shown anything pertinent in the boxes for 8 DOWN. All the words were boring like *native, bear, silt, caribou,* and so on. Nothing as blatant as the answer to the pacemaker clue.

What. Were. They. Missing?

Not only was Carrie infuriated that they'd hit another wall, but the UNSUB had called her out. Again. Practically yelling at her to keep up. Just like the note left for her in her files. She could almost hear him cackling at her failure.

Wasn't exactly the greatest way to start off her career here. If she failed, would anyone ever trust her again? Would her team?

She shook her head. All this self-doubt was ridiculous. Exactly what the person behind this wanted. Bullies always did that. Made their victim feel bad about themselves—like it was their fault.

Analyzing the killer's words should be her focus. This person was taunting them. Just like she'd suspected back in Fairbanks when she was investigating the mayor's murder.

Obviously, the UNSUB wanted to feel powerful. Intelligent. Above the law. Untouchable.

Well, they didn't know how driven and stubborn Carrie Kintz was. The gauntlet had been thrown down. It didn't matter what happened to her or her career. What mattered was solving the mystery and catching the killer before they hurt anyone else. But she needed wisdom.

If any of you lacks wisdom, you should ask God, who gives generously to all without finding fault . . . The Bible verse made her smile. James 1:5—one of her mother's favorites, regularly quoted when dealing with any or all of her six children. Carrie smiled at the memory. "Thank You, Lord," she whispered, clinging to the promise of Scripture. In the face of this horrible evil, God was still with her.

Taking a steadying breath, she turned back to the article and read it again. Now her team knew for certain there were eight dead. At least that's what their killer claimed. The person had to be stopped.

How was the question.

Kevin had checked in with the rest of their investigators, but they were all still occupied with other crimes. For right now, it was just the four of them. Was it enough? Was it possible the mastermind behind all this was creating havoc elsewhere to keep them scattered and shorthanded?

That was a horrid thought. But not outside the realm of possibility. She couldn't dismiss anything at this point.

"Maybe he just started using the crossword puzzles," Alan threw out as he picked up another slice of cold pizza. "Maybe that's why we can't find any others."

"I don't know . . ." She pulled out the evidence bag with the sticky note from the deceased with the hacked pacemaker. CLUE. 8 DOWN. The longer she stared at it, the more convinced she was. "I think there's more, we just have to find them. This killer is a planner. Thinks through every step. It's safe to assume there are clues for each of the eight they've already killed. The double meaning is intentional."

Alan tipped his head to the right and chewed another bite. He wiped his mouth with a napkin. "Yeah, you're probably right. But where do we look?"

"Can we get all the crossword puzzles for the *Anchorage Daily News* for the last five months? Think Mrs. Silva would send them over?"

"Worth a try. I'll give her a call." Alan squeezed Carrie's shoulder as he walked back into the squad room.

Her family back home was amazing. She'd hated leaving their tight-knit community. But the family God had given her here was beyond her wildest dreams. Kevin was not only a mentor but a father figure. Alan was like a big brother. Even the others within the ABI team had embraced her and made her feel at home. She hated the thought of disappointing them. What were they thinking after seeing this killer publicly humiliate her? Did they agree? Were they secretly thinking she had no business being an investigator?

Good grief. She closed her eyes for a long moment. No one was doubting her but herself.

Enough of the back-and-forth emotions. All the self-deprecation and pep talks in the world weren't going to solve this case. What she needed was a break. Close off everything else. Recharge. Focus.

Standing up, she grabbed her coat and headed for the door. "I'm going to take a quick walk to get the juices flowing."

Mumbles came from around the table. Kevin and Scott each had their heads buried in whatever they were reading.

Outside, the frigid air greeted her and large snowflakes drifted down from the sky. She shoved her hands into her pockets.

With quick steps, she walked the perimeter of the parking lot at the Alaska Department of Public Safety. It wouldn't be a long walk, but she was definitely feeling a bit more refreshed than she was a few minutes ago. The cold could do that.

With a shiver, she finished her lap and headed back toward the Alaska Bureau of Investigation building.

Out of the corner of her eye, she spotted a young man running toward her. She called out, "Are you all right?"

The kid smiled and stopped in front of her. "Yep. I'm good. Are you Carrie Kintz?"

That made her frown. "Yes."

"Here." He handed her a manila envelope. "I'm supposed to deliver this to you."

She flipped it over in her gloved hands. "Wait!" She had to catch him before he ran off. "Who asked you to deliver this?"

The kid shrugged. "A guy gave me fifty bucks to give it to you. Said you were outside, told me where." He turned and pointed. "He's right—"

"He's gone, isn't he?" With a sigh, she knew it was true.

"Yeah. Weird. Oh well. See ya!" He waved and began to run away again.

"No! Wait! Get back here!" she yelled. He wasn't going to get away without answering a few questions.

The kid stopped and turned and then walked back. "I've got to get back to work. Is something wrong?"

Carrie took the kid by the elbow. "I need you to come with me."

"In there?" He pointed to the building.

"Yes. Just for a few minutes. I need to ask you some questions."

"Cool."

His eagerness made her smile. They made their way inside, and Carrie gestured for an officer to come help her with the teen. "This young man might be able to help us with some information about a suspect. Would you mind finding Kevin and letting him know?"

The officer nodded and left Carrie with the teenager again. Curiosity was killing her. What was in this envelope?

She might as well open it while they were waiting for Kevin. Pulling off her winter gloves, Carrie shoved them in her coat pocket and pulled out her spare pair of disposable nitrile gloves. With careful movements, she peeled back the seal and pulled out a slip of paper.

A chill raced over her body.

It was a crossword puzzle clue. She pulled out a couple more of the small pieces of paper. They were all crossword puzzle clues. Carrie could only guess what they were all pointing to.

"Oh cool! A bunch of crosswords!" The chipper young man's voice broke through the fear that enveloped her. "You must be a big fan."

Carrie glanced at the kid, then to the clues in her hand. Slipping them back in the envelope, she pressed the flap down. "Not anymore."

◘ ◘ ◘

DOWN

8. Five letters. Bloop. Bloop. Bloop.

February 1—6:02 p.m.
Alaska Bureau of Investigation

Scott watched through the glass as Kevin questioned the messenger. It fascinated him how the older man morphed into a different person inside the interrogation room. Oh, he wasn't scary like all the TV shows portrayed the intimidating senior cop, but he was intense. Serious enough for fear to be apparent on the teen's face. As soon as he realized he'd been involved in something of great interest and related to a killer, the kid had sat straight in his chair and answered everything with a "yes, sir" or "no, sir." At least he had respect.

From what Scott observed over the last forty-five minutes, however, the messenger had no idea what he'd gotten himself into. He'd been hired literally moments before he delivered the envelope. He gave a simple description of the guy who'd hired him. Businessman, at least forty years old, in a long black coat with a scarf covering most of his face.

But then, when Kevin had drilled further about the man's age and appearance, the kid had said he was at least as old or older than the guy with the computer he'd seen as he walked in. Guy with a computer—meaning, *Scott.* Which made him laugh. Thirty and forty were a good deal apart. Kevin even showed him the sketch of the guy from the coffee shop, but the kid shrugged and said, "Maybe? Yeah, maybe not."

His observation skills might not be the greatest—why would they be? He had no idea at the time he was being asked to do something for a killer—but he seemed honest enough.

"What about his voice? Do you remember anything specific about it? Could you place it if you heard him again?" Kevin leaned forward.

"Nah. He didn't say enough, I don't think. And it was muffled by the scarf. I didn't think anything of it, I mean, duh, it's freaking cold out there if you haven't noticed." For the first time, the kid sounded defensive. Probably tired of all the questions, and he *had* been willing to cooperate.

"Hey." Carrie popped her head in the door. "Good news, the internet is back up. Can you join me in the conference room?"

"Sure thing." As fascinating as it was to watch an interrogation, he was ready to get back at it.

He followed her there and found Alan at the table, this time popping Doritos into his mouth. How the guy ever stayed as fit as he did with all the junk food he ate was beyond Scott's comprehension.

"Okay. Corey"—she paused and looked at Scott—"that's our forensic scientist."

"Gotcha."

"Once he had what he needed, he made us copies of all the puzzles. He'll work on the envelope and originals and see if there's anything else he can pull from them. I doubt there will be, but . . . This UNSUB is smart." She passed a stack to him, one to Alan, laid one out for Kevin when he returned, and then laid a set for herself.

"Corey even took the kid's gloves to see if the guy who asked him to deliver it left anything behind in the exchange." She shrugged. "You never know. Maybe we'll get lucky." Taking her seat, she laid each puzzle out in front of her.

Scott arranged his stack in front of him.

First thing he did was find the squares for 8 DOWN in each one. With a yellow highlighter, he marked the empty boxes. Then he took an orange highlighter and did the same with the clue for 8 DOWN. This would take some work. "Are you guys good at this? Crosswords were never my strong suit."

"I'll send you a few links to help." Carrie stared at her computer.

His own laptop dinged. When he opened the email, he found a link to crossword-dictionary.com, crosswordsolver.org, and a link that talked about the best crossword helps on apps and the web.

"All right. Guess we've got our work cut out for us." Scott stared at all the different puzzles.

Alan refilled his coffee cup and sat back down. "Last one to solve them buys dinner for the crew tomorrow?"

"Deal." He and Carrie responded at the same time.

Head buried in his work, Scott did his best to shift his computerized brain to pen and paper. How long had it been since he'd worked on a crossword? Didn't you need to work on the other words around the puzzle to have letters that fit into place? Maybe he should simply focus on the one clue. Might be simpler. If he got stuck, he could try some of the other clues.

But first, he had to know where the crossword puzzles were from. They were all clippings. Scanning the tops and bottoms, he found a few had the publication listed.

Washington Post, New York Times, People Magazine, Houston Chronicle, Los Angeles Sentinel, Chicago Tribune, AARP The Magazine, and the *Denver Post.* He groaned. "I hate to say it, but this guy was brilliant. Look at all the different publications he used." He was mumbling to himself, but the words were out there.

"I was just noticing that myself. Will that be hard to track?" Carrie peered over the top of her papers.

He allowed his shoulders to drop with the answer. "Yep. But I'll get to the bottom of it."

"Let's solve these clues and then tackle that." She bent over the papers again.

It was true. He needed to help them with what they needed in the moment. He could imagine that the timer ticking in Carrie's mind was focused on finding the bodies of the victims. Had it already been too long? Every second counted now that they had something to work with.

He wasn't as good at puzzle solving as they were, but he was a mad genius when it came to computer work. Maybe if he input all the clues into the computer, he could come up with some viable answers. Then it would all come down to word length and whether it fit into the profile.

He counted the puzzles to make a spreadsheet. Man. "There's more than twenty puzzles here." It ramped up his heartbeat. "Does that mean—?"

They sat in silence for a few seconds, the same horrified expressions on each face. They'd been thinking the killer had eight victims. Were they really looking for twenty bodies?

◻ ◻ ◻

DOWN
8. Ten letters. Where glucose likes to live.

February 1—11:34 p.m.
Downtown Anchorage

Griz grabbed the brown bag from the disheveled junkie and shoved it into his coat pocket. If it wouldn't have been so messy, he would have killed the guy right then and there.

But no. He'd have someone else take care of the supplier later. Griz had a higher purpose.

The world needed him. Needed his leadership. Needed his plans and ideas.

There was a new world on the horizon, and he was excited to bring it about.

His fingers wrapped tight around the package. Just a few more minutes and he could take another pill.

As he walked through the alley in the crisp cold of the evening, the sounds of nightlife covered up the swirling thoughts in his brain. He couldn't give in to temptation yet. Not when there were people around.

He had to keep up appearances after all.

Once everyone knew who he was and they celebrated him, he would look back at this time and smile.

People loved him everywhere he went. He tipped big. Bought rounds for everyone at the bars. Kissed babies. Played ball with the outcasts.

Yes. He was loved and adored.

When he rose to power, people who'd seen him here and there would recognize him and cheer.

All the pieces were falling into place.

The doorman at his building greeted him with a smile. He nodded at the man and headed toward the elevator. Once he was in his apartment, he could relax. The day had been grueling after all.

Each day he added more to his loyal group. He also added employees who could be erased quickly if need be. But everyone wanted to be a part of something great.

He was going to bring that about.

It just took time.

His fun little sideshow was taking up a lot of his energy right now, but he was getting attention again. Exactly what he wanted.

He breathed in a deep breath as he exited the elevator and unlocked his state-of-the-art apartment. With methodical movements, he pulled the bag out of his pocket, slipped off his coat, hung it up, dropped his keys on their specific hook, and picked up the remote that controlled everything in his home.

Time for some relaxation.

Tapping the remote, he turned on the fireplace and started his favorite jazz album playing through the surround sound. Then he poured himself a glass of his favorite scotch.

Griz watched the flames in the fireplace as they grew and diminished in their random pattern. He'd studied that for many hours. Controlled, yet scattered and unpredictable.

He was like the fire. No one could predict what he was up to next. They'd never figure out his plan. He was twenty steps ahead of anyone who was even close.

With long strides, he walked over to the exquisite leather couch and lowered himself onto it. He pulled out his little notebook, then popped a pill and logged it. He'd doubled up on doses without a single side effect. Long gone was Griz the addict. That man had been weak. Powerless. A mess.

But now? He was in control. He'd learned to dominate his own mind and used the drugs to give him clarity and brilliance. They only enhanced his magnificent mind.

The drugs . . . elevated him.

He glanced at his watch. The poor ABI team should be scrambling about now. He'd ensured that only a skeleton crew would remain to assist the new Ms. Kintz. Just like he'd ensured Scott would be there to help her. How long would it be before any of them figured anything out?

Griz laughed and took a slow sip. The liquid warmed his insides. They were no match for his brilliance . . . his skills. The thought was a pleasant one. He stood and stared at the fire again for a few more seconds. It was time to get some rest. Tomorrow was another new day.

He was only getting started.

CHAPTER TEN

DOWN

8. Ten letters. Counts your steps, measures your sleep, tracks your heartbeat.

February 2—7:08 a.m.
Alaska Bureau of Investigation

SPREADSHEETS NORMALLY SATISFIED SCOTT'S DESIRE for organization. But today, all he could think about was that there was a person—a body—attached to each line and clue. And he found it hard to stomach.

He was going to have to get over that. This case needed solving before more people died.

There had to be a better way to figure out these clues. Silence was interrupted only by the scratch of pencils on paper. Last night their little team had figured out six clues before the medical examiner called with another body. They were still waiting on the autopsy report.

Carrie cleared her throat. "Okay. Instead of all of us working separately on this today, why don't we put our brainpower together. If we get stumped on a specific clue, we'll set it aside and then come back to it."

"Sounds like a good plan." Scott threw in his agreement. "I know you guys are better on paper, but I'll input the clue into the computer and see what jumps out at us. It'll be even better if I can find the crossword key, but for some of these we don't have the name of the publication, and most don't have the dates on them."

"You search in the computer, and we'll go from there. I don't want to waste time looking for the dates, publications, and keys if we can just solve it faster ourselves." She picked up a puzzle. "First clue is: 'Related to metrical stress.'"

He typed it in. "Is the answer five letters?"

"Yep." Alan leaned over his paper with pencil in hand.

"*Ictus*." Scott gave them the word then went to Merriam-Webster's site. "Definition is: 'the recurring stress or beat in a rhythmic or metrical series of sounds.'"

Everyone appeared deep in thought over that.

Carrie looked to Kevin for guidance. He shrugged. "I think we put it aside. Maybe something will make sense to us later."

She lifted the next paper. "All right, next clue is: 'Creates a multitude of rubberneckers.'"

As soon as he typed it in, the screen flooded with suggestions all having to do with traffic accidents. So he went to the dictionary site again. "Definition of a rubberneck as a verb is 'to look about or stare with exaggerated curiosity.' The example, 'drivers passing the accident slowed down to rubberneck.'"

With his pencil held up, Alan squinted at them. "It's nine letters. *Collision* fits."

"Looks like the answer to me." Carrie wrote it in. "That goes all too well with our traffic light hack."

"Agreed." Kevin spoke up from the other end of the table. "We've got a clue matched to a case. One down."

"Next clue." She lifted another puzzle. "'Lawsuit due to negligence.'"

Once again, Scott typed in the clue. "First thing to pop up is *malpractice*."

"Eleven letters. That fits. But doesn't match any case yet." Carrie picked up another paper. "Next clue."

The next hour was spent filling in all the slots for 8 DOWN on the crossword puzzles. Several of them had multiple answers that would fit, but they'd hopefully landed on the correct answers. Now if they could just figure out how they were connected.

"Read us what we've got, Scott." Carrie leaned back in her chair and shoved her fingers into her tightly pulled-back hair.

"All right, here goes. First clue: 'Number 6 on the periodic table' was six letters. We filled it in with *carbon*. So far, we think that's a connection to the mayor's death in Fairbanks." He scanned the list. "Which also connects to the clue 'Silent killer,' which was an eight-letter answer. *Monoxide*."

Carrie grabbed a marker and went to another whiteboard. "Let me get these up here so we all have a visual."

Once she was done writing those down, Scott continued. "Next clue: 'Creates a multitude of rubberneckers' was nine letters. *Collision*. We're assuming that goes with the hack of the traffic lights. Clue: 'Lawsuit due to negligence' was eleven letters. *Malpractice*. We don't have a case for that one yet. Clue: 'It cuts like a knife' was seven letters. We went with *scalpel*. Another one we don't have a case for yet."

"Let me interrupt for a second." Alan's jaws worked on his ubiquitous chewing gum. "If this all has to do with hacking, then why a scalpel?"

"Good question." Carrie stared at what she'd written down.

Everyone's eyes went to the board.

She gasped and shot her gaze to Scott. "A hacker could get into hospital records, right? What if they put in the wrong procedure to be done?"

Kevin just about came out of his chair. "You might be onto something. I remember a death recently that had to do with surgery. I'll look for it. You guys keep going." He hobbled out of the room.

A new glint touched her eyes. They were getting some traction now, and she was clearly excited to be moving forward. Scott had to fight the urge to jump up and down and give her a high five, but it was too early in the game for that. He turned his focus back to the puzzles.

"Okay." He let out a breath. "Clue: 'A metronome for your ticker' was nine letters. *Pacemaker*. We're pretty sure that goes with the clue

Kyle gave me: 'The heart's pacemaker,' which was fourteen letters. *Sinoatrial node.*"

"Hold up." Alan shuffled some papers. "This other clue: 'Breaks. Pounds. Thumps.' It was five letters, and we answered *heart*. I think that one goes with the pacemaker."

With a nod, Carrie wrote it on the board and put a question mark in parentheses beside it. "Here's hoping we don't have another case that involves a heart." She turned to Scott. "What's next?"

He went to the next one. "Clue: 'Where glucose likes to live' was ten letters. *Bloodstream.* Don't have a case for it yet, but we're all pretty sure it has something to do with insulin. Which brings us to the clue: 'Sweet sugar high for your body,' which was seven letters, and the answer was *insulin*."

The marker squeaked as she wrote, and he went on. "Clue: 'Bloop. Bloop. Bloop.' Five letters. *Radar.* Again, no case. No idea what it goes to. Next clue: 'Snowed under.' Six letters. We went with *buried*."

"There was a controlled avalanche the other day. I haven't heard that there were any casualties." Alan shook his head. "Would someone really . . ." He let the words drop.

Scott didn't want to admit how much this killer creeped him out. Yeah, they called him the UNSUB. An offender. All the law enforcement terminology. But the fact of the matter was, he—or she—was a killer. Plain and simple.

He cleared his throat and began to finish out their list. "Clue: 'Irregular heartbeat' was eleven letters. The answer we came up with was *tachycardia*."

"I'm going to put this one in two columns. It might go with the pacemaker, but it might not. The victim didn't suffer from tachycardia." Carrie wrote it in the unsolved column and put a question mark beside it in the other.

"Well then, the next clue: 'Mishap and mayhem' was eight letters. *Accident.* Should we put that in the traffic light column?" He looked up.

Without answering she put it in both columns as well. Which

meant exactly what he dreaded—*accident* was too broad a term and could be used for any number of things. It wasn't encouraging.

He inhaled and went on. "This clue worries me: 'A pilot's home away from home' was seven letters. *Cockpit.*"

She leaned over the table and pressed her palms flat. "And another answer was *radar.*" Putting a hand to her forehead, she blew her breath out. "We need to contact the airport and the FAA. I haven't heard of any planes going down, have you guys?"

"No." They all answered in unison.

"Okay. Everyone take a quick break while I make a few calls. Maybe we can stop this one before it happens."

◘   ◘   ◘

DOWN
8. Five letters. Panic attack.

February 2—9:46 a.m.
Alaska Bureau of Investigation

Carrie stood with her hands on her hips and faced her little team. "The FAA is now aware of the threat and will pass it on to all pilots. But there are more than nine thousand private aircraft in Alaska. Plus the commercial planes."

Scott rested his head on the wall behind his chair. "We know that the UNSUB claims to have killed eight people. We know for certain that there are at least four, right? The mayor, the pacemaker victim, and the two because of the traffic lights hack." He held up four fingers.

"I'm not sure I'm following where you're going." Carrie focused in on him and lowered her brows.

"Do you think maybe he's blowing smoke? I mean, he wants us to take him seriously. He's smart and thinks he has all this figured out. There are other clue answers, like the *cockpit* and *radar* ones, that we don't think have happened yet. Should those be the ones we focus on? I mean, you can investigate something after the fact, but you don't always have the chance to stop things before they happen." He winced and looked doubtful. "I could be way off base, but that's what hit me when you went to call the FAA."

A tiny ripple of hope passed through her mind. "You've got a really good point. We've been looking for clues that connected with bodies." She picked the marker back up and pointed at him. "Let's finish getting through all the clues. Then Alan and Kevin—you two see if you can match them with any deaths in the past two months. Scott and I will do everything we can to prevent whatever might be coming next."

She didn't feel as confident about the scenario as she sounded. How could she prevent a murder when she wasn't even sure how he was going about them? Everything about this case overwhelmed her. What if she couldn't stop him?

Scott's voice refocused her thoughts. "Next clue: 'Reaction with aversion' was seven letters. We filled it in with *allergy*. Not connected to a case. Next clue: 'It's breath taking' was four letters. We weren't confident in our answer, but for right now we have *lung*. Also not connected to a case. Then we have: 'A different way to get where you're going,' which was six letters. *Detour*. Next: 'What claustrophobia can inspire,' and it was eleven letters. *Panic attack*. Then the last one: 'A breakdown in communication' was eight letters. This one was the weird one, but I found the key online and it says the answer is *no signal*."

As she wrote the rest of the information on the board, the urge to throttle whoever was behind all this grew.

"Hey"—Alan pulled the donuts closer to him and picked up a glazed one—"could the two answers *lung* and *panic attack* be connected? It was the claustrophobia that just put it together for me. My mom's got asthma and became claustrophobic last time she had pneumonia. Ever since then, if she has trouble breathing, she gets what the doc calls asthmatic panic attacks."

Carrie connected the two on the board. "It makes sense, that's for sure. I'll just keep a question mark here until we know. Good eye."

Kevin groaned as he got to his feet and shoved his crutches in place. "I have *got* to get a change of scenery. How about Alan and I go into the squad room to work for a bit. Dr. Blanchard or her assistant might have some more info for us, and we'll go through past death records and see what we can find."

"Sounds good." Claiming her chair again, she put the puzzles that they assumed went together in piles on the table. With a glance up to Scott, she redid her ponytail. "You up for this?"

He rubbed his hands together. "I am. Anything I can do to stop this psychopath."

"I'm with you. I can't bear the thought of more people dying on my watch." The last few words made her choke up. It took every bit of resolve she had to keep the tears at bay.

He reached across the table and laid a hand over hers. "I can see that this is a huge burden for you to bear. You don't have to take on the weight of it all by yourself."

She glanced out the door at Kevin and Alan. They'd been so good to her. Lowering her voice, she leaned a bit closer to him. "I can't let them down. Do you know what's at stake here? There are groups that have been wanting to defund the police for years. Their cries are loud and get attention. With the media coverage all over this and the offender specifically calling me out, it's my job to make sure the people trust us. If not—what will it come to? Chaos and protests in the streets?"

Another glance at Kevin was all it took to convince her that she was right. He'd mentored her, challenged her, and cheered her on. Neither one of those guys out there had let her down. She couldn't allow anything to happen that would put them or the department in a bad light.

Scott nodded. "Oh, I get it. I do. Our world has gotten crazier and more divided the last couple decades, but you've got to remember you're not alone in this. Let us help you carry the load. It's not nearly as grim as it was just yesterday. Look"—he motioned to the papers laid out across the table—"we have a lot more to work with now than we did."

"You're right." In her head she knew it was true, but her insides weren't cooperating. She closed her eyes for a second. Stress and anxiety were two top causes of burnout in law enforcement. Inhaling a long, slow breath, she practiced the method of square breathing she'd learned in training back home. If she had any say in the matter, she wouldn't allow the beast to take over.

Feeling calmer and focused, she opened her eyes and sent Scott a smile. "Thanks." Her gaze went back to all the puzzles in front of her. "I should be thankful that this guy is as arrogant as he is and dropped the clues in our lap."

"Yep. I know you have to try to get into his mind, but that is not a place I'd want to stay very long. This is . . . diabolical." He stood and straightened the papers around him, shifting things from one place to another. Then his face turned thoughtful. "Did you ever see the movie based on the Zodiac Killer?"

"No. I don't think so."

"It's an older film. Back in the early 2000s, I think? But I think I should watch it again. For some reason, this case reminds me of it. Arrogant killer. Taunts the media with ciphers and such. But they never caught the guy."

She remembered learning about the Zodiac Killer case back in her intense training. Could they be similar? Maybe she'd look into it.

The thought of not catching this offender was reprehensible. She wouldn't even consider it. Failure was not an option.

"Hey!" Scott ducked his head into her line of vision. "That's an awfully serious expression you've got there. I didn't mean to make things worse."

With a shift of her head, she forced her face to relax. He'd only been in her life for a few days, and yet it seemed right. She couldn't imagine working on this without him. "Sorry. I–I'm fine. I tend to allow my thoughts and emotions to show on my face. I was just digesting the thought of not catching this guy. I didn't like it."

"Look." He pointed to the clock on the wall. "Why don't we plan to go for an early dinner tonight. We can push all this aside for a bit, talk about normal things, eat a good meal, and then come back refreshed to tackle the monster. It will give us both something to look forward to. Say, four o'clock?"

They'd all been working just about around the clock. Which wasn't sustainable. She'd been here since six this morning. It couldn't hurt to get away for a while. Like he said, they could always come back. "It's a date."

"Perfect." He shifted back to his computer. "Now let me see if I can figure out how to track this guy. It's not as easy as they make it look on TV."

"Preach." She laughed and went back to the work in front of her. How many times had she told people what she did over the years and they compared it to one of their favorite shows? It was great that people were interested in what law enforcement did, but it'd be even better if Hollywood actually got it correct. Of course, then people would think it was boring since so much of what they did was tedious.

Oh well. Back to the case.

It would be a miracle at this point if their UNSUB had only taken four or five lives. The planning, the methodical thinking that had gone into each of these puzzles. The closer Carrie felt like she got to understanding the killer, the more it unnerved her.

Could there be a chance it was only five rather than eight? Even so, it was five lives too many.

The phone in the center of the conference table rang. She had asked Diane to only send calls that might be related to the case. The press had been relentless in their desire for a quote or information. Cutting off their access to her was the only way she could focus on solving this horrible mystery.

She picked up the receiver. "ABI, Carrie Kintz."

"I am disappointed in you," the distorted voice began.

The menacing tone sent goose bumps over her arms. This voice sounded deeper, angrier than the woman who called the first time. She hit Record and signaled Alan through the glass to trace the call. "Oh? Well, I'm sorry to hear that." Keeping her voice steady and calm were her focus for the moment.

"I hear you don't believe I told the truth."

What on earth? She schooled her breathing and tone. "Really? About what?"

"There were eight dead." The warbling voice grew louder. "Nine now, thanks to you, because you didn't believe me."

Steady and calm flew out the window. She came to her feet. "No. I'm sorry. I believe you."

"No more playing games, Ms. Kintz. You need to understand I mean business. I will outsmart you every step of the way. The Zodiac is a peon compared to me." It sounded like a robotic scream. Then silence.

"Hello?" She hoped he hadn't disconnected.

"Now for my first demand. I insist that you start having regular press conferences about me. Details are important, Ms. Kintz. Make sure people know my brilliance. If you don't, I'll have no problem eliminating a citizen of our great community every day. Maybe a child next time."

The line clicked.

"Hello?" Her heart felt like it was in her throat. But he was gone.

CHAPTER ELEVEN

DOWN
8. Eleven letters. Independent source of warmth; unrelated to your furnace.

February 2—11:03 a.m.
Department of Public Safety parking lot

CARRIE'S STEPS ATE UP THE parking lot. She'd made five laps around it already, and she'd only gotten madder and walked faster. The UNSUB had dared to blame her for his taking another life. If that wasn't bad enough, somehow they had a leak. How else could he have known that the team had discussed the Zodiac Killer and that they hoped he hadn't actually killed eight people?

As soon as she'd let everyone know about the call and they'd listened to the recording, Alan went to work checking for listening devices in the office. She'd nodded and stomped out the door. No one had even tried to stop her, which was a good thing. She was like a volcano about to blow.

Making her way around the parking lot once again, she spotted Scott heading toward her. His incredible smile made her stomach do a little flip, but it didn't calm the storm that brewed inside her.

What was she doing even thinking about having a relationship right now? Would this be her life from now on? How could she ask this of anyone? It was unfair, if she was honest.

On the other hand, she couldn't do this alone. It wasn't healthy, and she knew it.

"Hi." Scott jumped up and down a couple times when he reached her. "It. Is. Cold."

"Yeah." But she kept walking.

Keeping pace next to her, he rubbed his gloved hands together. "It wasn't your fault."

"I know that." The words spewed out whiny and defensive.

"Then why are you out here pounding the pavement when it's three below zero?"

"I needed to think."

"Okay. Well, let me help you. They used another burner phone for the call. Kevin called APD and found out where the burner phone used to call Mrs. Silva was purchased. So far, they've tracked the three burner phones to Washington State, Oregon, and California. All purchases made within the last two years. They're trying to get surveillance footage from the stores since they were cash purchases. Alan didn't find any listening devices in the offices. They've requested some assistance from the troopers next door since you guys are short-handed. They'll keep a sweeping device on twenty-four seven to ensure there's not anything."

"Well, if there aren't any devices, how did he know what we just talked about?"

Scott's jaw clenched. "Haven't figured that out yet." He turned and walked backward. "Look, I'm worried about you. It's seriously freezing out here."

She stopped, and her shoulders crumpled. "I really appreciate it, but I am so overwhelmed . . . I–I can't deal with this right now."

"Deal with what? The case? You've got all of us here to help."

"No." She blew out a breath, and it turned into an icy cloud. "Us. You and me."

He held up his hands. "No expectations here, Carrie. I'm here to help. Let's catch this guy, and then we can go back to being normal human beings. Deal?"

"All right." But she didn't like it. She didn't want to push him away. To be honest, she really liked Scott Patteson. But she felt engulfed by this case, leaving no room for feelings. Especially of the romantic nature. Carrie nodded her head toward the door. "Let's get back in there and see what the guys have found."

But as they headed back to the ABI building, a horrible thought took root. Could Scott be the leak? She hated to even allow that thought, but it was there whether she liked it or not.

No. Not Scott. No way he'd have the security clearance he had if he was in any way crooked. Right?

They entered the building, and she relished the warm air on her face. She headed straight for the conference room, where Alan was sweeping with a handheld device.

He frowned as she got closer. "Um . . . come over here, Carrie."

She stepped closer and took off her coat. "Okay." She hung it on the back of her chair.

He shifted the device to her coat. "Oh man."

"What?"

He put a finger to his lips.

Every hair on the back of her neck stood. It was her? She'd been the leak? How?

Alan set the sweeping device down and sifted through her pockets. Then ran his hand along the hem, the zipper, and then the hood. His hands stilled, and he grabbed a pair of gloves.

No one said a word as they watched. Carrie held her breath as Alan's hands traversed the seam of the drawstring in her hood. Out slid a tiny circle.

Smaller than any bug she'd ever seen.

He reached for an evidence bag, and Kevin shook his head, then slammed his hand on the table.

Alan walked into the squad room and grabbed his stapler. When he came back, he smashed the listening device with the stapler and then swiped all the pieces off the table into his cup of coffee. "There.

That should render it unusable. But why didn't you want it taken down to Corey?"

Kevin's eyes were steely. "For Corey to find anything, it would have to still be in use. As soon as our UNSUB knew we'd found the bug, he'd have turned it off and erased all data. And I couldn't take the risk of a listening device down in the lab. We've obviously given this guy too much information already."

"It's highly doubtful Corey would have been able to trace it anyway." Scott stood with his hands in fists at his sides, clearly agitated. "This guy's tech is more sophisticated than your average criminal's. But"—he paused and went to his computers—"it does give us a hint. He's got money. Lots of it. And that gives him access to anything. I'll get on and see what's available on the dark web. This just might help us track him down."

¤   ¤   ¤

DOWN
8. Six letters. Destroying the flow of traffic.

February 2—noon
Underground tunnel, downtown Anchorage

They found the bug. Yay for them. Didn't matter anyway. It had served its purpose and put them on edge. It also told them he was serious. And smart. And that he would stop at nothing to get what he wanted.

What he deserved.

There were plenty of other plans up his sleeve to accomplish his goals. The world had no idea what he was capable of doing.

Last night, he'd stayed glued to the computer monitors watching all the news stations. The world was deteriorating right before their eyes. When were people going to wake up?

They needed a leader. They needed *him*.

He was the only one who could save the world. He'd start here. With Alaska. Then people would see what he accomplished and would want that for themselves.

A buzz on his watch reminded him of the time. He pulled out his little notebook, popped a pill into his mouth, and logged it. He'd worked on the perfect blend and timing.

All those psycho-psychiatrists and patsy doctors over the years telling him he had mental health issues. They said he was troubled. Diagnosed him with every single thing they could find in their medical books from depression to psychosis. Then told him he was an addict after they shoved pill after pill down his throat. The roller coaster his life had been because of them was brutal. But he had survived. On his own.

Because of his own brilliance. Once he'd finally understood his true potential, he'd realized he was unstoppable.

Everything inside him was working at one hundred percent, and his mind hummed with ideas. He'd never felt so alive.

Footsteps alerted him, and he searched the security monitor. Glenn. The kid was needy and proving not to be the asset that Griz had hoped. Another disposable. He spun in his chair and waited.

"Hey." Glenn closed the door behind him. "I've got bad news."

"Well?" He waited.

The kid shuffled his feet. "Cal OD'd last night."

Griz bit the inside of his cheek to contain his temper. "Cal was weak. Are you going to be weak?"

Glenn lifted his pathetic face. "No."

"Dispose of the body."

"I can't. The police came, and I couldn't do anything about it."

He growled.

"But I made sure there was nothing on him. I promise."

He stared the kid down for several seconds. "Fine. I have two messages that need to be delivered."

"I can handle it." The skinny young man straightened.

"Good. When you're done, we'll talk about a promotion."

◻ ◻ ◻

DOWN
8. Five letters. Welts that appear whenever I come near, but it's not because you hold me dear.

February 2—3:39 p.m.
Alaska Bureau of Investigation

"What do you think?" Carrie leaned on the table and looked over Scott's shoulder.

"All the burners were purchased by young kids. The one that made the first call—the woman. The one that was sent to the editor of Anchorage Daily News. The one that made the second call. The security footage is weak and none of them get a shot of their faces. Stores should start saying, 'no hoodies allowed.'" He sighed as he leaned back in his chair. "Sorry. I don't know how you deal with this day in and day out."

"I had a feeling we wouldn't get anything, but at least we tried." She plopped into the chair beside him. "This case infuriates me. Especially since he's claimed that he's killed people and we don't have all the bodies. Kevin already put out a bulletin that all deaths in the city have to be reported here to see if we require an autopsy before the families do anything like cremation."

He swiveled in his chair and faced her. "That's good. I know grieving families won't want to deal with it, but it's for the safety of everyone. Frankly, I'm not too keen on you doing these press conferences, but if Kevin says you should, then I guess you have to."

"It's not my first choice either, but we'll play this little game if it helps us to catch our man."

"Still convinced it's a male?"

"Yep. It's just a hunch right now, but Kevin says he feels the same way. Not that we'd rule out any female leads. It would be great if we had *any* lead at this point." She reached across the table and grabbed the rumpled sketch of the guy from the coffee shop. "I wish we had more to go on with this guy than just a sketch and my suspicions."

"I was hoping that messenger kid would identify him, but that was wishful thinking, wasn't it?"

She let out a short *humph*. "I've found I do a lot of wishful thinking . . . not that it helps much."

The now-familiar *step, thump, step, thump* of Kevin on his crutches made her turn to the door.

Paper in his teeth, he stopped and then tossed it on the table. "Alan and I have some cases to follow up on."

She scanned the sheet. "This is great. If we understand more about the murders he's already committed, then we might be able to figure out what he's going to try next."

Kevin took the seat on the other side of her. "I'm now talking to you as your superior. You need to get out of this office for a while and focus on something else. Why don't we trade off getting dinner. You and Scott go first. Take an hour. Then Alan and I will do the same. We're looking at long days until we catch this offender."

She glanced the other way and shared a look with Scott. Hadn't they made plans for dinner tonight? That seemed like eons ago. "Sounds good. We'll go now and beat the rush. I'm starved."

"No talking about the case," Kevin warned.

She shrugged into her coat and pulled her hat down over her forehead. "No promises."

Scott grabbed his coat. "You don't have to tell *me* twice. I've seen Alan eat, so if we get to go first, that means there might actually be food left in the city for us."

The guys laughed and ribbed each other, but she kept walking toward the door. She absolutely hated leaving things undone. She was going to have to get over that if she wanted a career as an investigator. There were some cases that detectives worked on for years. The thought was unpleasant and made her cringe. Of course, *she'd* never had an unsolved case. Then again, she'd never been in charge of a case any bigger than a stolen vehicle before.

Quick footsteps sounded behind her and she glanced over her shoulder. Scott. She let out a breath.

Better apologize now and get it over with.

"I'm sorry for my moment of—well, let's just say it. I freaked out a little bit. About us. When I get overwhelmed, sometimes . . . I lash out. It was unfair for me to take my frustrations out on you."

"Ice cream sounds good."

"Huh?" Was he even listening to her?

He winked at her. "Sorry, I wasn't making light of the situation. I promise. You and me? We're good. Everyone's entitled to the occasional freak-out moment here and there. We're all under a lot of stress. It doesn't change how I feel about you. Or how I see you as an investigator."

Whoa. How he felt about her? While she had to admit she was attracted to Scott and had high hopes for a future, for some reason his admitting it made her nervous.

"So, like I said, ice cream sounds good." Scott's deep voice penetrated her thoughts as they exited the building. "Relax. You're overthinking. We're supposed to get away from all this and hit refresh."

He was right. She needed to block everything out for a bit and relax. She could play along. "Ice cream. In the dead of winter? Alaskans." She laughed. "You know, I read an article before I moved up here that said there was an urban legend about Alaskans eating more ice cream per capita than anyone else on the planet."

He clicked the auto-start button on his key fob. "That's not an urban legend. That's fact. How about we make a fast run for burgers and then get some ice cream?"

"Sure. Why not."

"You don't sound enthused. Let's make a bet?"

"Okay. What are the stakes?" It felt good to smile and laugh and be normal.

"Loser has to buy ice cream for the whole team for a week." He eyed her with a challenging grin.

"You're on. What's the bet?"

"I bet you that there will be a line outside Cold Stone when we get there."

"*Pfft.* Yeah, right. It's not even ten degrees outside! You're on." She thrust out her hand to shake his.

"You're gonna lose . . . I give you fair warning now." He opened the passenger door of his SUV for her, and she climbed in.

"We'll just see about that."

Once they were out on the road, he drove through the streets like he knew them inside and out. Of course he did. He'd lived here his whole life. As he drove, he pointed out good places to eat, his favorite coffee huts, and places she hadn't even realized were tucked into little corners, and the distraction melted away the stress of the day. The seat warmer on high didn't hurt either.

He pulled to a stop next to a nondescript building. "Hope you like burgers. These are my favorite. We'll have to eat them in the car, though, is that all right? They don't have indoor dining."

"I don't even see a restaurant." There wasn't a sign or anything on the building.

"You have to know it's here. Look, you tell me what you want, and I'll venture into the cold." He listed off the choices. Not a huge menu, but the more he talked, the hungrier she grew.

"I'll have a double cheeseburger, extra cheese. With mushrooms and onions." Her mouth watered as she said it.

"Want to split some loaded fries?" He waggled his eyebrows at her.

"Sounds amazing."

"Be right back." He hopped out and raced across the tiny parking lot.

Ten minutes later, he emerged with two large paper bags, the steam off the tops clearly visible in the frigid air.

He opened the driver's side door, and the amazing smell of grilled beef, cheese, and onions overtook her senses. Pulling his door closed behind him, he handed her one of the bags.

"I have to admit, a friend of my family owns the place, but these are the best burgers in the city."

She licked her lips. "I believe you. The smell alone has my stomach turning cartwheels because it can't wait." On a whim, she grabbed his free hand. "My turn to pray."

After probably the quickest prayer ever, she tore into her bag. But when she saw the size of the burger, her eyes practically popped out of her head. "This is *huge*."

He shrugged, a big bite in his mouth making him look like a chipmunk. He chewed for a few seconds and watched her. "Good luck. But save room for ice cream."

"Watch me." She kept the wrapper halfway up the sides because it already looked like the best of the best—which meant she was going to need twenty napkins before it was all said and done. Biting into the massive double cheeseburger, her taste buds thanked her, and her brain swirled with so many thoughts she had to close her eyes.

"Good, huh?"

When she had swallowed and opened her eyes, she laughed. "You've been watching me this whole time?"

"Oh yeah. Had to see your reaction. It was worth it."

"This is the best burger I've ever had. Make sure you tell the owners I said that. Seriously. I'm going to have to work out five extra times a week, because I see an addiction in my future."

"I thought pizza was your favorite food?" He shoved a fry dripping with cheese, bacon, and sour cream into his mouth.

"It is—was. Burgers were always my second fave. But this might edge out the pizza. Although that stuff from Moose's Tooth was the bomb."

He laughed at her. "Nice lingo."

"I'm from North Dakota, ya know. That's how the crazy kids talk back there."

Their dinner passed in lots of talk about food, their favorite restaurants, and the craziest things they'd ever eaten. Both of them scarfed down the burgers and fries in record time.

"Ready for that ice cream?" He gathered up all the trash as she wiped her hands with every last napkin in the vehicle.

She groaned and put a hand to her stomach. "I definitely want to win that bet. But can we drive over there and let our food settle a bit before we tackle dessert?" With a glance to her watch, she noted that it wasn't even 4:45. Perfect timing. Who was going to be out for ice cream right before dinnertime?

"Sounds like a plan. But don't say I didn't warn you."

Scott began to pull around the parking lot when she did a double take. Movement over by the building had caught her eye. That man. She knew his face. "Turn around." She gripped Scott's arm.

Without question or hesitation, he did as she asked, but by the time the SUV had come full circle, there was no sign of anyone.

"What is it?" Scott leaned over the steering wheel and stared out the windshield.

"Nothing." With a shake of her head, she tried to eliminate the chill that had wriggled its way up her neck. There was nothing to see. Her mind must have conjured it up.

"Let's get that ice cream. I'm ready to win the bet." She forced a smile.

But in her mind, clear as day, she'd seen the man from the coffee shop. Watching her. Again.

CHAPTER TWELVE

DOWN
8. Nine letters. Like diabetes and the flu. Oh, but not this time.

February 2—4:43 p.m.
South Anchorage

WITH A FLICK OF HER thumb, she opened her laptop and stared at the screen. She hated writing papers. Especially after a long day. Rubbing her eyes, she determined to put at least an hour into the project before class tonight. The sooner she started, the sooner she'd finish. And the sooner she finished, the sooner she could graduate and get out of her thankless minimum-wage job.

If she'd listened to her mom, she wouldn't be here. But there was no sense dwelling on the past. Or telling her mother she was right.

The moment helped her to laugh it off and she began to type about early childhood education and the effects of screen time on children under ten. She'd been researching the topic for weeks now; she practically had what she wanted to write memorized.

Her computer buzzed underneath her fingertips, and then the lights started.

Horrible. Flashing. Pulsing. Strobing. Bright . . . too bright.

No. No . . . *No!* She closed her eyes against it.

But the damage was done. The seizure took control until her body betrayed her and flung her violently out of the chair.

◻ ◻ ◻

DOWN
8. Eight letters. Once it's broken, your body can't fix it.

February 2—4:52 p.m.
Cold Stone Creamery, Anchorage

"I can't believe it." Carrie stared at people standing outside the Cold Stone Creamery in freezing temperatures, waiting in line for ice cream. The irony was not lost on her. "You win."

"I sure do." He put his vehicle in Park and shifted in his seat. Laying his hand on the back of her headrest, he locked eyes with her. "As much as I'd like to revel in my victory, I think it's time you told me what you saw. It was the guy from the coffee shop, wasn't it?"

Her jaw dropped and then she snapped it shut. "Did you see him?"

"No. But the only other time I've seen you react like that was at the coffee shop." He leaned back against his door.

How could he be so relaxed? It unnerved her. "It's probably the stress. I must have been imagining things."

"I doubt that."

It was her turn to shift to face him. "Why?" She hated how the question came out. Full of anger. It wasn't his fault; he just happened to be the only one in her line of fire right now.

"Are you in the habit of imagining things, Ms. Kintz?" Apparently, she hadn't fazed him. He was calm and, as always, sweet.

With a huff, she expelled all her pent-up energy. Her head went back until she was staring at the headliner of the SUV. She clasped her hands in her lap. "No. I'm not. In fact, it's never happened before."

"So stop doubting yourself."

She turned her head, and they stared at each other in silence.

Blinking, she could think of no smart retort. He was right. Again.

"Want to talk about it?" He laid a hand over the steering wheel. "I can step in line and grab us some ice cream. Then we'll have plenty of time to talk."

She pursed her lips and blew out a breath. "Let's talk first. Ice cream can be the reward."

"All right." His relaxed grin made her feel at home.

For several seconds, she just studied his face. The firm jaw. The dark hair that fell over his forehead when he took off his hat. Brown eyes with crinkles at the corners, testifying to the fact that he'd laughed and spent a good deal of time in the enduring Alaska sun. Brown eyes that made her feel safe. Scott was the first guy she knew who would be there to catch her when she fell, to cheer her on, even take the proverbial bullet for her. But how could she know all that in such a short amount of time?

"You've got great instincts."

"What?" Was he reading her mind? Heat rose up her neck and into her face.

"The question is, why do you doubt them?"

"Huh?" Wait. Was he talking about her instincts about him? Could he tell she was starting to have feelings for him that scared her? Was she that obvious?

"You're a natural at this job. Kevin sees it. Alan sees it. I see it." He paused. "Shoot, I even think your UNSUB sees it. That's why he's trying to get at you."

Flicking her gaze back down to her lap, she allowed his words to sink in. Logically, they made sense. But emotionally? The words were tougher to accept.

"It might sound ridiculous, but I think the doubts come from my own expectations."

"I get that. I'm terrible at placing expectations on myself that I can't achieve."

"You and me both." She lifted her hands and shook her head. "And what's worse, I put higher expectations on myself than anyone else does. Growing up, if my dad expected me to do something, I'd do it, but I had to make it harder than he said. Just because." Words began to flow out of her. "I feel so inadequate at this job. Not because anyone has made me feel that way—well, not at the department. We won't talk about my taunter. But I wear it like a cloak.

"And I've had this picture-perfect life. I have an amazing family—faithful, strong, loyal. Believers. When I wanted to go into law enforcement, they all cheered me on. When I dreamed about getting into the FBI and pursuing profiling, they told me nobody would be better. I've never suffered any major loss. Never had anything crushing happen to me. I was the good kid in school. Always had straight As. Existed in my little Christian bubble in my Norman Rockwell–worthy hometown. Never threatened."

The more she said, the more the puzzle became clear in her mind. "It's like I feel guilty for having such a great life. Like, I don't deserve this. I haven't done anything to earn it, and that means I'm probably not capable. Or worse, I must be messing it up royally. Then this case shows up. He figures out all my fears and puts them on public display. I'm the new guy. I can't possibly solve this case. I can't even keep up." A tear slipped down her cheek. She hadn't even realized she was crying until she swallowed and choked back the tears.

Scott reached across the seat and grabbed her hand. The warmth from his fingers seeped into her own. "I'm going to say something that might come across as Christianese, but I want you to hear me out."

Swiping at her cheek, she chuckled. "Go ahead—Christian bubble, remember?" She made a circle with her hand in front of her face.

"That's the enemy talking, and you know it."

She moaned. "I know. And ever since I've been here, I haven't found a church home yet. My schedule is nuts, and I've been putting my faith walk on the back burner. My grandma would fly up here and scold me if she knew the truth." She shook her head. "Gracious, what am I saying? She'd bring the whole family up here for an intervention and tell me that I needed to get down on my knees, repent, and get back in the Word."

He laughed. "It's not bad advice. But I think you already know all that. Look, a huge move like that has got to be tough. Can't say that I've ever done it myself, but I've had friends who said it took over a year for them to feel settled and comfortable and normal again."

Tilting her head, she watched the man before her. "No judgment? I'm impressed."

It was his turn to put up his hands in surrender. "Hey, I've got my own issues that give me all kinds of grief. But I do have a great church home. I'd love for you to join me sometime. Lots of professionals our age, which is great, but there's also an amazing core group of people older than us, willing to pour into and mentor the next generation. I don't know how Pastor Garry created that climate for building relationships, but it's incredible."

"You know what? I might take you up on that. It'll probably have to be after we catch this serial killer, but hopefully soon."

"Deal." He shifted again. "I'll even throw in another run for burgers after church."

"Now how could I pass that up?"

He put his gloves back on. "Want to get some ice cream now?" Somehow, he was able to sense just how much soul baring was enough for her.

"Sounds perfect." She slipped on her gloves as well.

His cell buzzed. He removed a glove with his teeth and used his fingers to swipe at the screen and answer. "Hey, Mac."

She could tell by his body language it was someone he knew really well. Motioning to the creamery, she whispered, "I'll go get in line."

He gave her a quick nod, and she exited the warmth of the vehicle. To go stand in the cold. Laughing, she had to admit that she was craving ice cream. Maybe she was adapting to her new surroundings better than she'd thought after all.

"Carrie." Scott's voice called to her as he jogged over to where she stood. When he came close, he tipped his head and reached for her elbow. She stepped toward him, and he put his hand on her back, pulling her even closer.

The intimate gesture diminished all the cold air around her. "No ice cream?" She pointed to the line he'd pulled her out of.

"I'm sorry. My boss, Mac . . . well, he was . . . He lost his wife and daughter up in Fairbanks during the 26 Below attack."

She put a hand over her mouth. "Oh my goodness, that's awful."

"He's asked me to come see him. I know we need to get back to the investigation, but would it be okay if I dropped you off? Could you spare me for an hour or so?"

"Of course. It sounds important. Besides, I need to get caught up on whatever Kevin and Alan have been working on. There's plenty to keep me busy. Let's go." She started back to the car.

His hand on the small of her back made her smile. All the old-time movies had gentlemen doing that. It made her feel special. Protected. Cared for and important. "Thanks for this, Scott."

They reached his SUV, and he opened the passenger door for her. As she moved to step in, he stopped her. Their gazes collided, and for a moment she thought he was going to kiss her.

But instead, as he closed the space between them, he stared deeply into her eyes and dipped his chin. He was crouching a bit, reducing some of the difference between their heights.

"You are a wonder, Carrie Kintz. I'm looking forward to getting to know every little detail about you." He spoke softly, touching her cheek with his gloved hand.

Only inches separated them, and she held her breath, savoring the moment.

With a smile, he stepped back, and she blinked. Then she ducked into the car, and he closed the door.

◻ ◻ ◻

DOWN
8. Seven letters. A taking or attack.

February 2—6:06 p.m.
Hillside East, Anchorage

Mac fiddled with his mug and swiped at the tears in his eyes. "Give me a minute."

Scott's heart ached for his friend. He couldn't even begin to imagine what the man had gone through losing his wife and daughter. By a cyberterrorist too. It was like a slap in the face to his boss at Cyber Solutions.

Jason had been sent up to Fairbanks to assist the Emergency Ops Center while Mac and his family had been whole and intact back in Anchorage. Then his wife and daughter went up to the pipeline for a school project and got caught in an explosion. A diversion for the guys who hated the government and wanted to take over the world.

It wasn't fair. None of it was.

Mac was a shell of the man Scott had known for years. His friend was in great need of a haircut. A shaggy beard had taken up residence on his face. And it looked like he hadn't slept since November.

Which he probably hadn't.

Mac had been the steadiest, most reliable, and most trustworthy man Scott had ever known. The man was a rock. Mentor to many. Head of their Cyber Solutions office. Nothing had ever shaken him. Until November. It was hard to see what had become of him.

"They didn't catch whoever was behind the attack up in Fairbanks, Scott." He lifted his gaze to Scott, and the anger there was palpable. "The man responsible for killing my family is still out there." He gritted his teeth.

Scott took a sip of the intense coffee Mac had given him. He couldn't blame the guy for needing closure. At this point, it was best to just listen. He waited quietly for his friend to say more.

"I know you're probably thinking that I'm just a grieving husband and father who's become obsessed. But it's true. I need you to go back to the ABI and figure out how to tie it all together."

"Mac—"

"I don't need your sympathy or words telling me I need sleep or I need to grieve or I need closure or whatever. I've heard it all before. But it couldn't have been more perfect for you, out of all the guys at Cyber Solutions, to be placed there for this case. I told Tim you were the guy. You understand loss."

The hint at Maria stabbed him. It had taken years to rid himself of the heartache she'd left behind. Mac knew this. Why would he bring it up now?

Scott held up a hand. "That's all in the past. It took me a long time to get over it, so yeah, I understand, Mac. But why do you think they didn't catch the guy? Weren't there arrests at the cabin the prophetess lady had hidden in? And a bunch of dead accomplices?" He stopped cold. So much for listening. As soon as Mac put him on the defensive, he started spouting. "I'm sorry. You asked me to listen, and I—"

"Don't apologize. I get it. I shouldn't have brought up Maria. But I really need you to pay attention."

"Okay." He leaned back on the couch. "I'm listening. I promise."

Going over to a draped object in the corner of the room, Mac removed the blanket to reveal a large corkboard with notes in all different colors and string connecting them to other notes.

Scott got up from the couch to get a closer look. His eyes went wide as he began to read. How much time had this taken?

Mac cleared his throat. "As you can see, I've done my homework. Jason and Darcie up in Fairbanks helped me with some of the information. The rest, I've pieced together on my own."

"How? Where did you get the information?" His mind spun with thoughts and questions as he examined each note.

"I went to the Fairbanks Correctional Center. Darrell Collins had a lot to say about the guy who was actually behind it all."

"Who's Darrell Collins?"

"One of the guys they arrested at the cabin. Along with Kirk Myers—Jason's brother."

Scott remembered Jason's brother being involved. He'd been an addict for a long time, and Jason had searched all over for him. But this was the first time he'd gotten a name for the other terrorist. "Are you certain this Collins guy wasn't just trying to say that he was innocent to save his own skin?"

"Positive. This is the mastermind—from Collins's testimony. I hired a professional sketch artist to work with him until it was exact. Collins confirmed it." Mac opened a file folder and pulled out a sketch. "I can't keep this up on the board because it makes me crazy, but I feel like his face is etched into my brain anyway."

"Don't get me wrong, I want to help any way I can—especially if they haven't caught the real guy. But how do you know you can trust this Collins?" Scott looked at the sketch, swallowed hard, then did his best to keep his expression clear. Pulling out his phone, he snapped a picture of it. He couldn't say anything to Mac, not yet, but the sketch looked a lot like Carrie's coffee-shop creep. The implications were more than he could fathom.

He took pictures of the board next, just to show Mac he was serious about listening to him. And also because Carrie needed to see it. All of it. Just in case it was connected.

Dear Lord, I hope we're wrong. The magnitude of the situation made him feel sick to his stomach. Mac was talking, and Scott forced his mind to pay attention.

"There's so much that doesn't add up. But I guess I believe Collins because his story has never changed. They've had psych evaluations done three times, and they've come back clear every time. He's constantly working on appeals. He's openly admitted his participation— and his motive."

Scott crossed his arms over his chest and stared at his friend. Was he obsessed and going overboard, or was there truth in all this? He owed it to Mac to find out the accuracy of the guy's claims.

"Okay, so let's say this Collins guy is telling the truth. What about Jason's brother? Everybody knows he was a mess. He's been mixed up with radical groups for years. What does he say?"

"He claims Darrell was the mastermind, but it doesn't ring true. There's plenty of evidence to prove Collins couldn't have done a lot of what went on with the cyberattack. Kirk's hiding something. Every time I've talked to him, I see it in his eyes. The way he smirks. He's covering for the real mastermind. The man who murdered Sarah and Beth." Mac's jaw clenched and unclenched in rapid succession. "I'm sorry. It's still fresh, but I owe it to them to get to the bottom of it."

Scott stepped closer and laid a hand on his friend's shoulder. "Look, we're computer guys. We can't get to the bottom of it like the police can. Have you gone to them with your suspicions?"

"Multiple times. I'm telling you, there's someone behind all this that's blocking me at every turn. What if he's connected to your serial killer?" His friend's eyes were desperate. Bleary and full of pain. "I need your help, Scott. But be careful. This guy is still out there. And I'm pretty sure he's got friends in high places."

If he hadn't been in on the discussions at the ABI about the mayor's murder being connected to their serial killer and her possibly being connected to the cyberattack, Scott would have thought this was all quite a stretch. But Mac was a smart man. And then there was the sketch. Not a coincidence.

Scott couldn't tell him anything to get his hopes up, but he stored each little nugget to discuss with Carrie and the team later. For several seconds, he ran over in his mind the best way to respond. "I'll look into it. I don't know how much I can do since our hands are full with this serial killer, but I'll do what I can. I promise. Right now, I've got to get back to the ABI."

He turned to go, but then looked over his shoulder. "Is it all right with you if I share your suspicions with Carrie?"

The tension in Mac's face eased for the first time since Scott had walked in the door. "Yeah. Thanks. That'd mean a lot to me."

Scott dipped his head in a nod and walked toward the door. Mac followed. Scott tossed an arm over his friend's shoulder. "Promise you'll try to get some sleep tonight?"

"I'll do my best." His voice was low and scratchy.

As he climbed into his SUV, Scott went back over everything he'd seen and heard. Far-fetched as it seemed, he suspected Mac was right.

He wasn't sure which was worse—the serial killer on the loose or the cyberterrorist. If Mac was onto something and it was the same man behind it all, then they were up a creek without the proverbial paddle.

Scott doubted *he* would get any sleep tonight.

CHAPTER THIRTEEN

DOWN
8. Seven letters. Leave stranded.

February 2—8:02 p.m.
Alaska Bureau of Investigation

"WE'VE GOT ANOTHER BODY." ALAN spoke from the door of the conference room, catching Carrie's attention.

"Does it match any of our clues?" She went to the whiteboard.

"No. It's an OD."

Scribbling in a new column on the board, she wrote down the specifics Alan gave her. "Ask Dr. Blanchard to call if she finds anything—and I mean anything—out of the ordinary."

"You got it." He rushed out of the room and back to the phone at his desk.

Staring at the board, she wished she could magically snap her fingers and all the pieces of this puzzle would come together. More than anything, she wanted to take down this guy.

Voices out in the squad room shifted her gaze to the door. Scott was back. As he strode toward the conference room, she couldn't help but smile. God had given her an amazing gift by bringing him into her life.

"Hey." His voice was a bit breathless. "I've got a lot to talk about, do you have a minute?"

"Sure." She sat in her chair. "I hope it's about our case."

"Uh, not exactly." He drew out the words, sat down, and looked over to Kevin. "I could really use your insight here as well. Alan's too." Carrie called him in.

For the next half hour, Scott shared everything he knew about Mac, his friend's suspicions, the pictures of the board, and then finally, the sketch.

Carrie gasped when she saw it. "That's him. The man from the coffee shop." She bolted from her seat.

"I had a feeling it was when I saw the sketch."

"I need you to send that to me so I can print it out." She paced around the conference room. "And you say that Darrell Collins—one of the men in prison for the 26 Below cyberterrorist attack—said this man is the mastermind?" Her hands flew to her hips, and she shot a glance at Kevin.

His face was hard and serious. "I don't believe in coincidences, and neither do you."

"I need to get up to Fairbanks. I want to interview Collins and Myers myself. Scott"—she turned back to him—"you're going to come with me. You're the connection to Mac and Jason and can call them if we need them, right? I'd like to meet Jason and Darcie as well, but we need to fly—there's no time to drive all the way up there, investigate, and drive back. Not with a serial killer on the loose."

Scott raised his hand with a sheepish grin on his face. "I can help with that. My dad's got a plane, and I have a pilot's license."

That was an unexpected surprise. But she'd take it. "Kevin, if we try to do it all in one day, do you think you and Alan will be able to handle everything here?"

"We'll do our best. We've got team members out all over the state. Hopefully some of them will be back soon."

The phone rang at Alan's desk. He rushed over and answered it.

Carrie drummed her fingers on the table while she waited for him to come back. Good news would be nice, but she doubted that with every fiber of her being.

"Three more bodies." Alan's voice was hushed as he glanced down at the paper in his hand. "One is from a private plane crash that happened several days ago. One is an epileptic. Doc believes it was a grand mal seizure. And the other, she's not sure. It happened at the hospital, and the docs there were baffled."

Shooting her gaze to the board, she studied the clues they had. Then it hit her. "Look! These two right here—'reaction with aversion' and 'lawsuit due to negligence'—how much do you want to bet the body from the hospital was an allergic reaction?"

Alan and Scott joined her at the board. Scott pointed. "These two. 'A pilot's home away from home' and 'Bloop. Bloop. Bloop.' *Cockpit* and *radar*." He rushed back over to his computer. "Both of these could be caused by hacks."

◌ ◌ ◌

DOWN
8. Seven letters. Bone to break if you want to get to the heart of the matter.

February 2—9:00 p.m.
Alaska Bureau of Investigation

Scott chewed on his thumbnail as he watched the TV screen in the conference room. Carrie was outside, about to give a press conference. She'd invited the press and intentionally kept them outside in the cold because that would keep it short and to the point. Kevin would stand behind her as a known and seasoned investigator. And she wouldn't be taking any questions. Not tonight.

The station went to a "Breaking News" banner, and the anchor announced the press conference.

Then there she was. Center of the screen behind a small podium bursting with microphones.

With a lift of her chin, Carrie spoke. "Good evening, ladies and gentlemen. I'm coming to you tonight on behalf of the Alaska Bureau of Investigation, the Alaska State Troopers, and the Anchorage Police Department. I am Special Agent Carrie Kintz, and I am the lead investigator on our serial killer case. It is a team effort to keep our citizens safe, and I'd like to thank you all for your support during this extremely difficult time." She paused and cleared her throat.

"I'll keep this brief. We have a serial killer on the loose. With seven confirmed dead, we are using every resource we have to track this offender. I implore all our residents to be vigilant. He's not coming after you with a gun, a knife, or some other violent weapon. Whoever he is—he is using our own technology against us. That said, we are advising you to power down your electronics whenever you can. Don't rely solely on technology to accomplish your daily tasks. Keep an eye on your family, friends, and neighbors. We're up against a brilliant psychopath and ask you to not call 911 unless it is an emergency. Please do not call the troopers, APD, or the ABI unless you have information that can help us track down this killer. That's all for now. Thank you."

"How did the victims die?"

"Are we in danger?"

"Do you have any suspects?"

The questions were thrown out simultaneously, but she stepped away from the podium as more volleyed at her from every direction. The news station went back to the "Breaking News" screen and then back to its regular programming.

Carrie strode back into the squad room, removed her winter things, and tossed them on her desk.

Scott watched her step purposefully toward the conference room and run a hand through her hair. Her nose was red from the cold.

"How'd I do?" She made a face at him.

"I thought it was great."

Alan sat on the edge of the table, his arms crossed over his chest. "It wasn't exactly what he demanded, but I agree with Scott. You did great."

"Hey, I threw in the word *brilliant* before I called him a psychopath. That was the only thing I could do without lying. Which I refuse to do."

The phone rang and the air in the room practically sizzled as they stared at it. Scott hated to think it was their killer, but everything inside him said it was.

Carrie shook out both of her arms and then reached for the phone. "ABI, Carrie Kintz." Her jaw dropped as she reached for the speakerphone button, then her lips clamped shut as she hung up. Her face a deep shade of red.

"It was him, wasn't it?" Kevin stood at the door, propped on his crutches.

"Yep." Her lips disappeared as she sucked them in.

"What did he say?" Scott stepped over to her, wanting to give her some sort of support.

But she moved over to the board. "Five words. 'I am not a psychopath.'"

◻ ◻ ◻

DOWN
8. Five letters. Perforation kills.

February 3—7:51 a.m.
Alaska Bureau of Investigation

They'd connected seven deaths to their serial killer now. As an investigator, she should feel some relief. But as a human being, she only felt sick.

The twenty-six-year-old woman with epilepsy had been at home in front of her computer when it happened. The laptop had been delivered to them late last night, and Scott found the evidence. It had been hacked to display intense, seizure-inducing light patterns. For twenty minutes.

Apparently, she'd been working on a paper for night school. The lights had engaged and sent her into a grand mal seizure, during which she fell and struck her head. She bled out and was found the next morning by her roommate.

The private plane victim had never had a chance. Flying at night with cloud cover, the forty-three-year-old male was a seasoned pilot. Their best guess—until Scott could get his hands on the computer from the plane—was that the killer had reprogrammed the navigation system and sent him hurtling straight into a mountain.

And then there was the thirty-year-old female from the hospital. Scott had dug through the hospital's computer systems for five straight hours last night and found that someone had tampered with her records. She'd been given a penicillin-based antibiotic when she had a severe allergy to it. Something simple like that never happened anymore, but the records had been completely swapped with another patient's. In the ER, they'd simply pulled her file and gave her medicine. The hospital was overflowing, and they didn't find her until it was too late. The family had been on the news talking about lawsuits and malpractice. It wouldn't ease their pain to find out the truth, but at least it would help the health-care workers who'd tried to save her life.

Staring at all the pictures on the board—now connected with the creep's crossword puzzles—she wanted to throw something out the window. There were two more people he'd claimed to have killed.

"Penny for your thoughts, boss." Kevin hobbled into the conference room.

The teasing in his voice lightened the tension in the room. "Boss? Really? How did I go from rookie to boss?"

"You're in charge of this case, aren't you?" He grinned and took his seat.

"You say I am, but we all know I couldn't do this without you."

"That's not true, Carrie. I have every confidence in you." He shuffled through his notes and slipped his reading glasses on. "Are you and Scott headed up to Fairbanks today?"

"Hope to. But last night was long on work and short on sleep. For all of us."

Scott ambled into the room and let out a loud yawn. "Coffee. Need coffee." He dropped his gear on the table and went straight for the coffeepot.

She couldn't help but laugh at his antics. At least he wasn't a grump when he didn't get sleep. "How many hours did you squeeze in? Of actual sleep?" She quirked an eyebrow at him.

"Two and a half. You?"

"Three." Blinking against her gritty eyes, she headed toward the coffee too. "I should probably drink a few more cups."

The phone in the middle of the conference table rang.

"I got it. You guys get some caffeine." Kevin leaned forward, grabbed the cord, and tugged the phone toward him. "ABI. Kevin Hogan."

She filled her travel mug two-thirds of the way with coffee, then went to the fridge and grabbed the bottle of Hershey's syrup she'd stashed there. She squirted a good bit into the cup. A little more sugar. A lot of half-and-half. And she gave it a good stir.

Scott just watched her and shook his head. "Whatever works, I guess."

"Don't try it till you knock it," she muttered.

Scott bit his lips together, his shoulders shaking with laughter.

"Wait, I said that wrong, didn't I?" She chuckled. "See? That's why this is necessary. Half a bottle of syrup and all." She took a sip. "Mm." She headed back to her seat.

Kevin hung up. "That was APD. They just sent over three more bodies to Dr. Blanchard. Found within the last hour."

"Three?" She just about spit out her coffee.

"Yep. No visible signs of murder or a struggle, but they're sending everything they have to us just in case it's our serial killer." Kevin shook his head. "I really hate this guy."

"Me too."

◻ ◻ ◻

DOWN
8. Seven letters. Used to blow the snow.

February 3—1:20 p.m.
An unidentified bunker, Anchorage

Psychopath. She'd dared to call him a psychopath. He stomped around the room, waving the gun at his side.

White-hot anger tinged his vision. He was *not* a psychopath. That suggested he was mentally ill. In truth, he was more advanced than any of them could ever hope to be.

"Let's just see what you think of me, Agent Kintz, by the time I'm done with you!" Spittle flew from his mouth as he screamed the words at the human-shaped target on the wall. Then, lifting his favorite Glock, he aimed at the target and squeezed the trigger. Again and again until it was empty and the target was full of holes. Four in the head. Eleven at center mass.

Tilting his head to the right and then the left, he cracked his neck and rolled his shoulders. There. That was better.

He discharged the empty magazine, shoved in a full one, and holstered the Glock.

With methodic movements, he picked up his brass and straightened the cellar. Then he slid his suit coat back on, slicked back his hair, and took long strides down the hidden hallway.

Back in his private office, he studied the files on his desk that had led to the bodies on the floor. He was surrounded by imbeciles.

His plan was perfect, but he was having trouble finding people as good as the ones he'd had up in Fairbanks.

The Members were also getting restless. Of course, once he laid out his full demands to the media, they'd all know how brilliant he was. And cheer.

Using the Narcotics Anonymous meetings as a cover to find his minions over the years had been perfect. He understood the mind of an addict. Knew how brilliant they could be if given the right opportunity. And most importantly, he knew how to take advantage of the fierce loyalty they could exhibit.

Everyone needed a cause to be passionate about. He gave them that.

But sometimes, they stepped off the path. Got greedy and selfish. Or simply lost control of their addiction.

In those instances, he had to eliminate them.

Too many of late.

No one understood his brilliance anymore. Griz popped a pill and logged it in his little book.

Footsteps sounded behind him. He turned a slow circle in his chair and faced his guest. "Ah, Peter." He offered a seat by holding out his arm. "I'm glad you could join me."

Peter surveyed the room. "I take it you need me to get rid of them." He tipped his head toward the bodies.

"That would be lovely, yes. But that's not why I asked you here."

"I'm all ears." The man had been a mess when Griz found him ten years ago. He'd looked nothing like the brother of Griz's youth. Gaunt and hooked on several different street drugs, Peter had been the definition of a junkie. Now look at him. Dressed in all black, the man oozed mystery and a hint of danger. His little brother had grown up.

"Are you still loyal to our cause?"

"Of course."

"Willing to come fully aboard with me now?" Peter had taken a higher offer to be a bodyguard a few years back. It had made Griz furious at the time. Back when family loyalty still meant something. But he'd gotten over that. Especially now that Peter's boss was dead.

"What's your offer?"

"Double what you were making. Plus bonuses for a few special projects. I appreciate the work you've done so far with the ABI agent."

Peter nodded and leaned forward. "Contract?"

"Of course."

"I assume that once you accomplish the Members' goals, you'll need a right-hand man."

"Do as you're asked, and you can be that person."

"I'll expect to see the contract this evening. I'll take care of the mess here and return at five sharp."

"I look forward to it." The two men stood and Griz shook his brother's hand.

Surveying the bodies on the floor, Peter tsked. "Haven't lost your touch, I see."

Griz glared at him. "Just get them out of here," he growled.

"They'll be gone in twenty." Peter nodded and pulled out a small flip phone, making a call.

With a sigh, Griz sank into his chair and rubbed his temples. Had he made a mistake involving his brother again? No. He couldn't think that way. The power he desired was in his grasp. Peter was just like everyone else in his life. Blood or not, he would serve his purpose.

And then he would be eliminated.

CHAPTER FOURTEEN

DOWN

8. Nine letters. Used to measure conductivity.

February 3—4:22 p.m.
15,000 feet above the Parks Highway

"Relax." Scott patted Carrie's knee and then looked back to the Cessna 206's controls. "I'll adjust our altitude so that I can always see where we're going. I won't rely on the instruments for everything."

She clasped her hands in her lap. "It's not that. I trust you." A long sigh escaped her lips. "I just can't shake the details of this case. The blatant disregard for human life. Our UNSUB doesn't seem to have any qualms about killing people. Not that serial killers ever do, but this guy—I don't know what it is about him. And we still have no idea why. No demands have been made other than the fact that I'm supposed to give press conferences. And considering I ticked him off pretty good last night with my psychopath reference, he might change his mind."

"Somehow, I doubt that. This guy wants attention."

"Well, I can't wait until the day when all this is behind us. I want this guy caught."

"Me too." They hit a bit of turbulence and Scott gripped the yoke with both hands. "I'm going to learn as much as I can from Jason while we're up there. His team handled quite the cyber mess."

"After reading the reports, I'm amazed they were able to get the power back on the way they did. It was divine intervention for sure." She lifted her briefcase to her lap and pulled out a few files. "I called ahead to the prison and made arrangements to meet with Mr. Myers and Mr. Collins. I'm going to read up on their files before we get there."

"Sounds like a plan." He adjusted the plane for the cloud cover. "We have about forty-five more minutes of flight time."

While she studied the files, Scott used the time to pray for guidance and answers. He couldn't help taking a few sneak peeks at her as well. She used different colored highlighters as she went along. For what, he wasn't sure; he'd ask her about it later. He smiled at the thought. Their camaraderie was so easy and natural. He could feel not only mutual attraction growing between them but a genuine trust and friendship as well.

Add that to the fact that she was in law enforcement—something she thought was a detractor for most men—and he was smitten.

He was pretty certain she wouldn't pull the wool over his eyes. Carrie was bent on finding the truth. He'd found her to be honest about everything, even if something wasn't flattering for her.

Their conversation from yesterday after their hamburger run flooded his mind. Had that really been less than twenty-four hours ago? So much had happened since then.

It had taken a lot of courage for her to open up to him and be vulnerable. The fact that she held up this well under the pressure amazed him. Perhaps one day, he'd share his past too.

That's the thing. Everyone had a past. The good, the bad, and the ugly. He had just as much trouble getting over his as Carrie seemed to have with her own expectations.

His mind wandered to his family and thoughts of the future. It was nice to think about something other than this case. But as he landed the plane in Fairbanks, he had to corral his thoughts. "Back to business," he mumbled.

Carrie was in the middle of taking off her headset and shot him a questioning look. "What did you say?"

"Nothing important." He pointed. "There's Jason, and that must be Darcie." He shut down everything and did his postflight check while she gathered their things and spoke with the two on the ground. Jason greeted him with a hug and three pats on the back. "Good to see you, man."

"You too." Scott lowered his voice. "I saw Mac the other night. We need to talk about that if we can spare a minute or two."

"Gotcha. Our conversations have been . . . peculiar, to say the least." Jason held out a hand to Darcie. "I'd like you to meet my fian-cée, Darcie. Darcie, this is Scott, another of my accountability broth-ers. As you know, he works at the Anchorage Cyber Solutions office."

Scott stepped forward and hugged Darcie. He spoke in her ear. "If you have problems with this geek, you let me know."

She laughed and squeezed him. "I most certainly will take you up on that."

They all piled into an SUV with Jason behind the wheel. "As much as I'd love to catch up and have this visit be all warm and sunny, I'm afraid we've got some bad news to share."

Scott's stomach plummeted. With a huff, he grunted. "I should have known. Go ahead. Lay it out."

"Darrell Collins was found dead at the prison an hour ago. And Kirk—my brother—is gone."

◻ ◻ ◻

DOWN
8. Six letters. To accuse, put on trial for; or TNT.

February 4—8:30 a.m.
Fairbanks Emergency Operations Center

Scott paced the large room and sipped his coffee. Yesterday had been brutal. They went to the prison and found that Kirk's records were completely gone. The paper trail that usually followed inmates from trial to conviction to sentencing was nowhere to be found. Just like the man. Vanished.

How did a man vanish into thin air?

The warden and several security guards seemed just as confused. They had promised Carrie they would testify in any court that Kirk had been an inmate at the prison.

But it wasn't just his physical records that had disappeared. Jason said that his brother, Kirk Myers, was gone from all databases and search engines. The state troopers had no records. The APD had none. Not even the FBI.

No law enforcement agency had one single fact about him.

They'd spent the entire day scouring each state Kirk had traveled to, every rehab facility he'd been in, but whoever was behind this had been thorough. There wasn't even a birth record for Kirk, no elementary school records, no high school records. Absolutely nothing.

"Good morning." Carrie's voice beside him made him jolt. "Sorry." He lifted his shoulders and stretched. "No, it's okay. I didn't realize how tense I'd gotten." He turned toward her and smiled. "Good morning to you too."

"You know what this reminds me of?" She walked toward Jason's computer.

"What?"

"Did you ever see that old movie with Sandra Bullock . . . from the early nineties, I think. *The Net?*"

"Yeah. That's a classic for us cyber guys." He leaned on the desk. "What about it?"

"It always freaked me out that you could erase someone like that. You know, if you didn't see people all that often. On paper—or computer—you just disappear." She shrugged. "It's like Kirk. There are a few people who knew he was actually there at that prison. Jason and his family obviously know he exists. But think about it. Today we're even more reliant on digital records. Everything's on the computer—our medical records, banking records, communication, everything. That's why we get so frustrated every time we have to deal with a company's customer service and they say, 'It's not in the computer,' and we want to scream, 'I don't care if it's not in your computer, this is what actually happened.'" She released a growl and then took another sip of coffee. "But"—she paused and looked at him, her eyes narrowing—"to make records disappear at a law enforcement agency? That takes more than someone with mad cyber skills."

"What do you mean?"

"We keep paper copies. You've seen it. We have physical files for every case, on top of the digital files. And evidence boxes that get logged and stored securely."

"Yeah." His brain filed that piece of information. "So what you're saying is—"

"Someone had to be hands-on to erase Kirk." She finished his sentence.

He jumped up from his chair and looked around the room. "Maybe that's how we do it."

"How we do what?" She followed him.

"We don't track the guy's digital footprint. We track the physical one. Someone has to have left a trace in one of the places Kirk was erased. Probably multiple someones. We scan security footage, lift fingerprints, do whatever it takes."

"Do you have any idea the manpower it would take to accomplish that?" She shoved her hands into her jeans pockets, her face grim. "Every law enforcement agency in the country is shorthanded. I just don't see it happening."

"At least allow me to look at the security footage." There had to be something they could do to stop this guy. Their best leads yet had either vanished or been killed.

Darcie and Jason entered the main room, each carrying two boxes.

Jason set his boxes down on the desk. "Here are the master files. I sent everything digitally to you on our encrypted server, so you'll have that once you go back to Anchorage, but while you're here, you might as well go through what we have."

Darcie set her boxes down and headed to her office. When she came back out, she carried a flash drive and handed it to Carrie. She opened her mouth and then shut it. After another breath, she opened her mouth again. "I haven't said anything to anyone but Jason, but I haven't been able to get past the feeling that someone else was involved in the 26 Below attack." She shared a look with Jason. "I have no proof. Nothing but a feeling. But I've put some notes about Darrell Collins and what transpired between us on that flash drive. I know Kirk testified that Darrell was the mastermind, but in my humble opinion, there's no chance of that."

Scott's shoulders tensed. His pulse quickened. His conversation with Mac came rushing back. "Why do you say that, Darcie?"

"Why don't we all sit down." Jason dragged some chairs over so they could sit in a circle.

Carrie pulled out her phone. "Do you mind if I record this?"

"Not at all." Darcie tucked her curly hair behind her ears. "Darrell was a rich, spoiled brat. He didn't get the job—my job—and was upset. He admitted to hiring someone to hack the EOC and plant ransomware. All to make me look bad. He'd been trying to get rid of me since I got here. But he was adamant that he didn't have anything else to do with the attack."

"I thought he kidnapped you and held you at gunpoint?" Carrie leaned closer.

"He did. But I think he'd been trying to find something—maybe to clear his own name? He'd obviously gotten in over his head. All he wanted to do was buy his position and power. There's no way he was smart enough to pull all of it off."

They dug through the physical files for three hours. Finally, Carrie looked at her watch. "We need to get over to the trooper station. They've got some info for me too. Then we should head back. We've got a serial killer to hunt down."

Scott helped pack up the boxes. "You're the boss." He grinned at her when she swatted his arm.

Jason laughed as he stepped closer and grabbed the boxes. "I saw that."

Yeah, well. He wouldn't deny it. He liked Carrie. A lot.

They drove over to the state troopers' office, and Scott waited in the car with Jason and Darcie while Carrie went inside. The lack of sleep was catching up to him, so he leaned his head back. If he could rest his eyes for just a few minutes, he'd be good to go.

His phone buzzed in his pocket and woke him up. He rubbed his eyes and pulled it out, glancing at the time. Ten till two. A fifteen-minute catnap. Not bad.

He swiped at the screen to open the phone, then touched the mail app. The encrypted email from Jason was there. Plus several others from the office. He scrolled down to see how much he would need to catch up on once this was all over and found an odd one.

It was encrypted from an undisclosed sender. He touched it.

The email opened, and a video with music started playing the song "Maria" from *The Sound of Music*.

He muted it as fast as he could but hadn't missed the words that scrolled across the screen.

Laughing, Darcie turned her head to see him in the back seat. "Was that from *The Sound of Music*?"

It took him several seconds to calm his heart rate. He faked a smile. "Yeah. I like musicals."

"Since when?" Jason's frown from the driver's seat was clear in the rearview mirror. Then realization. "That was—"

"Doesn't matter. It was just a prank." Scott cut him off and jumped out of the SUV. "I need some air." Slamming the door behind him, he stomped off into the parking lot.

Someone was digging into Scott's past and wanted to make sure that he knew about it. Their killer, no doubt. He rubbed his face. This was a problem. Just like the song alluded to. He'd have to show the video to Carrie. Which meant . . .

He'd have to tell her the truth.

CHAPTER FIFTEEN

DOWN

8. Four letters. TV show featuring a plane crash.

February 4—2:46 p.m.
Flying over the Alaska Range

THE SILENCE INSIDE THE PLANE was deafening. Carrie worked on her laptop while Scott checked the plane and then got them off the ground and up into the air. She'd tried to start up a conversation at first, but his answers were sharp and stabbing, his expression brooding. So she went to work. But now, they were almost back to Anchorage, and she couldn't bear it any longer.

She packed up all her things, ready to go once the wheels touched down, and then shifted in her seat to see him better. "What's bothering you?"

He shook his head, his lips a firm line.

"I take it you don't want to talk about it." She kept her voice calm. "Well, I don't like to keep secrets because I know how damaging they can be. I care about you, Scott. Please let me in."

His long sigh echoed through her headset.

"I can be patient. Take all the time you need. But I'm not getting off this plane until you tell me."

He darted a glance at her. "Stubborn woman."

"Thank you. I'll take that as a compliment." Pressing her lips together, she stared him down and waited.

"It's not that I don't want to tell you. I *need* to tell you. But it's not going to be pretty. It's not a short conversation, and I was trying to figure out what I would say if you told me you didn't want anything to do with me after this." He gave her a long glance, his eyes full of emotion. "I care about you too. A lot more than I should after knowing you all of ten days."

Heat spread through her limbs, and her heart pumped faster. "Now that we've got that out in the open . . . let's talk."

He tipped his head toward the windshield. "How about I land the plane first?"

"Deal."

Once they were on the ground, Scott did all the postflight checks. Then they carried their belongings to his car in the parking lot. They climbed in, and he cranked the heat.

With his body facing her, he grabbed her hand. "I'm sorry."

"For?" Why did it sound so ominous?

"For being such a grump on the plane. I was processing and hoping and praying you wouldn't kick me to the curb when this is all over."

Even though her heart was preparing to be torn in two, she lifted her chin. "Whatever you have to tell me must be pretty bad. If you haven't noticed, I can handle bad."

"I hope so." He rolled his shoulders a couple times and released a breath. "Here goes. Just . . . please know that I would never intentionally hurt you."

Even though they still held hands, hers felt cold and prickly. "Okay. I believe you." Dread pooled in her stomach.

"Seven years ago, I worked for the governor's office. I was the IT guy, and I met a young intern." He coughed and swallowed. "We dated. She started coming to my church. Got involved with several charities. She was always volunteering her time when she wasn't working. She could quote Scripture and participate in great theological discussions with our Bible study group."

"Seems like a great match for you." Why did her voice squeak on the end? "Go on."

"By all appearances, she was. After almost two years of dating, we were engaged and planning our wedding. I thought I knew everything about her. She definitely knew everything about me. But it was all a charade." He turned his head to the windshield and stared out to the parking lot.

"What happened?"

"Long story short?" He looked at her, tears glistening in his eyes. But he blinked them away. "She was living a double life. She was married to another man. I knew her as Lisa Jones, but her name was actually Maria, and she had been using me. An elaborate scheme. She stole hundreds of thousands of dollars from more than a hundred donors to the governor's office."

"How did she do it?"

"The office she worked in was always having computer problems. I was the IT tech of choice . . . at her beck and call. I mean, everyone had computer problems. The government's tech isn't always the greatest. So I didn't think anything of it. But the police figured out that she had mirrored my log-in and duplicated my keycard. Interpol actually got involved because Maria and her husband were wanted in six different countries. They were fluent in five languages."

"Wow." It was hard to believe he hadn't seen it, but she shouldn't judge. She had training in criminal profiling and law enforcement. He didn't.

"They stole more than five million dollars over the course of ten years. They were geniuses at fake identities and hacking into computer systems. All those times she acted like she didn't know what she did to make the screen go blank, I believed her. She looked young and innocent. Wouldn't even allow me to kiss her until we were engaged. I talked to her parents—or whoever they were—over Skype several times, and they were extremely conservative and devout Christians. At least, they had me fooled." He swiped a hand through his hair. "She played me."

"What happened?"

"Oh, one day I got a visit from the FBI, and they showed me video of her with her husband. After that, even though it broke my heart, I helped them take the duo down. I was a mess. She begged me to come visit her in the jail, and I did. But I couldn't bear to look at her, so I said my goodbyes and walked out. I was living in Juneau at the time, and I couldn't get out of there fast enough." He licked his lips and smacked them together.

"I came home to Anchorage and looked for a new job. The FBI and the governor both gave me impeccable references and kept my name out of the news. Cyber Solutions hired me on, and a month later, my pastor recommended I start seeing a therapist. And I did. It took me five years to put it all behind me. I haven't trusted my judgment in women ever since and haven't even been attracted to another woman until you."

This was definitely not what she'd expected. But at least it wasn't about her. She'd been so worried about losing him, and they'd just gotten to know one another. She squeezed his hand. "I don't have any words that would mean anything right now."

"I'm not expecting you to." He tugged her closer and kissed her forehead. A sweet and intimate gesture. "But there's more."

The way he said it made her stiffen. "Okay."

He released her hand and pulled out his phone. He swiped at the screen, then tapped it a few times and showed it to her.

As the familiar song played, words scrolled across the screen.

You abandoned her. Then look what she did. That's on you. And it's not over.

She furrowed her brow. "I don't understand. What did she do after you left her in jail? And what does it mean that it's not over?"

"They found Maria's husband and another man dead. Somehow she escaped police custody during a transfer to Interpol. Of course, she's their number one suspect. They've never found her."

◻ ◻ ◻

DOWN

8. Eight letters. Club.

February 4—7:08 p.m.
Palmer, Alaska

"I'm doing this for the greater good. It's the needs of the many outweighing the needs of the few." Griz spoke to the screen. "One day, you will understand."

Peter knocked on the doorjamb.

Griz cut off the recording.

Dressed in his typical all black with black leather jacket, Peter held a package. "I just picked this up for you."

"Good. Thank you."

"Might I ask you a question?" His brother clasped his hands behind his back. A knowing smile on his face.

"Of course. Doesn't mean I'll answer if I don't want to, but go ahead. Ask." He leaned back in his chair.

"You're a brilliant man."

"Thank you."

"And I pride myself on being quite smart myself." He licked his lips with satisfaction.

Griz nodded but kept from rolling his eyes at the man. His own IQ was over 160. Peter wasn't even close to the genius level. It'd been a source of contention between them when they were younger. But he'd humor him. "Your question?"

"I know you are completely committed to the Members' cause. I also believe you are the born leader for us." He started to pace back and forth, a sly grin ever so slightly lifting his lips.

What was he up to?

"To show your power and your brilliance, I think you have another plan in play—an alter ego, if you will. A plan to destroy the law enforcement agencies from the inside out and have the media singing your praises. *You* meaning the leader you."

Griz wasn't sure he liked where this was going. "Spit it out, Peter."

"Funny how Collins is now dead up in Fairbanks, and Kirk's disappeared. That took some expert planning." He rubbed his chin, then looked Griz straight in the eye. Planting his hands on the desk, he leaned forward. "Are you the serial killer they're looking for?" His smile stretched across his face now. "Because I think you're the only one brilliant enough to pull it off, *brother.*"

"Are you wearing a wire, Peter?" Griz came out of his chair. "Bull should have searched you before allowing you back here." He marched around his desk and stripped the man of his jacket, then his shirt. "Take off your pants. Shoes and socks too." Once he was satisfied, he handed Peter's clothes back. No wire. "Get dressed."

"Now that you see I'm clean"—the smile was still there, accompanied by admiration and awe in his eyes—"will you answer my inquiry?"

Griz chose his words carefully as he walked back around to his chair. "Close the door and lock it."

"Yes, sir."

"Where do your loyalties lie? With the Members?"

He put a hand to his chest. "Of course with them. But only if you are at the head. My loyalty is to you. I've been watching everything you've done with great respect for your work. You saved my life. What you've built here is incredible." He dropped his hand and leaned forward again, his hands planted back on Griz's desk. "I want to be a part of it. Everything we accomplished up in Fairbanks was because of you. I will do whatever you ask. All the way to the very end."

"That's good to hear." Even though they were brothers, it didn't mean Griz could trust him fully. Especially with the job that he had for Peter. But over time . . . he'd find out.

"Thank you."

Griz studied the man and a new piece of his plan formed in his mind. "You understand the purpose of the killer?"

"To prove he's smarter than everyone else. More powerful. To show once again that people shouldn't trust the current authorities. What we need is a real leader. It's also an amazing distraction."

He couldn't help but smile at that. "He is indeed smarter than everyone else."

CHAPTER SIXTEEN

DOWN
8. Nine letters. An old drug used to treat irregular heartbeat.

February 5—6:05 a.m.
Alaska Bureau of Investigation

TELLING CARRIE ABOUT MARIA HAD lifted a huge weight from Scott's shoulders. It's not like he'd wanted to keep the secret forever, but it wasn't exactly a topic to bring up on a first date. It also didn't say much about his discernment when he'd been engaged to a fraud.

Sure, Maria had been a pro at conning people, but it still stung that he hadn't seen it. Of course, he hadn't been the only one. No one in the governor's office had figured it out.

A chime from one of his laptops brought his thoughts back to the case. This particular search was just giving him more of the same information. The advanced tech used by their UNSUB was readily available on the dark web. Of course it was. He'd found ways to obtain a bug similar to the one used in Carrie's coat many times over now. So much for tracking down the purchaser this way. Why was it criminals seemed to have no problem finding access to weapons and illegal surveillance equipment?

He knew the answers. Money. No moral compass. They didn't care about abiding by the law. That's why stricter laws rarely curbed criminal activity. Even less in the cyber world. The further technology advanced, the more hackers rose to the challenge.

Case in point, just look at what he did for a living. The need for cybersecurity continued to grow exponentially. But it was easier staying on the corporate side of things, where cyber threats were all about money and keeping up with the latest updates.

Diving into this darker world with the ABI team sobered him. People were dying. Somehow he had to help stop it. But how was the question of the year.

He swiped a hand over his unshaved jawline and started another search. Getting into the mind of this cyber genius was vital to stopping him.

He sent a quick message to Tim and Kyle over at Cyber Solutions, hoping his boss would allow the younger guy to assist with this case. If Kyle could work on tracking down the bug the killer used, then Scott could work on much more pressing things. Like finding the hacker behind the crossword puzzles and tracing the digital footprints of the hacks that had been done to kill the first victims, which would hopefully lead them to their killer.

Scott stood and stretched. Another cup of coffee was in order before he tackled anything else. While he was filling his cup, Carrie strode into the room with three file boxes. "Whoa. Need some help?"

"Nah. They're not heavy. Not even full. I asked the APD to keep the evidence for each case separate." She set everything down, removed her coat, and headed straight to the coffeepot. "I received all the autopsy reports from Dr. Blanchard, and we've got everything the police have from their investigations."

"Sounds like you've got your work cut out for you. Just tell me what you need me to do." He took a sip of the strong brew and leaned against the wall.

"First"—she took her coffee over to the area she'd claimed the past few days—"I wanted to ask you a question."

"Shoot."

"What are you going to do about that video? Are you trying to trace it? I mean, we're pretty certain our killer sent it, right? To distract us?"

Since they were the only ones in the room, he walked over to her and squeezed her shoulders. "That wasn't just one question. That was four." He walked back to his seat and winked at her.

Her face softened for a moment. "Behave yourself, Mr. Patteson."

"Yes, ma'am." Her reaction was enough to boost his spirits for a few hours.

"And yes, I know it was four questions"—she smirked—"but they all need an answer. My mind doesn't stop spinning when it comes to cases."

He swallowed another swig of coffee and picked up a pen. Back to business. "In all seriousness, yes, I'm pretty certain that video was from the killer. Yes, I think he wants to distract us. But I think it's even more than that. He wants to invade our lives and our privacy. Make us uncomfortable so we focus on ourselves rather than preparing for what he's going to do next."

"Now you're thinking like a profiler. You're right. He wants to get under our skin."

"Yep." He tapped the pen on the table. "And last, I already traced it as far as I could. Then, *bam*, dead end. Not that I expected to find anything else."

"Okay. Well . . ." She put on a pair of nitrile gloves and pulled the first box toward her. "Would you mind helping me with this until the guys get here? I know we're asking a lot of you and you're having to ping-pong all over the place."

"I don't mind." He stepped closer as she pulled all the evidence bags out of the box. "Just tell me what you need me to do."

"Put on a pair of gloves if you're going to touch any of the evidence." She picked up the folder that had been on top. "Our victim is a thirty-three-year-old female. Wealthy. Smart home. They found her in her panic room. According to Dr. Blanchard's report, she was an asthmatic. Had an attack in the panic room that led to her death. The police reported that both inhalers stored in the panic room"—she lifted the evidence bag containing the inhalers—"were completely empty. The air ducts were covered with plastic wrap beneath the register. Her fingers were bloody from what the police concluded was her trying to remove the grates. No fingerprints. No DNA. Other than our victim's, of course."

He didn't like the implications. "Is there access information in the file to the victim's home? I'd like to see what I can find in the code."

She searched. "Yep. Right here. I'm pretty certain this was also our guy." Handing him a file, she went back to looking through the evidence. "I can't imagine dying this way." Her voice held a sharp edge to it.

Scott removed his gloves and went to his computer. For thirty minutes, neither one of them spoke.

"Our killer activated an intruder alert on her system two hours before she died. She went straight to the panic room. He shut down the ventilation system. When she started running out of air, she tried her inhalers, but they were both empty. How much do you wanna bet, the guy emptied them?" He slammed his hand on the table. "Sick—" he stopped himself before he said something he regretted. "I am not in the habit of using foul language or getting violent, but this guy?" He growled and clamped his mouth shut.

Carrie nodded, her face pale. Inhaling, she closed her eyes. "I know." She must be trying to keep calm. He wasn't sure how she did it.

Blowing out her breath through a small circle in her lips, she opened her eyes again. "I think we have the basic gist of this case." She put the file back in the box. "After we go through the others, I need you to find how he gained access. I don't need every person with a smart home or smart thermostat or smart fridge panicking and thinking that he's coming after them next."

"Got it." But at this point, their team had no idea who he would target next. That was the problem. How could they prepare people for this so they could prevent it?

Opening the next box, she lifted the folder and examined it. "Looks like this one isn't our guy. It's another overdose." Her shoulders slumped a bit. "I hate these. Totally preventable. He was young too." She shook her head as she read the rest of the file and placed it in the box. "You're welcome to take a look just in case, but I'm going to move on to the next box."

"All right." He glanced at the file and the evidence and didn't see anything that would point to a malicious cyber hack leading to an OD. So he replaced the lid.

"This one might be our guy." She waved Scott over. "Twenty-five-year-old male. A detonation for a planned avalanche went off and he was on the mountain, skiing." Tilting her questioning gaze up to him, she bit her lip. "Is there a way to hack the detonation?"

"If it's controlled by a computer, anything can be hacked." He took the file. "Let me work on this one first and see what I can find. It should be easier than the smart home case."

"Sounds good. I'm going to make detailed notes and see how these connect with our clues and if there's any connection between all the victims."

Two hours later, the entire team was assembled in the conference room with the good news that three more investigators would be returning that day. It boosted everyone's spirits as each worked to figure out how to stop their serial killer.

Quiet permeated the room until someone had an idea or lead to follow. Then back to quiet. By one in the afternoon, every person was on at least their fifth cup of coffee.

"I've got something." Alan stood from his chair. "A clue to one of the crosswords was 'Snowed under.' The answer was *buried*. It took me a bit, but I tracked down the original crossword puzzle. It was in the *Washington Post*. But that's not the most interesting part. It was in the paper *two days* before our avalanche victim died."

All eyes snapped to Alan.

Carrie gasped. "Wait. What? It was in the paper *prior* to the death?"

"Yep. That's not even the best part. There was another crossword in the same paper the very next day. Guess what the clue was for eight down?" Alan slapped the file on the table. "'The opposite of a natural avalanche.' Answer? *Planned slide.*"

The air in the room changed. Carrie held up her hands. "Okay. Everyone stop what you're doing, and let's find the original date for each of the crossword puzzles our UNSUB sent us. Scott, call your boss and beg him to let us have the young guy from your office that loves these things. Just for a few days. In fact, let me talk to your boss. If there's any chance at all that we can stop the killer before he strikes, we have to do it. He's taken nine lives that we know of. He's not messing around."

CHAPTER SEVENTEEN

DOWN
8. Five letters. Last, strangled breath.

February 6—8:29 a.m.
Alaska Bureau of Investigation

CARRIE CLENCHED HER JAW. THE news station had stated that a press conference with the serial killer's demands would air at 8:30 a.m. Right now the screen read "Breaking News."

The second her phone read 8:30, the station went live. The ashen-faced reporter stood in front of a single microphone with papers in her hand. She was visibly disturbed. The woman swallowed and then cleared her throat.

"My instructions are to read word for word what is on these pages." She dipped her head, and her hands shook.

"'These are nonnegotiable. You've seen what I'm capable of bringing to pass. This is for the good of the people. My demands are simple. Our state must go into executive session and vote to secede from the United States of America, making Alaska its own country, reliant on no one. We are tired of the idiots in Washington, DC, making decisions for us. They have no right to oppress us or take from us what is rightfully ours. Then every person—and we do mean every person—in any capacity of government in this state will resign immediately after the secession so that a new leadership can take its place.

"'We are not to be trifled with. Our numbers are many. You cannot stop us, so don't try. What is best for Alaska has been researched for years. Most of you won't even realize you've been oppressed until we free you. This is the only way. The United States is corrupt. The government is corrupt. Do you really want your children and your grandchildren to grow up in this world?

"'To quote from the *Dubuque Herald*, November 11, 1860:

There is a natural right, which is reserved by all men, and which cannot be given to any Government, and no Government can take it away. It is the natural right of a people to form a Government for their mutual protection, for the promotion of their mutual welfare, and for such other purposes as they may deem most conducive to their mutual happiness and prosperity; but if for any cause the Government so formed should become inimical to the rights and interests of the people, instead of affording protection to their persons and property, and securing their happiness and prosperity, to attain which it was established, it is the natural right of the people to change the Government regardless of Constitutions. For be it borne in mind, the Constitution is an agreement made among the people that the Government formed by it is to be just such a Government as it prescribes; that when it recognizes a right to exist, it must protect the person in the enjoyment of that right, and when it imposes a reciprocal duty upon a portion of the people, the performance of that duty it will have enforced. When a government fails in any of these essential respects, it is not the Government the people intended it to be, and it is their right to modify or abolish it.

So, if the rights of the people of the United States as

recognized by the Constitution are not secured to them by the Government, and the people of any State have no other means to redress their grievances except by separating themselves from their oppressors, it is their undoubted natural right to do so.

"'You will be given seven days to put this into action. That is fair and generous. Each day I do not see progress made—or if you try to stop me—another innocent citizen will die. I expect press conferences every day to show you are being diligent with what you've been given. You have my demands.'"

The screen went black.

"What happened?" Carrie looked to Scott, who was at his computer.

"I don't know. But the station is off-line."

The phone rang.

She picked it up, dreading whatever the news might be. "ABI, Carrie Kintz."

"This is Tom Spivak from the APD. A bomb just went off at the TV station. We're presuming there are no survivors."

◻ ◻ ◻

DOWN
8. Twelve letters. The opposite of a natural avalanche.

February 6—9:15 a.m.
Underground, Anchorage

Tapping a key, Griz started the video call.

Faces appeared on the screen.

"You've gone too far." His rival in the last vote didn't wait for a greeting or anything else. "It's one thing to kill people for the cause, but entirely different to take lives for the fun of it. What made you think the Members would support such atrocities? We will not abide by this and will denounce you to the media. The Members will not align themselves with the likes of you."

A cacophony of voices filled the air as every face on the screen chipped in its two cents.

Griz released a long breath and waited for them to finish. Once it was quiet, he stared at them.

"Are you quite done?"

Several grunts were the only answer he received.

"I don't need your permission to do what has to be done. The Members are nothing without me and you know it. Do you not remember what we accomplished just a couple months ago?"

"You're crazy." A voice from the bottom corner piped up. "And a murderer."

"I make a motion to remove this heinous man from our midst." Another voice threw out.

"Second!" Multiple voices at the same time.

Griz noted each face.

"All in favor?" His rival raised an eyebrow.

"Aye!" Every person raised a hand.

"It's unanimous. You are hereby terminated and will no longer be associated in any way with the Members. Our cause will go on without you. And we will gladly give your identity to the authorities."

So that's how it was going to be. Stupid weaklings. "I give you all fair warning: if any one of you turns against me with the police, FBI, ABI, any news media, or *anyone* . . . or reveals even the tiniest bit of information about me? You. Will. Be. Next. They can't protect you."

He watched as faces blanched, winced, hardened, and realization took hold.

"I have no problem with killing every last one of you. But I could also do much worse. Need I remind you what I know about each of you? I'll leave you with one last question: do you want to live or die?"

□ □ □

An hour later, he stared into his reflection. Straightening his tie one last time, Griz checked to make sure his appearance was perfect. Then he walked behind his desk and sat in the large leather chair. He picked up the remote and hit Record.

"My son. There is so much more to your story. You will have a great deal more than I have, because I am making certain of that." He smiled at the camera. "There is a reason for everything that I do. You might not understand now, but you will when you are older.

"My great-grandparents lost their family land and legacy when the United States government came through and stole it to build roads. My grandfather was then forced to grow up in a tiny apartment in the city because there was no work for men who were uneducated and only understood farming. The government—who'd promised to help—left them in the cold. Because of this and the slum they were forced to live in, my grandfather's brother was killed in the street. Trying to sell bread, he was hit by a car. A rich person's car. A man who worked for the United States government, and who was never held accountable for murdering a hardworking man.

"My disdain for the government doesn't stop there. My father and mother inherited that tiny little apartment. My grandparents died of disease that happens when too many people are cooped up in one place. My father worked three jobs trying to get us out of there. He had a heart attack and died. Then two weeks later, we received a notice that our building had been condemned and would be torn down. A check for one hundred dollars was all they gave my mother."

Mention of the woman who'd raised him burned the back of his throat. Griz took a sip of water. It was important for the boy to know the truth.

"We lived on the streets for a few months while she looked for work. The government gave handouts to all kinds of people who didn't deserve them. But us? No. The system was broken and had been broken for a long time. My mother went to a man who was on the city council for help. What did he do? He raped and murdered her. What's even worse? He never spent a single day in jail for it. "I don't want to focus on the negative, son. But it's time you knew the truth. That man will never hurt anyone again. In this family, we are strong men. You will be . . . one day soon. And you will be by my side." He could picture it now. All the wealth he'd accumulated was for naught if he couldn't pass it down and give the next generation a new and lasting family legacy. A world to be proud of.

"It won't be long before you and I are reunited, and I can give you everything you've ever dreamed of. We will build a heritage together. One that will last for generations. And the government, which has allowed career politicians to cause division and chaos to reign supreme, will be taken to task. I can promise you that. Things will be different soon. Your mother won't be able to keep you from me any longer."

He pressed the pause button. His mind was jumping in too many directions. It was getting harder and harder to tame all the brilliant thoughts in his mind. Perhaps another pill was in order. They helped him focus. He'd keep track of it in his log and see if there was any difference in his perception. If it was too much, he'd back off.

As he went to the cabinet in the corner, the words of his father flooded his mind. *"Your genius is once in a lifetime. It won't be appreciated for a long time, but be patient. The world will burn at your command."*

Griz had clung to those words after his dad passed. Closing his eyes, he could almost feel the fire.

CHAPTER EIGHTEEN

DOWN
8. Five letters. Smartwatch stat.

February 6—6:23 p.m.
Alaska Bureau of Investigation

SETTING THE PHONE HANDSET DOWN, Carrie grimaced. "Well, guys. It's been fun." With a swallow, she pushed the next words out. "That was the FBI. They're on their way over." Helplessness overwhelmed her. The taste of failure was bitter in her mouth. But this case had blown up into something much larger than a murder case or even a serial killer case.

Kevin didn't appear the least bit ruffled. "Hold on, Carrie. That doesn't mean they're taking over. They're simply coming to our office. Correct?"

"That's what they said. But I doubt it's a social call or their cheerleaders coming to boost our spirits with their pom-poms and tell us what a phenomenal job we've done." The sarcastic tone from her own lips made her wince.

Nobody said a word for several seconds.

"Sorry." She cleared her throat. "I shouldn't take out my frustration on the very people who've been here day and night. Forgive me. Please?"

With his crutches stashed under his arms, Kevin made his way to her. "No need to apologize. We're a team, and we all feel it. Don't worry, we've got your back. Remember, you're in charge." He gave her a salute with his right hand, which made her laugh.

"Thank you for that." She glanced over at Scott.

A deep frown creased his forehead. "Could they really come in here and take over?"

"If they deem it a federal case, hands down, yes."

"But is this federal since it's just Alaska?" His strong arms crossed over his chest and reality hit her. She'd gotten used to his presence. Wanted—no, *needed*—him here.

Kevin sat back down and shook his head. "It could go either way. It's a serial killer case—but right now, he's only killed in Alaska, as far as we know. But the killer's demands were for an entire state of the Union to secede. It's"—he rubbed his forehead—"frankly, it's weird and insane, and I can't quite wrap my head around what this guy is thinking."

If the lead investigator for the ABI couldn't figure out their UNSUB, she could give herself a break. Logically, her head could think it, but the inner turmoil wouldn't stop churning up the feelings of guilt and failure.

Within fifteen minutes, she found herself welcoming three FBI agents into their little conference room. It had felt large when it was just the four of her team, but now? Everything felt inadequate.

The agent she'd met previously—Mike Hudson—was obviously in charge. After everyone officially exchanged names, he stepped toward her. "As you can imagine, red flags popped up all over the place when our serial killer insisted on having his demands read over live television and then blew up the station. The director of the FBI and the governor of Alaska have asked us to take over this case."

As much as she wanted to stomp her foot and argue with the man, she kept her cool. "We've invested a lot of hours into this."

"I understand, I do. But we have greater resources and manpower."

His look wasn't one of scolding; it seemed like he'd had to go through this before and could relate. At least, that's what she would keep telling herself.

God, I need Your help. Keep my mouth shut so I don't bite anyone's head off. It would be good if You could help me act like a professional, too, and not a petulant child who's just had her favorite toy taken away.

"You do," she agreed, "and we can appreciate that."

"That being said, we will take over the larger case as it pertains to this UNSUB and his demands to take over Alaska. We will need all the files and evidence but would also appreciate your team continuing to assist."

She frowned at that. "What do you mean by *assist*? At crime scenes?"

"No. We will handle that. But if you would continue to research and study what you can here, we would love to hear your opinions."

He was tossing her a bone, and she knew it. "All right. We'd be honored to assist."

Once the FBI left with all the case files and evidence, Carrie deflated like a balloon. "Well . . . alrighty then." She took her seat and glanced up at the board they'd worked on. With new determination, she tapped the table. "Our cyber serial killer is still out there. Now that we know his motivation, we can stop him."

"What do you have in mind, boss?" Alan grabbed a Little Debbie brownie from their stash of snacks in the middle of the table.

"The crossword puzzles. That's got to be the key to stopping him. If he's arrogant enough to publish them before he kills his next victim, then we have a chance, don't we?"

"Yes," all the guys echoed. They were on board.

She turned to Scott. "I know you've been here to help us with this case and since it technically doesn't belong to us anymore—"

"Nope. Don't say it." He held up his hand. "I texted Tim while the FBI was here. He agreed that I should stay. Kyle, too, since he's a genius at crosswords. You can't get rid of me that easily."

◻ ◻ ◻

DOWN

8. Three letters. Carbon monoxide.

February 7—11:13 a.m.

Alaska Bureau of Investigation

It was frustrating to no end that the FBI had taken over the cyber tracing for each of the hacks. They'd taken his data, but he'd kept a copy for himself. The more he studied it, the more it puzzled him. Different IP addresses all over Russia.

That was too easy. Why would their UNSUB—who demanded they acknowledge his brilliance—point them to Russia unless it was a joke? A way to insult the ABI by pointing to the "scary" adversary known for its hacking prowess. That seemed beneath him.

But it was the FBI's problem now. Let their team of cyber guys mess with it, and he could help Carrie try to stop the next murder.

The phone rang and she reached for it without even looking up. In less than a minute, she had hung up and was looking around the room. "Dr. Blanchard. Gotta love her for giving us a heads-up. They've got another body. It was a fifty-five-year-old male with an insulin pump. Cause of death? A faulty pump—sent too much insulin into the body."

Alan flipped through the puzzles. "Two matches in this stash. Time of death?"

"Today."

Scott began searching online. They'd combed through crossword puzzles from every publication they could gain access to. "I bet there's more."

"What makes you say that?" She leaned forward.

"He's arrogant. That's why. And he's taunted us time and again that we can't figure it out. There has to be a pattern in how and when he places the clues before he strikes. If we can figure that out, we can apply it to new clues."

"That's what we'll do." Alan darted back to his seat. "I'm going to scan every crossword I can from the past three days and get Kyle to help me solve them. If Scott can find a way to get into the crosswords before they're published, we just might have a window to stop him."

◻ ◻ ◻

DOWN
8. Three letters. The diagnostic test used to diagnose epilepsy.

February 7—9:10 p.m.
Northeast Anchorage

"Everything's in place. I've done my part. Now back off."

As Carrie played the video again, she listened closely and wrote down each word. She hadn't been able to get her mind off the fact that the FBI had taken her case, so when she came home, she'd started going through the digital files the ABI office in Fairbanks had given her. Without the mayor alive to defend herself, it was hard to justify what Carrie heard and saw on those videos.

Three suspicious phone calls, all time-stamped the day prior and the day of the 26 Below attack.

Four different security videos showed the mayor sneaking confidential files out of the office, taking them home, and burning them. Why would she keep incriminating videos? Had she been killed before she could destroy them? But that didn't make sense either. A smarter person would have disabled all security feeds at the office and home before taking the files.

It was all a bit too neat and tidy.

The mayor's staff had all testified that there was no way the woman would have been involved. They each said she was tough and maybe not the most likable person, but she wouldn't have betrayed her city, her state, or her country.

It didn't make sense.

But after the press conference the other day, there was no doubt in Carrie's mind that their serial killer was somehow connected to Fairbanks. His demands were simply an escalation of the verbiage used by the terrorists in the 26 Below attack. Had he been part of the group behind the attack and just derailed a bit? Well, a lot. Or was he a fan of their work and decided to take it up a notch on his own?

She pulled out her laptop to look up her psych professor from college. Professor Hatcher understood the criminal mind better than anyone Carrie had ever met.

After doing a quick search, she found the professor had retired to Hawaii.

She glanced at the clock. Would it be rude to call her tonight? It was an hour earlier in Hawaii, so not *too* late.

She swiped through her contacts on her phone and found Professor Hatcher's number. If she'd changed cell numbers, the time concerns would be a moot point.

She tapped the screen to call and then put it on speakerphone.

"Hello?"

Relief flooded her at the familiar voice. "Professor Hatcher? This is Carrie Kintz."

"Carrie, my dear. How are you?"

"I'm doing okay—well, other than the case I'm working on. I work for the Alaska Bureau of Investigation now and could use a little of your wisdom. I'm sorry to call like this, but I'm running out of options." She bit her lip. Was that rude? She hadn't spoken to the woman in years.

The beloved professor chuckled. "No need for idle chitchat with me, Carrie. I bet you are working on the serial killer who wants Alaska to secede, aren't you?"

"Yes, ma'am. How did you know?"

"Dispatch with the *ma'am* talk, dear. And don't call me *professor* either. I'm retired. Call me Diane." She cleared her throat. "I've had any number of students call me over the years for things like this. And this case is everywhere on the national news. How can I help?"

The next hour flew by as she filled the woman in on all the details of their serial killer and then read the most important pieces of information from the files of the attack in Fairbanks. Leaning back, she huffed. "It's frustrating. It sounds like our UNSUB has completely derailed—but I'm convinced the two are connected."

"Oh, me too, dear."

"Really?" The confirmation of her instincts made her want to jump up and cheer.

"Yes. Let's review." Professor Hatcher was back in teaching mode. "You mentioned this Kirk fellow—the brother of someone important in Fairbanks—who was an addict. In his file, he spoke of surrounding himself with like-minded people. How many ODs have there been since the killing spree started?"

Carrie searched through her computer. "Two . . . wait"—she'd missed one—"three."

"As expected. Kirk, who was obviously higher up on the food chain during the cyberattack in Fairbanks, was chosen because addicts are drawn like magnets to others like themselves who have achieved greatness. Whoever is at the top of this proverbial food chain is also an addict. That's how he supplies his workforce."

"Wouldn't that be stupid?" She backpedaled. "I'm sorry . . . I mean, wouldn't that be risky?"

"Think back, Carrie. You took several classes from me studying the mind. Not just the criminal mind. Many of those drawn to drugs have addictive personalities, yes, but they are also often high-functioning and brilliant minds. Many of them walk a very fine line between a normal person and a sociopath or even a psychopath. Criminals aren't all dumb, and cops aren't all smart." Shuffling happened on the line, but Carrie waited to see what would come next. "Bottom line is that addicts attach to addicts. Once they find support, they cling to it. Relish it. Often even worship it."

It made sense. But that didn't make it any less disturbing. "Our UNSUB has a brilliant mind. There's no question about that. Drugs involved? Definitely. Found like-minded addicts?" She said it all out loud as she wrote.

"One thing has to be very clear, Carrie."

"Okay?"

"Why don't you pull out your book, *Inside the Criminal Mind*. I'm assuming you still have it?"

"Yes, of course. Give me a sec." Carrie ran to her bookshelf and pulled out the worn book. "I've got it."

"Chapter thirteen, dear. 'Criminality Is Primary, Drugs Secondary.'"

"Yes, I found it." Carrie smiled. "I know exactly what you're going to say because it's underlined, highlighted, and starred in my copy. 'Drugs do not cause crime. Drugs magnify existing features of the user's personality.'"

"And what conclusion does that bring us to?"

Her thoughts rumbled around in her brain until they fell into order. "Yes, our serial killer is brilliant. He has to be if he was part of the 26 Below attack and designed all these new deaths. But he's also an addict. He's surrounded himself with addicts, but when something doesn't go his way, he just gets rid of them. Easy enough. They're drug addicts, right? He's controlled his addiction for some time. But something happened—perhaps the EOC and authorities up in Fairbanks stopping him too soon, or maybe the power coming back on before he could realize his grand finale? I don't know. But something triggered him into derailment. He needed . . . what? What does he need?"

"Attention, my dear. He needs attention. Especially a high-level acknowledgment of his intelligence. Didn't you say that one of his demands was a requirement that you hold press conferences and talk about him?"

Oh! "So when the media attention died down after Fairbanks and he was no longer front-page news, he spiraled."

"That would be my guess, and not the first time in history we've seen this behavior in a psychopathic serial killer. But let's jump ahead." She paused for a long moment. When she resumed speaking, her voice held a hint of trepidation. "Carrie, I believe this offender has passed the point of no return."

Carrie's breath caught in her throat. "Which means what, exactly?"

"He's totally unpredictable. Out of control. Oh, he'll probably still send the crossword clues because that's part of the game to him, but his timeline has most likely sped up. He's going to kill more than he said he would. He's taking more and more drugs to keep him going, so he'll be stepping outside of his own parameters more often. Someone is going to push him over the edge. And when they do . . ." She was silent for a moment, then cleared her throat. "I'm afraid he's going to continue to escalate until you stop him."

CHAPTER NINETEEN

DOWN
8. Two letters. Overdose abbr.

February 8—5:12 a.m.
Downtown Anchorage

LIFE DRAINED OUT OF HIM. He could feel it as much as the cold from underneath him burned his skin with its icy tentacles. He didn't deserve this. He'd done everything asked of him. Hadn't he?

Was there life after death? Why hadn't he thought of that before now? The drugs helped him survive in the moment but hadn't solved his problems.

The new job was supposed to take care of things.

Griz promised.

But now . . . there was no hope.

That woman was here too. Her voice smooth and silky. She must be the boss.

"You know this is best. I'll make the phone call." Her voice was always so calm.

"No. You've done enough already."

"Griz!" The raised voice was *not* like her. But the following whispers he couldn't understand. Maybe she was upset that Griz had eliminated him too. Maybe she was sorry. Sorry for all the pain she'd caused.

Numbness overtook his body. He couldn't move. Couldn't breathe.
He blinked. Maybe someone would notice him lying there and call
for help.

He blinked one more time.

But his eyelids refused to open again.

◻ ◻ ◻

DOWN
8. Seven letters. Gridlock.

February 8—10:14 a.m.
Outside Providence Alaska Medical Center

Just the man he wanted to see. He lowered the small pair of binoculars and set them in the seat beside him.

Griz stayed back with the car running as he watched the man hob-
ble his way across the parking lot. He'd have to cross the road here to
get to the parking structure. An easy enough target.

Griz pulled on a black knit cap and then his hood up over it. He
lifted his scarf almost up under his nose and parked his sunglasses on
his face. Waiting. Waiting. Waiting.

Then the man began to cross Health Drive.

With his right foot, he stomped on the gas and sped up around
the curve in the road. He slammed into the man. Crutches crunched
under the vehicle as Griz sped away.

His adrenaline pumped. He couldn't contain his smile. It was perfect. Much better than behind a computer screen.

He darted into the Elmore Road parking lot, parked the car, and
then ran across four lanes of traffic to University Park. Sirens wailed
in the distance.

But it didn't matter. He disappeared into the trees.

◻ ◻ ◻

DOWN
8. Eight letters. Falling sickness.

February 8—11:23 a.m.
Alaska Bureau of Investigation

"ABI, Carrie Kintz." She took a sip of water after she answered.

"Ms. Kintz, we need you to come down to Providence Alaska Medical Center as soon as you can." The voice held urgency.

She squeezed the phone to her ear with her shoulder while she stood up and grabbed her coat. "What's happened?" With a glance around, she realized the guys had left the room.

"Mr. Kevin Hogan was struck by a vehicle outside the hospital. He's not doing well and has asked for you."

Her heart seemed to stop in her chest as she wrote the information down. Hanging up the phone, she put a hand to her abdomen. She needed to breathe. "Guys?" Her voice cracked.

Alan and Scott raced toward her from the squad room. Scott was at her side in seconds. "What's going on?"

"It's Kevin. He was hit by a car and is in the hospital." The shaking started once she got the words out. "We need to get up there."

Scott wrapped an arm around her shoulders and led her to the door. "Let's go. I'll drive."

Having his strength helped steady her. But even with his arm around her, she wasn't sure her legs would hold her upright. They kept moving, and she forced herself to breathe.

Out in the squad room, everything was a blur. Two of the ABI team—Susan and Brad—were settling back in after being gone for two weeks. Alan filled them in on what was happening, and then her little crew of three left the building.

Once they were outside, she couldn't even feel the cold. What was wrong with her? *God . . . help!*

In the vehicle, Alan and Scott kept up a steady stream of conversation, but all she could think about was Kevin. All the time he'd poured into her. His patience. His guidance. He was one of the very best men she'd ever known. *God, please save him.*

The guys gave her space as her thoughts went from memories of all the moments with her mentor the past few months to short prayers shot heavenward. She didn't want to talk anyway.

At the hospital, they raced in, showed their badges, and a nurse led their troop to a curtained-off area.

The nurse gripped her arm. "To warn you, he doesn't look good, and he's about to head into surgery. Two minutes, tops."

With a nod, she braced herself as the nurse pulled back the curtain. Covered in blood and bruises, Kevin turned his head ever so slightly toward them.

Alan walked to the far side of the bed. "Our thoughts are with you." His words were low, and Carrie saw a tear slip out of the tough guy's eye. "Besides, you haven't finished putting our rookie here through her paces." The forced smile only made the tear race down his cheek.

She couldn't imagine what Alan must be feeling. He'd worked with Kevin for years.

Inching closer, Carrie steeled herself. Kevin needed them strong right now. Not a blubbering mess. So she went into investigator mode. "Did you see who hit you?"

"Co . . . vered . . ."

"The guy's face was covered? In a disguise?" She scribbled that down. "Anything about the vehicle?"

"Black." Kevin winced and shut his eyes. "Taurus."

"Don't worry. We'll check all the security cameras and see what we can find." She reached out and gently touched Kevin's hand. "I'm praying for you."

He moved it a bit under her fingers. "You'll . . . catch him."

She pinched her lips together, willing herself not to cry. "I know. And you'll celebrate with us."

"Carrie"—with the slightest tug on her fingers, he urged her closer—"take care . . . of the team."

She gulped against the tears and nodded. "We'll be waiting for you. You focus on doing what the doctors tell you." Forcing a smile, she squeezed his fingers.

"Time's up. We've got to get him into surgery." The nurse from before had two other staff with her and they started messing with IVs, tubes, and the bed.

When the three of them didn't make a move to leave, the nurse came back to her. "He's going to be in surgery for hours. Why don't you head to the waiting room—or better yet, get back to your office and figure out who did this." The woman shook her head. "I hate what our world has come to." The words were mumbled as she went back to her patient.

Carrie looked at Scott and then Alan. "Let's head back to the office."

Not a word was spoken for a good ten minutes as they made their way out of the hospital and to the parking lot. Then her cell phone rang. "Carrie Kintz."

"Hudson here. We've got another body—smartwatch hack seems to have been the trigger. Guy took too much heart med when his watch said his heart was beating too fast. I'll send over some info. Oh, and there was a note: 'You can't stop me.'" A bunch of noise rose in the background. "What've you got? Sorry, Ms. Kintz, gotta run."

"Thanks." But he'd already hung up. She turned to the guys. "Another death. This one caused by a smartwatch hack." She gave the few details she had and looked out the window. It was hard to think about the case with Kevin facing life and death. But she had to. That's what he would want her to do.

They climbed into Scott's vehicle. Her phone rang again. "Maybe that's more information." She swiped at her screen. "Carrie Kintz."

"Where are my press conferences?" The voice wasn't distorted this time. She touched the record button then put the call on speaker-phone so the guys could hear and made a signal for Alan to begin a trace. "I specifically asked for press conferences. Oh, that's right, you allowed the FBI to take over. Imbeciles. That was a bad move on your part, Ms. Kintz."

That voice. It made him sound normal . . . human. And that angered her. "Did you try to kill Kevin Hogan this morning?"

A low chuckle was the only response.

"You despicable—"

Scott grabbed her arm and shook his head.

"Are we reduced to name-calling now, Ms. Kintz? Tsk, tsk, tsk. That's so beneath you. Now back to the problem at hand. I want a press conference. With all the details."

"I'm not in charge anymore, so take your demands to the FBI." If she could keep him on the line a bit longer, they might be able to trace it.

"But they're no fun. I wanted you to be the one to solve the case. I've practically laid it out for you. Tell your boyfriend and Mr. Sanderson that I said hello. I've got eyes everywhere."

"I—" Three beeps interrupted her.

The call dropped.

CHAPTER TWENTY

DOWN
8. Ten letters. Brain bleed, can be caused by a smash to the skull (or so I've heard).

February 8—11:56 p.m.
Underground tunnel, downtown Anchorage

"I SEE YOU'RE GOING ABOUT attaining your political aspirations by taking a different route?" The smooth voice washed over him.

"Maria." Griz kissed her cheek. "It's so good to see you." His tolerance of her insistence at being in the middle of things was wearing thin. But she still had her uses. He could fake it a little while longer. With a glance over her shoulder, he narrowed his gaze. She'd brought a friend. That broke every rule in his book. "Who's this?"

"You can trust her. Met her in Russia. A wiz with disguises. You might even find her useful at some point." She put her hands on her hips. "What? Are you remodeling?" Lifting a white sheet off a chair, she scrunched up her nose. "You don't have the best taste. Why don't you let me help with that?"

"Perhaps I'll hire a decorator." Which was nonsense since they were in a closed-off tunnel underneath the streets of downtown Anchorage.

"Suit yourself." She shrugged and stepped forward onto the area rug. "I'm about to head out. Just wanted to make sure you didn't need me to do anything else before I go. And, of course, I came for my money." One perfectly shaped eyebrow rose.

Of course she had.

He turned to the safe and pulled out an envelope. "Here's what we agreed upon, plus a little extra."

She took the envelope with a smile and began to count it, which only made him angrier.

He lifted his gun, fired two shots at her friend, and the other woman crumpled to the floor. Blood bloomed on her chest like a poppy. Maria was right. This woman had been useful. Calm spread through his limbs and he inhaled. He was in control again. It felt good.

"Why'd you do that?!" Maria's scream as she lunged toward him hurt his ears.

He sidestepped her and grabbed her arm with his free hand, twisting it behind her back. He pulled her up against his chest, the barrel of the gun pressing between her spine and ribs. "You shouldn't have brought her here. You know the rules. Would you care to join her?"

Maria shook her head, and he let her go. She tripped, lost her balance, and fell to the hard floor. Her dark hair hung around her face in waves. She glared at him, the rage in her eyes unmistakable, but she kept her mouth shut. Good girl.

Pressing a button, he spoke into the speaker. "Come in, please." He shifted his gaze back to Maria. "You can leave."

With a huff, she got to her feet. She shoved the envelope of money into her bag and stomped out.

The side door opened, and Peter entered. His eyes widened a bit, but he didn't say a word.

"Take care of the body. Then clean up the mess." Griz holstered his weapon and went back to his chair. "We're going to have another meeting this afternoon at two, and I'd like you to share your ideas with the group." He sat in his chair and watched Peter for any signs of weakness, emotion, or anything else.

"I'd be honored." No reaction. No flinching. He rolled up the rug around the body, bagged it up, and threw it over his shoulder.

"Wonderful. We'll go far together, Peter."

The man walked out the way he'd come. Peter was the only one not getting on his nerves these days. Maria . . . he swiped a hand over his face. She was becoming a problem. Too cocky. She'd changed in the years since he'd recruited her as an intern at the governor's office. Brilliant girl—she'd even had *him* fooled with her con. At least for a while. She'd remained a valuable asset through the years.

But now, she was pushy. Asking too many questions. Making insinuating remarks about their history, jobs they'd done together. Griz frowned. It was almost like she thought she had something on him. He stroked his chin. If she thought their years of working together gave her some kind of in with him, she was mistaken.

Peter returned and pulled the blood-splattered sheets off the furniture and checked the floor.

"It's time for you to step into a higher position, Peter."

"I'm willing to do whatever you need." The man in black faced him, his eyes darkening.

◘ ◘ ◘

DOWN
8. Four letters. All alone in the middle of nowhere.

February 9—7:15 a.m.
Alaska Bureau of Investigation

Scott leaned back in his conference room chair and rubbed his face. Yesterday had been a long day without any good news regarding Kevin. They were waiting for him to wake up after surgery, but the surgeon informed them that it was going to be touch and go for a while.

So the team knuckled down and stayed at the office all night, fueling themselves with fast food and coffee. Two more ABI investigators were supposed to return today from Barrow, and that would give Alan and Carrie a breather from trying to manage the office in Kevin's absence.

More than anything, Scott wanted to help them figure out how to stop the serial killer. Second to that, he wanted to take away the pain he read in Carrie's face. She'd admitted that she'd never had a major loss in her life, and Kevin's life hanging in the balance was rough on her. But they all plowed through as best they could.

By about four in the morning, they'd finally found all the dates and publications of the crosswords the killer had sent them. Alan and Kyle continued to scour every crossword puzzle they could get their hands on, and their board now contained at least four crossword puzzles with a clue positioned at 8 DOWN for each death.

He checked the clock. They'd made a lot of progress. But was it enough? Carrie excused herself to the restroom, and they were all going to regroup at seven thirty this morning. That gave him a few minutes.

He needed more coffee. Even though he'd had enough caffeine the past twenty-four hours to fuel him for a normal month, with the lack of sleep, this was the only option.

The scent of something freshly baked wafted over to him. He stood and stretched and saw Susan headed their way.

She held up a plate of cinnamon rolls. "Don't mind me, I'm going to leave these here for you guys. We've got to head out for another case. Would you let Alan know I'll call him from the car?"

Scott nodded and grabbed a warm roll, devouring it. The cinnamon-and-sugar-laced dough melted in his mouth. Chasing it all down with a swig of coffee, he felt a bit more alive.

Carrie walked in with Alan not far behind. "What is that divine smell?"

"Susan brought cinnamon rolls." Scott grinned and reached for another one.

Their team of three situated themselves in their seats, the room quiet for a few minutes as they enjoyed the warm pastry and coffee. Finally, Carrie pointed to the board, licking icing off her lips. "I think it's safe to say our UNSUB is escalating his timeline."

Kyle walked into the room. "Sorry I'm late, but I solved the last of the clues." He held up some papers and took a seat.

Carrie stood and stepped closer to the board. "Excellent. Let's review what we've got, and then we can add what you've found, Kyle."

The younger man nodded and grabbed a cinnamon roll.

"The first two deaths were weeks apart. Five clues were in the crosswords: *carbon, monoxide, alarm, space heater,* and *gas.* Only two of those clues were published prior to the mayor's death." She drew a circle around the first group. "Then our next deaths were the two from the hacked traffic lights. We've found five crosswords: *collision, pileup, snarled, wrecks,* and *accident.* All these were published before it happened. The last one was four days prior."

Alan drummed his fingers on the table. "As much planning as he put into all this, he didn't settle into a groove until after that. Because all the others had at least four clues published no less than four days before he killed them."

"Until a few days ago." Scott held up his hand and studied the spreadsheet on his computer. "The victim whose insulin pump was hacked and the smartwatch hack"—he sent Carrie a look—"both of those have at least four clues all published the day before."

As the weight of that information sank in, Scott ran the numbers through his mind. He didn't like the shortened timeline. Especially now that they'd figured out the pattern.

The phone in the middle of the table rang, and Carrie reached for it. "ABI, Carrie Kintz." She paused and listened. "All right, thank you." Then hung up the phone. "We've got another body. Twenty-five-year-old female stranded up on the Parks Highway."

He wanted to growl. "Let me guess, her car was hacked and shut down."

Kyle pointed to his computer. "That would match what I found.

Detour, no signal, lost, alone, abandon. All published February seventh."

"She died yesterday." Carrie deflated and fell into her chair. "Our UNSUB said he would kill somebody every day. Looks like he wasn't bluffing."

The room went silent. Scott glanced from one person to the next. Everyone appeared exhausted. But more than that, they looked defeated. Scott couldn't blame them. He was fighting that feeling as well. There had to be a way to stop this guy. Why couldn't they find it?

Carrie bolted up and placed her palms on the table. "Okay, here's what we're going to do. It's a little unconventional, but I don't care. We're going to look for every crossword puzzle published today, we're going to solve eight down, and we're going to stop this guy from whatever he has planned tomorrow." Her voice was choked with emotion, and tears streamed down her cheeks, but with a swipe they were gone. "Let's get to work, because if the killer continues to speed things up, we won't have the luxury of a day's head start. He might publish the clues the day he plans to take a life. And I, for one, can't allow that to happen." She ran out of the room.

Scott followed her out the front doors of the building. Neither of them had a coat, and it was hovering just above zero this morning. "Carrie—"

"Leave me alone, Scott. I've got to deal with this on my own." She was stomping her way across the parking lot. "Unless you're a wiz at crossword puzzles, you might as well go back to Cyber Solutions."

CHAPTER TWENTY-ONE

DOWN
8. Six letters. Pulled a switcheroo on.

February 9—11:11 a.m.
Alaska Bureau of Investigation

THE MORNING PASSED IN SILENCE as the air sizzled with tension. Carrie had snapped at Alan and Kyle multiple times, while Scott kept quiet in the corner. With the others working on the crossword puzzles, he was determined to trace the killer's connection to the puzzles. The whole reason Cyber Solutions had been called was to help with the cyber side of things—if he couldn't trace the digital footprint, what good was he doing? When Jason was sent to Fairbanks, he'd helped the Emergency Operations Center stop the terrorists. What had Scott done?

Not much in comparison.

So far, he hadn't helped catch the guy, and he hadn't stopped the serial killer from going after more people. How many more lives would be lost?

The spiraling of his own thoughts shook him to his core. His group of accountability brothers would remind him this was an attack. The enemy was on the prowl.

When was the last time he'd contacted them and let them know the depth of the situation he was in? Or had a solid night's sleep?

When was the last time he'd spent time seriously seeking the Lord's guidance?

Lord, forgive me for relying on myself in this mess. I need Your help to see the way through this evil. In my own strength, I am useless. Only You can help us stop this person.

Bolstered with a renewed sense of energy, he refocused and studied his notes from the phone calls he'd made earlier, confirming what he discovered. Some publications—like the *New York Times*—had an editor just for their crossword puzzles. Of course, the *NYT* was known for the great puzzles that increased in difficulty as the week progressed. Other publications used services to purchase their puzzles.

Whoever was behind all this was pretty smart, and Scott hated admitting that. He not only seemed to submit puzzles to be used by some of the larger publications, he then hacked in and changed the 8 DOWN clue right before it went to print. For other publications, he'd hacked the servers that provided the crossword puzzles and either changed the whole puzzle or simply the clue and answer for 8 DOWN.

Which was not an easy feat.

It was the same with the hacker's digital footprint. Random and all over the place. He never hacked the same way twice.

Back to square one.

His email icon bounced in the corner. He clicked on it and saw a new email from the editor of the *NYT* crossword puzzle. It had been a whim that Scott attempted to reach him, and he wasn't expecting to hear back. But the email asked for Scott to call ASAP.

He grabbed his cell and went into the squad room, dialing the number as he went.

The editor answered.

"This is Scott Patteson in Anchorage."

"Thanks for calling me so promptly." The man cleared his throat. "Our puzzles are heavily guarded, as you might imagine, because of their popularity. I was just doing a scan of tomorrow's puzzle and found something odd. Since you contacted me and are working on that serial killer case, I wanted to let you know."

"Hey, that's great. Shoot it over to me."

"Sorry. I can't send it to you. Not before it's published. But I can tell you the clue for eight down. Will that help?"

"Yes, please. Any clue or hint is a step forward and helpful."

"There are eight spaces. The clue is: 'Surgery. Too bad you won't make it.'"

"Yikes. That's not subtle at all." Scott scribbled it down on a sticky note. "Do you have the answer?"

There was a brief pause and the sound of keys clacking. "Um. No. The clue was changed. But our master answer key did not change the previous correct answer, which was 'avocado'."

"And the original clue was . . . ?"

"*Aguacate.*" The editor sniffed. "Um, look. Should I not print this? Replace it with something else?"

"No!" Scott said it a bit too loud. "We don't want him to think that we've seen it yet."

"Will do. But if it turns out to be your serial killer's clue, our readers are going to complain about it."

"I hear you. But we've got to catch this guy."

There was a long pause. "Just this once. If we get another one, I'm not printing it."

"Thanks for your help."

The line disconnected, and Scott raced back to the conference room. "We've got a lead."

"Thank God. We need something." The desperation in Carrie's voice leaked out with the words.

"That was the editor of the puzzles from the *New York Times.*"

Kyle whistled. "Wow, dude. How'd you manage that?"

"I have no idea." Scott shrugged. "But the puzzle that's going to print tomorrow has quite a straightforward—albeit disturbing—clue."

He stuck the note to the board. "Eight spaces. Clue is: 'Surgery. Too bad you won't make it.'"

Carrie pulled out a fresh legal pad. "Okay, that gives us at most two days to stop him. So what are the ways he could hack a surgery?"

"Easy." Alan grimaced. "Hack the medical records and input the wrong procedure."

"Wouldn't the surgeon and the patient know? They discuss it before going into the OR, right?" Kyle munched on granola.

"Could an emergency surgery switch surgeons at the last minute, and the new team get wrong information? They're always frantic in the ER—at least from the shows I watch." Carrie laced her fingers together, pressing her knuckles against her mouth for a moment in thought. "What else? We have to think evil but on a large scale. This guy has a twisted imagination. At this point, no idea is too crazy."

"A member of the medical staff is blackmailed? Forced to give the wrong anesthesia or drug?" Kyle shrugged. "I hate to pull from TV, but I've seen that done too."

"What about a transplant? The patient and the surgeon think they're doing a specific surgery, and then the organ is not the correct one? Or the right blood type?" Scott brainstormed. "I'm just spitballing."

"You might be onto something." Carrie searched on her laptop. "I wonder if we could talk to the hospital administrators to get their insight."

"That's a great idea." Alan reached for his phone just as Carrie's cell rang.

"Carrie Kintz." Her face paled and she bit her lip. "We'll be right there."

Scott held his breath and waited. Another call from the killer? What now?

She visibly swallowed. "That was the hospital. Kevin has too much internal bleeding. They can't stop it. His son is in Virginia and can't be reached. We've got to get up there right away." Her lips smashed together. "They think he's only got a few hours."

◻ ◻ ◻

DOWN

8. Six letters. Create havoc, punnily enough.

February 9—4:13 p.m.
Wasilla, Alaska

"I did everything you asked. Now where's my husband?" The woman dared to hold a gun on him.

"Susan . . . you know this isn't over. Your husband is fine." Griz showed her his phone screen where a video flashing "Live" played of the man. There was a shift in the shadows behind the weeping woman in the corner. His backup had arrived right on time.

"Rob." She sucked in her lip and then shook her head. "I never should have given in to you." Tears dripped down her cheeks. "Never. It was against my better judgment. Against my training and everything I knew as an officer of the law." Her demeanor changed. The weak, sobbing wife was replaced by the ABI agent. "You're a monster. I'm not letting you get away with this."

With a brief glance over the woman's shoulder, Griz stepped to the side right before a shot rang out. The bullet plowed through Susan's chest, propelling the woman face down to the ground.

"No need to thank me." Maria stepped out of the shadows, wiped down the gun, and laid it on the table, a smug expression twisting her face. "I took care of the husband too. Nice job making the video seem live." She sidled closer and gave him a sly grin. "What are you going to do without someone on the inside?"

Oh, she thought she was so smart. "Do you think if I still needed her, we'd be here right now?" He glared at her. "Besides, who says she's the only one I had on the inside?"

Her lips pinched. "Well . . . you know where to find me if you need me." Without waiting for a response, she left as quietly as she'd entered. He'd finish her later. At least she'd been useful one last time.

The little hiccup was a bit ahead of schedule, but it didn't matter. He'd enjoy moving up the timeline.

¤ ¤ ¤

DOWN
8. Four letters. Chest flexors.

February 9—4:31 p.m.
Anchorage Police Department

Kevin was dead. Her case had been taken away. And their serial killer who wanted to take over the state of Alaska had gone off the rails.

Carrie had shed enough tears in the past hour to dehydrate herself. But she couldn't allow any more. No. More. She blew her nose and took a settling breath. What were the facts? What was the evidence telling her? That's what needed her attention.

Their UNSUB had driven the car that hit Kevin. He'd as much as admitted to it the last time he called. Who else would do something so malicious? Now she was headed in to talk to the officer in charge of the hit-and-run investigation. She gripped the steering wheel of her car. She could do this. Kevin had believed in her. Tears pricked her eyes again.

"No," she muttered and closed her eyes. "Stop. Crying. Think, Kintz. Get a grip. Every person on your team is doing their part. You do yours." It wasn't the most rousing of self–pep talks, but it would do for now.

Scott, Alan, and Kyle were back at the ABI doing whatever they could to figure out the killer's next step. She'd given them an earful, that's for sure. No one would have crossed her with the temper she'd spewed. She'd deal with that later. They were all grieving, but there was a killer she was determined to stop.

Kevin had been a good man. One of the best. He deserved to be honored and respected. Not run over like an animal.

Carrie got out of the car and clicked the lock button. As she walked toward the square government building, her eyes scanned the parking lot. Her guard couldn't be down for a moment.

Once safely inside, she approached the officer at the front desk and asked if she could speak to someone in traffic about Kevin's case. Thankfully, she didn't have to wait long. A tall man with graying temples and a serious expression approached her.

"Officer Klein, ma'am." He stepped up next to her and held out his hand. "You're here about the hit-and-run at Providence?"

"Yes, I'm Carrie Kintz with the ABI. The victim was my boss." She swallowed back the tears that threatened to clog her throat as she shook his hand. "He, um, he just passed away." She lifted her chin and forced the emotion aside. "I need to know if you've found the vehicle yet or any evidence?"

The officer put his hands on his belt. "We found the car a few hours ago in the Elmore parking lot. They've been over it for DNA and fingerprints but came up with nothing."

She shook her head. It wasn't surprising, but she was still disappointed. "Nothing?"

"We did"—he reached over to the counter and picked up a file— "find this note." He pulled out an evidence bag. "I was just about to call you when Stevens let me know you were here."

She took the bag and read what was inside.

Press conference, Carrie. Now. Or someone else from your team dies.

◻ ◻ ◻

An hour later, she stood outside the ABI. If he wanted a press conference—fine. She'd give a press conference.

The light on the camera went on, and she dove in.

"Today one of the finest to wear a badge for the Alaska Bureau of Investigation passed away. Agent Kevin Hogan was the victim of a hit-and-run traffic incident yesterday outside Providence Alaska Medical Center." Carrie swallowed, fighting the tightness of her throat. "An exemplary officer, Agent Hogan worked with the ABI for twenty-three years. He was dedicated to keeping every Alaskan safe and died in the line of duty. He was highly decorated during his years of service. He was caring and compassionate, intelligent, and dogged in the pursuit of justice. The ABI has lost not only a top agent and supervisor, but a mentor and friend." She inhaled and slowly forced the breath out through her nose, fighting to stay calm and emotionless.

But then the rage began to boil. "We believe the serial killer is also behind the hit-and-run that killed Agent Hogan." Nausea clawed at her throat. She swallowed again and pressed forward. "Even though our unidentified subject is smart and calculating, we *will* catch him. The FBI is relentless in their pursuit, as are we."

She paused, looking at her papers. The words blurred together. She trembled with anger and looked back up at the press. It was time to throw in a dig. "The evil behind all this would like to run the show. That's not going to happen. To catch the person or persons behind this, we need everyone's help. We are Alaska strong. If you have any information, please use the tip line for the FBI's office or call us here at the ABI.

"A sketch of our suspect is being circulated as we speak. If you have any information on this person or his whereabouts, contact us immediately." She grabbed the paper off the podium and shoved it toward the camera. "I repeat, this is our number one suspect. With your help, we can stop him. Thank you."

Cameras flashed. The press corps surged forward, yelling questions. But Carrie ignored it all as she stalked back into the ABI building. Her hands shook and the rest of her body followed suit. What she had just done was stupid. She hadn't followed protocol. Hadn't followed the FBI's script. She'd hear about it and probably get fired. But she didn't care.

This guy wanted attention? He just got it.

CHAPTER TWENTY-TWO

DOWN

8. Six letters. Too much of this gave you hyperglycemia and the stroke that took you too soon.

February 9—4:48 p.m.
Alaska Bureau of Investigation

HER CELL PHONE BUZZED. CARRIE looked at the caller ID. Unknown number. She was pretty certain it was either the FBI or some other bigwig calling to chew her out. Best to get it over with. "Carrie Kintz."

"Ms. Kintz, please hold for the governor."

She bit her lip. Nerves zipped through her body. Oh boy. Here it came. Walking back into the squad room, she braced herself.

"Ms. Kintz. I must ask that you refrain from any more press conferences without my permission. Allow the FBI to do their jobs."

"But, sir, if I may—" A new boldness rushed over her, and she plowed ahead. "The killer left a note in the vehicle that ran down Kevin Hogan and demanded that I hold a press conference or he was going to kill yet another member of my team. I could not allow that to happen."

"Yes, the FBI informed me of the extenuating circumstances around the press conference. At which you went off script." An audible sigh.

"I'm sorry, sir—"

"I highly doubt that, Ms. Kintz. Be that as it may, I've made my-self clear. I'm sick and tired of this killer getting his way. In *my* state. From what I've been briefed on the situation, you know that this suspect was somehow involved in the terrorist attack in Fairbanks. I don't have to tell you that the whole country—perhaps most of the world—is now watching this unfold. *Again.* The great state of Alaska is not about to kowtow to some crazed psychopath. Do I make myself clear?"

"Yes, sir." She spoke with as much respect as she could force through her vocal cords.

"We do appreciate your commitment to the Alaska Bureau." The governor paused, then added, "Keep up the good work."

The line disconnected.

Well. That could have been worse. She shoved her phone in her blazer pocket. One thing was certain, she'd hate to be in the gover-nor's shoes right now. Blogs, news sites, and social media had been blowing up with everyone discussing what they would do, how they would handle the threats, how the world was corrupt with politi-cians. No one trusted anyone anymore. It was causing even more division, which was exactly what their UNSUB wanted. She blew out her breath and went back to the conference room.

¤   ¤   ¤

She was wrong. It was much, much worse. Two hours later, she'd found out just how much her little stunt had ticked off everyone and possibly messed up the whole case. The FBI apparently sent out a memo to all hospitals, law enforcement offices, and all the media and press, that Ms. Carrie Kintz of the ABI was not to be talked to. The FBI was handling the case.

Kyle and Alan had both gone home a half hour ago. She couldn't blame them. No one had slept in more than twenty-four hours. The team planned to meet again at six in the morning. But what could they do?

She'd been blacklisted from everything. The head of the Department of Public Safety—her *boss's* boss—told her to lay low in the office for a few days and let the other investigators handle anything that came in. Carrie tapped a pencil against her desk. She might have compromised the case because of one impulsive move. The killer was probably setting up his next victim, laughing at her stupidity. What a mess.

Wouldn't Kevin be proud of her now.

◻   ◻   ◻

DOWN
8. Eleven letters. Blood and belly accessory that makes you feel safe (but you're not).

February 9—7:54 p.m.
Northeast Anchorage

Scott knocked on the door of Carrie's town house and waited for her to answer.

The door swung open. She smiled, but it didn't reach her eyes. "Ooh, you brought pizza." She dragged him in by the arm. "Hurry up and get in here."

He chuckled and looked around. A plush navy-colored couch sat along one wall with a dark brown coffee table in front of it. A thick rug with swirls of dark gray and white complemented the light gray walls. A couple of candles flickered on the end tables flanking the couch, filling the room with a warm hazelnut scent. "You've got a nice place."

"Thanks. I still have a lot I'd like to do, but it's home." With a shrug, she padded toward the kitchen in her slippers. "I appreciate you coming. And appreciate you even more for bringing food."

"Anytime."

They filled paper plates in companionable silence, and she pointed toward the dining room table with her head while she grabbed glasses and napkins. "Join me?"

"I'd love to."

She set down her plate and two glasses, then moved papers around so he would have space to eat.

After they prayed, he took a bite of pizza and studied the paper on top. "Whatcha working on?"

Pulling her knees up to her chest, she rested her feet on the chair and wrapped an arm around her legs. The other hand held a huge slice of cheesy pizza. "I was compiling a list of all his points of contact with us. Trying to figure out if there was any other clue I missed. I know I'm off the case, but I could at least call the FBI if I found anything. What matters at this point is that someone stops this guy."

"Agreed." He took another bite and chewed, tilting his head to read the sideways piece of paper. "Let's go over it together and see if anything sparks."

She finished off the slice, wiped her hands on a napkin, and pulled the paper closer. "First, there was the space heater up in Fairbanks at the mayor's cabin."

"Gotcha. Space heater. Okay, what's next?"

"Then I received the cryptic phone call saying people were dying. There was the note found on the forehead of our pacemaker victim—he was the fourth. Following that, the UNSUB tipped off the media with his cryptic little message, then kidnapped the editor's son and had her run his letter. After that, he somehow left a note in my file that said, 'try to keep up.' Still trying to figure out how he managed that. A couple days later, I saw the man in the coffee shop." She took a sip of her root beer. "He then sends another letter to the paper about eight down and says his demands will be next. I get the phone call with him demanding I do press conferences so everyone can know how brilliant he is. You get the email with video. He follows that up with another phone call to me after my press conference telling me in no uncertain terms that he's not a psychopath. He sends his whacked-out-full-on-crazy demands for Alaska to secede to the press. Then, the phone call—not distorted—with him reprimanding me and telling me that he has eyes everywhere."

"The one where he called me your boyfriend." Even though it had been an eerie call, he would take the title.

"Yep." She sent him a sideways glance but didn't keep contact as red rushed into her cheeks. "Then the note in the car he hit Kevin with was next."

"Okay, so where are we with all this? Any ideas?" He studied the paper. "Did it help to write it all out?"

"Yes and no." She reached for another slice of pizza and stared over his head as she ate. "Maybe there's something else in all the videos from Fairbanks."

"Let me help. It'll be another set of eyes."

"Sure. But let's finish off this pizza first." The first real smile he'd seen from her since Kevin died filled her face.

"Deal."

They talked about mundane things for a few minutes. Which was nice. Different, but nice. The whole time they'd known one another, they'd been entrenched in intense situations. It didn't bother him one bit, now that he analyzed it. Neither one of them had a chance to keep any walls up and they were able to simply be real. That's what he'd needed. There was no reason for them to rush.

He helped her clean the table and they took turns washing their hands in the kitchen sink. As he stood close to her side, the citrusy smell of her shampoo filled his senses. He dared to make the most of the moment. "I like the way your hair smells." It was cheesy, and he knew it.

Carrie turned toward him. Brown eyes tired but sparkling. "I like *you*, Scott Patteson." She stood on tiptoe and kissed him on the lips. Every nerve in his body sparked to life. Apparently, she didn't mind his lack of suave words.

She pulled back and giggled. "My grandmother would tan my hide if she saw that." Putting her fingers to her lips, she paused. "I've never done anything so forward in my life."

"Mm, I enjoyed it." He was afraid to kill the moment but had no idea what to do next. Kiss her again? Give her a hug? He took a chance and grasped her hand in his. Her blush deepened, but she didn't pull away. "I like you, too, Carrie Kintz."

"Sounds like we're in seventh grade all over again." Lacing her fingers through his, she led him to the couch. "But I don't mind if you don't."

"Not a bit."

He'd never bought into romantic mumbo jumbo. Plain talk was his preferred way to communicate, even when it was uncomfortable. But he couldn't deny the attraction he felt or how right it felt to be with her in this moment. In every moment, actually—even the hard ones. And they'd had plenty of those over the last few weeks.

He ran his thumb along hers and took a breath. "This might be a conversation for another day, but I'll chance it . . . where do you see this going?" He reached over and tucked a strand of her hair behind her ear with his free hand.

"Honestly?" She glanced at him, eyes squinted.

"Honesty is the best policy. And I *did* ask." He grinned at her, hoping and praying that he wasn't scaring her off.

For several seconds, she studied his face, like she was searching for something.

He found himself fascinated watching her lips pinch and then relax. Over and over. It was distracting, and he needed to focus.

Carrie smiled and squeezed his hand before letting go. "To be honest, I don't believe in casual dating. One, I don't have time for it. Two, I don't think it's wise to go out with someone that you couldn't see as a potential lifetime partner."

"So . . . ?" He held his breath and waited for her to finish the thought.

"You wouldn't be here if I didn't see a future." She blew out a quick breath and bit the corner of her lip. "There. I said it. Too forward?"

"Not at all. I asked the question, remember?" He trailed a finger down her cheek. "Ever since I met you, I've wanted to have this discussion with you, but, well—"

"A psychopath derailed those plans." The words came out with a bit of finality. Her expression fell, breaking the moment. "Speaking of which . . ." She cleared her throat and pulled her gaze away. Lifting her computer onto her lap, she opened it and scooted closer to Scott. "We should probably get back to the case."

He didn't mind the proximity as their legs touched, even though she'd closed the door on their personal discussion. At least he knew there was hope. Because his heart was getting more attached every moment he spent with her.

"Okay, here's the videos the APD and state troopers gathered from the mayor's office and home."

He blinked several times to get himself back in the game.

"They're pretty certain she was in on either planning the terrorist attack or helping whoever did it."

They spent the next few minutes watching the mayor from a camera above her desk. It was trained on the mayor's back and the empty chair on the other side of her desk, clearly aimed to capture anyone who came in to talk with the mayor. A few more minutes ticked by on the video. As Scott watched, an uneasy feeling settled over him. There was something about her movements that unnerved him. Something way too familiar.

Then Carrie switched to another video. The woman's side profile flashed in a frame. Scott felt sick. The resemblance was uncanny. "Stop. Replay that one."

She did.

"Again?"

"Okay." Carrie waited. "What do you see?"

"Is there more video?"

"Yep."

"Let me see it." He hated the churning happening in his gut.

Neither one of them spoke for several moments.

After two more videos, he was convinced. "Has the forensics team gone over these for timestamps?"

She furrowed her brow and frowned. "I would assume so. I didn't ask. Why?"

"Because that's not the mayor. That's Maria."

CHAPTER TWENTY-THREE

DOWN

8. Five letters. Inhaler output that can't save you this time.

February 10—5:04 a.m.
Hilltop Ski Area, Anchorage

GRIZ THREW DOWN THE SMASHED and mangled laptop.

Killing via computer hacking was satisfying and thrilling and he didn't have to be present. Killing people with a gun was powerful and quick.

But this?

It allowed him to vent and let all the rage out. Everything inside of him pumped and cheered.

He stared down at the man who had sneered at him. A naysayer. His rival.

Now he was face down, covered in blood, his arms and legs at odd angles.

Taking off one of his gloves, Griz reached down a hand and pressed it to the man's throat.

No pulse.

He wasn't surprised. Twenty blows with a blunt object would do that.

Griz slid his glove back on, pulled out a handkerchief, and rubbed at the man's throat. It wouldn't be good for a forensic specialist to lift his print, now would it? With a chuckle, he walked back to his warm vehicle. He climbed into it and began whistling a random tune. Everything was moving along. Better than he'd hoped.

The governor was scrambling, the FBI was lost, and poor Ms. Kintz and her team had been sidelined.

Perhaps it was time to change the plan again. These games were much too fun. Freeing. Exhilarating. And frankly, he was tired of the pressure and responsibility that had been his burden to bear for too long. Pleasing everyone simply wasn't in his wheelhouse.

He didn't need that stress.

He didn't need the others.

He was more powerful like this anyway. The perfect villain. Smarter than everyone else. No one could stop him. Why hadn't he thought of this before?

Popping a pill into his mouth, he swigged it back with some bottled water.

A new idea began to form at the edges of his mind. Hm. This would take some preparation.

He did love a good plan.

Yes. It was time to watch the world burn.

◻ ◻ ◻

DOWN
8. Seven letters. Private health data now in my possession.

February 10—8:36 a.m.
Alaska Bureau of Investigation

"Yes, sir. I understand, sir." Carrie hung up the phone. Surprise, satisfaction, and a little embarrassment were making her feel jittery.

Scott stared at her, his eyebrows almost touching his hair. "Well?"

"I can't believe the director of the FBI just called me." She grimaced.

"What did he say?" Alan shoved a donut in his mouth. "The suspense is killing me."

"Well . . ." She flicked her gaze from one to the other. "While he praised me for my good work on the case at the beginning, and he appreciated our tip last night"—she connected with Scott—"he asked me nicely to step back and take a day or two off. You, too, Alan."

"And me?" Scott leaned back with his arms crossed.

"They want you back at your regular job. They said the timestamps are real and there's no way someone else was impersonating the mayor."

"That's a bunch of garbage." Scott's head wagged back and forth. "They're covering for someone or something."

"Now who's been watching too much crime TV?" Alan laughed as he shoved things into his bag. "You don't have to tell me twice to go home. I love you, Carrie, but after the loss of Kevin and the lack of sleep and the craziness of this case? The FBI can have it. I'm going home."

"I love you, too, you big lug." Carrie whacked him in the arm as he passed. "See ya tomorrow?"

"Yeah."

"Okay. Be careful." Once he was gone, she closed the door. "You staying?"

"Of course." Scott grinned at her.

"You might get in trouble."

"I don't care. My boss doesn't answer to the FBI or anyone else."

"Good." She picked up the phone and dialed the ME's office. "Dr. Blanchard, please." She waited for a few seconds and then the doctor answered. "Sorry to bother you, Doc, just wondering if you by any chance have any new bodies?"

"I was actually thinking about calling you. We do have another body. I wanted you to see it before I let the FBI know."

Carrie felt the blood drain from her face as the ME filled her in. She hung up and looked at Scott. "I need to get over there right now. There's a woman. She's been shot twice, execution-style. I don't remember a clue about a shooting, do you?"

"No, but one could have slipped past us."

Carrie grabbed her purse off her desk and fished around for her keys. "True. That wouldn't be good though." Her frown eased a little. "The good news is they believe they have an identity for this one. They're waiting for verification. Lisa Jones."

"What?!" The word burst from Scott.

Carrie's head whipped up in surprise. His face was white, hands trembling. "Are you okay? What's wrong?" She stepped toward him, but he held up his hands.

"What was that name you said?"

Her gaze searched Scott's face. Then slowly, details of their conversation about Maria came back to her memory. Her heart broke a little for him. "Lisa Jones. That is—"

"Maria." Her name came out as a whisper. He closed his eyes for a moment, and she watched him breathe. In and out. "I'm coming with you. I can identify her."

CHAPTER TWENTY-FOUR

DOWN
8. Five letters. I watch you when you're sleeping, I know when you'll awake.

February 10—9:15 a.m.
Alaska State Medical Examiner's Office

SCOTT HAD NEVER BEEN IN a medical examiner's office before. He'd never been in a morgue. Never seen a dead body before.

But here he was. Walking beside Carrie at the Alaska State Medical Examiner's Office. It was a bit more overwhelming than he expected.

Dr. Blanchard had a team of highly qualified people working for her, so it was even more impressive that she was the one taking them back to see the Jane Doe. The one they suspected was Lisa Jones. *Maria.* Something in how the woman explained the situation showed that beneath the surface, her wheels were turning. It was her job to stay objective and state the facts. Investigate the evidence in the deceased the way only a trained medical examiner could. Keeping professional distance was necessary, but Scott began to understand how difficult that must be for these hardworking doctors.

They weren't cold, unfeeling individuals. They probably all had families, loved ones, lives outside this intricate and horrible world of crime and chaos. How did they separate their work from the world they went home to?

It wasn't a question he wanted to ponder too long. He couldn't do it. Plain and simple. Walking the long, sterilized hallway gave him too much time to think. He rubbed a hand down the side of his jaw.

He was here for one reason. To determine whether or not the Jane Doe was Maria. Anything he could do to help Carrie and her team with the case was his paramount concern. He'd just have to swallow his discomfort and look forward to the time when he could get back to his computers and scanning code. That was more his speed.

The doctor shoved her hands into her white coat pockets and stopped in front of a wall of stainless-steel doors.

He'd seen the likes of this before—on all the television crime dramas he loved to watch. The key was, he liked to *watch* them. On TV. Where it wasn't reality.

Not experience them. The sights. The sounds. The smells.

This was completely different.

The scent in the room was unlike anything he'd ever encountered. Very chemical. It burned the back of his throat, but the alternative wasn't something he'd want to inhale either.

The silence that permeated the huge room unnerved him. So quiet, he could hear the hum of . . . the lights? Or was it the large wall of refrigerated space in front of him?

Whatever it was, it enhanced the sense of . . . *sterile*. He felt oddly disconnected. Unfeeling. As if he were outside his own body, watching the scene unfold.

"This is our Jane Doe." Without any emotion, the doctor pulled open the door and slid out the long metal tray holding the body.

Scott swallowed.

Carrie stepped up next to the body as the doctor pulled a white sheet from over the face.

He saw the woman's forehead, and he couldn't get past the gray of her skin. The pallor of death was disgusting.

Carrie motioned him toward her, and the contrast of her pink skin—full of life—compared to the woman on the table made his stomach turn.

So much for guys being tough.

He stepped forward, swallowing the burning acid that crept up his throat. He rounded the table and winced.

That face. He'd know it anywhere. "That's her."

"Are you certain?" Carrie sidled closer.

"You know this woman?" Dr. Blanchard's voice couldn't tear his gaze away from Maria's lifeless form.

He nodded. "This is Lisa Jones. The ID you found with her was the alias she gave me." With a sniff, he looked up. "She should have records under that name. We worked at the governor's office together seven years ago. We were also engaged until we broke up five years ago." He inhaled sharply then eased the breath out slowly. He could get through this. *Lord . . . I don't even know how to pray right now. Please help.* "When we broke up, she told me her real name was Maria. Maria LeCourt. There might be other records of family or information under that name."

Dr. Blanchard walked over to a desk where a computer sat. Her face remained impassive. "And you are positive that's her?"

Scott rubbed his jaw. "Does she have a tattoo on her right wrist? A pastel blue butterfly?"

Dr. Blanchard looked at her papers, running her finger down a list of something. Then she went to the body and lifted the side of the sheet. She pulled out Maria's lifeless limb and turned it over. There it was. What she'd called her silly youthful mistake. The butterfly was stark against the paleness of her skin. Scott glanced at Dr. Blanchard and nodded once.

She slipped Maria's arm under the sterile white sheet and went back to her computer.

"Thank you for the information." The woman typed into the computer.

"I need to leave." Scott glanced down at Carrie.

She took his arm and led him a few feet away. "Do you need us for anything else, Doc?"

"No. You go on. I'll send all this info on to the powers that be."

The entire walk out of the building and to the car, he couldn't hear a thing. Couldn't feel a thing.

Not even Carrie's hand on his arm.

Once they were in the vehicle and she'd started it up, she turned toward him. "Talk to me, Scott."

He blinked. "My mind is spinning. As awful as it was seeing a dead body for the first time"—he shook his head, still feeling bile in the back of his throat—"it was even worse to have all the anger and betrayal from all those years ago force its way back into my thoughts."

Carrie reached over and took his hand. "It's never easy to confront the past, especially when someone resurfaces like this."

He cringed and then cracked his neck. "Not a pleasant experience. Maria was a wrecking ball to my life and one I'd prefer to leave in the past." He squeezed her hand, then let go and stared out the window. He could feel Carrie's eyes on his profile, but he couldn't talk anymore. Not right now. The whole experience had taken whatever energy he had left.

Oh, God, help me!

◻ ◻ ◻

DOWN
8. Seven letters. North, south, east, or west, you can't escape me.

February 11—12:02 p.m.
Alaska Bureau of Investigation

Back at the ABI, Carrie left Scott alone for the first hour or so as he processed and worked through whatever haunted him after the visit to the ME's office. She understood it all too well. The first time seeing a dead body on a slab was always shocking, but there was a lot of history between Scott and the woman who was now deceased. Besides, giving him space wasn't a problem. She needed a moment herself. All the deep emotions that had surged forth when he talked about being betrayed by that woman were overwhelming.

Their conversation had brought her awfully close to spilling her own heart out. Everything in her ached to comfort him, to reveal just how much she cared about him. But it felt too raw. Too soon. Something she couldn't deal with right now.

To combat it, she dove into work. She'd been needing time to go through all her notes and see if she could come up with some sort of plan. Everything else could be put on hold until the killer was caught.

Alan was home with a supposed migraine, which was fine since there wasn't anything more they could do on their case. Deep down, though, she knew he was grieving the loss of his longtime friend and colleague. Alan might be all tough guy on the outside, but he wasn't immune to grief. Kevin's death was hitting him hard. But Alan wasn't alone in his sadness. The whole station was in a state of mourning. Nothing would be the same, even after the case was solved.

Carrie looked at the stacks of papers and files surrounding her. At least now she had time to find the top of her desk. The head of the ABI wanted them to keep a low profile because of their affiliation with the serial killer case.

Every other investigator in the office was busy with the craziness that occurred when winter and long darkness drove people to do stupid things.

"Hey, Kintz!" Brad's voice brought her gaze up.

She stood and stretched. "What's up?"

"Have you seen Susan?" Hands on his hips, he looked even grouchier than usual.

Now that she thought about it, she hadn't registered who was in the office the past couple days. "I don't think so." Had she been so obsessed with the case she didn't even notice when a colleague wasn't around?

His frown deepened. "No one has heard from her. No word from her husband either. I assumed she'd been assigned another case since we've all been running ragged, but nobody has seen her." Grabbing his coat, he tipped his head toward Carrie. "I'm going over to their house to check on them. Let Kev—" He stopped and grimaced. "If anyone needs me, have them call my cell."

"You got it." Brad's slipup was just one more reminder that Kevin was gone for good. It was like the knife already plunged into her heart was being twisted over and over again.

Needing a change of scenery, she headed back to the conference room. Maybe Scott would welcome her presence.

At this point, she needed him more than ever. And not just here working on the case. But how could she tell him that?

His phone was ringing as she entered the room, and he glanced up at her. "It's Jason." He lifted his cell to his ear and answered.

Carrie listened to Scott's side of the conversation. First, he filled in his friend on everything that had happened. When he got to the part about having to identify Maria, she didn't miss the hostility that grew in his voice.

Then he was quiet for several minutes as he listened.

Whatever the guy said, it had a calming effect on Scott. Which was good. His demeanor changed, his tone of voice was back to normal, and his words were those of appreciation.

Seeming to be back to business and talking about the case, Scott did a lot of nodding and typing on his laptop.

Carrie released a breath she hadn't realized she'd been holding. She took a seat and waited for him. From what she could tell, they'd moved on to discussing how a wrong surgical procedure could kill a person and how it could be done remotely. She only understood about half of the terminology and acronyms Scott used in his side of the conversation and hoped that they would be able to figure it out.

It didn't matter who got the credit. It didn't matter whose case it was anymore. All that mattered was stopping the killer.

Even if that meant ticking off the FBI. That thought made her wince. Was she willing to lose her job over it?

Without hesitation—yes! She might not be as fulfilled doing something else for a career, but to know that she'd been able to keep the guy from killing anyone else would be enough for her. After all they'd been through. After losing Kevin.

Scott set his phone down and sent her a serious look.

"What'd you find out? Does he have anything to help us?"

"Darcie got on the line too and shared all her knowledge from being the emergency operations director. With the HIPAA laws and the fact that we have hunches and circumstantial evidence at best, our hands are tied. Not to mention that we're technically no longer on the case. But Jason and I both agree that it has to be a transplant or heart surgery that our UNSUB is going to try to hack. It's the only way to ensure death, because surgeons can overcome a lot of wrenches thrown into the mix when lives are on the line."

"All right. How many of those can there be? Let's start calling the hospitals. Someone has to listen, right?"

"I don't know." He blew out a huge breath. "You're more versed in this than I am."

She opened her mouth, but her phone rang.

Unknown number.

Unease crawled up her spine as she swiped to answer. "Carrie Kintz."

"Too bad the FBI took you off the case. They'll pay for that mistake." That voice. It was the second time she'd heard it undisguised. She put it on speakerphone and hit Record.

"It doesn't matter what happened to me. You'll be caught. That's what matters." She shared a glance with Scott. His face mirrored the determination she felt.

"Oh, I highly doubt that." The light chuckle was gravelly. "Besides, it's happening now."

Coming out of her chair, she lifted her chin. "*What's* happening now?"

"Don't play games, Ms. Kintz. I know you saw the clue. Oh, I'm sorry. Didn't you want to be the one to stop me?" Laughter filled the line until three beeps cut it off.

He was gone.

And they were too late.

CHAPTER TWENTY-FIVE

DOWN
8. Three letters. Anaphylaxis treatment that you don't have.

February 11—12:22 p.m.
Downtown Anchorage

HE PACED THE TINY STUDIO apartment, hands clasped behind his back, waiting for his prey. Griz had it laid out perfectly.

Once he'd finalized his new plan, everything seemed brighter. Happier. Having thrown caution to the wind, he didn't care about anyone's rules anymore.

The governor had everyone in the state scrambling. From politicians to law enforcement to every hoarder and prepper. Fear hung over the state like a thundercloud. Citizens were terrified of a serial killer on the loose.

That was the realization that had changed everything.

The power he craved wasn't in the control he thought he desired. No. It was in the chaos.

The chaos *he* created.

No one could catch him, much less stop him. So why not take matters into his own hands and ramp things up a notch or two or . . . three hundred?

The lock in the door clicked, and the knob turned.

Griz swung around to face it.

The door opened, and Peter entered. His gaze swept the room, shock reddening his face. "What are you doing?"

All the evidence was laid out. "With your dedication to the cause, I'm sure you understand what has to happen next. You're going to take the fall."

"Of course. I understand." Peter lifted his chin. Then in the next split second, he had his SIG pointed at Griz's chest. "But not before I kill you first."

Two shots rang out.

Griz fell backward. The white-hot pain in his shoulder competed with the blow to the chest. Blackness clouded the edges of his vision. His head rolled to the side, and he held his breath, listening. What was that traitor going to do next?

Several seconds passed. A shadow fell over him and kicked his leg. Every ounce of training kicked in, and Griz refused to react.

The trilling of a cell phone broke the quiet. "What? Yes. I'm done here. I told you I'd do it . . . " His voice trailed off then was cut off by the simple click of the door.

Griz gritted his teeth and squeezed his eyes shut as he sat up. Blood oozed from his left shoulder. Just inches outside the bulletproof vest's coverage.

He ripped off his shirt sleeve and shoved it over the wound with his right hand.

The bullet to the chest would have been deadly. Peter's aim was true. Too bad he didn't know Griz had protection.

He would have chuckled had he not just had the wind so thoroughly knocked out of him.

After a short respite, he got to his feet. The shoulder injury was a problem, but not one he couldn't handle.

This was going even better than he'd planned.

◻ ◻ ◻

DOWN
8. Six letters. I know where you are in your car.

February 11—12:35 p.m.
Alaska Bureau of Investigation

Carrie covered her face with her hands, trying to calm her racing heart. The phone call she'd received was enough to send her over the edge. But she had to stay focused. Who did she tell about this new development? She hadn't heard anything about a replacement for Kevin. The thought twisted her heart.

She had to go to the FBI. Even if it took begging and pleading. If push came to shove, she could even remind them that the call was in her jurisdiction and threaten to follow this lead. Sure, it would effectively derail *any* hope of a career at the FBI. But they had the chance to stop this madman and bring some semblance of closure to every life he'd touched; it was worth it.

Dialing the head of the Anchorage FBI, Carrie closed her eyes and prayed that he would take her call and listen.

"Ms. Kintz. Please tell me you aren't impeding our investigation." His voice was clipped, but at least he answered.

"Director, I don't want to hinder you in any way, but you need to hear this. Right now." She pressed Play and let him hear the call.

"Play that again?" A muffling sounded.

She did as he asked. *Please, oh, please, let him listen and take it seriously. God, we need Your help.*

The seconds ticked by as she waited.

"I'll have two agents at your office in five minutes. We'll have a plan by then."

The call disconnected and she released her breath. With a glance at Scott, she grimaced. "Let's see what happens next."

She raced to her desk and grabbed everything she needed just in case they allowed her to help. She would be ready. With her badge, her weapon, and her go bag, she watched the door.

In less than a minute, two agents waved at her from the front.

"Scott!" She called to him, and he ran toward her.

When they met the FBI, the agent in charge had his hands on his hips. "We don't have a lot of time and things are dicey with privacy laws. But the director called every hospital personally so they would take the threat seriously. All non-lifesaving surgeries on the docket have been put on hold as the hospital personnel double- and triple-check all records. But there are currently ten surgeries in process at three different locations. That's where we are focused. As we speak, the hospitals are being given the information to get to the surgeons in the operating rooms." The agent turned to Scott. "Can you trace a signal? If a computer were online at this moment?"

"If I'm given access, yes." Scott's voice was clear.

"Good. Get on that right now." The agent turned to the other man with him. "Get Patteson everything he needs." He headed toward the door. "Ms. Kintz, if you'll accompany my team, we're headed to one of the sites now. If you receive another call, we want you with us. Just in case."

She nodded and followed him with a glance over her shoulder at Scott.

His face was grim, but he dipped his chin at her.

Somehow, they had to stop this beast.

◻ ◻ ◻

DOWN
8. Six letters. The poison in your blood, creating a silent death. I did that.

February 11—12:53 p.m.
Alaska Regional Hospital

Agent Parnell's radio crackled.

Carrie crouched with the other FBI agents in the hallway outside the operating room at Alaska Regional Hospital. Her quadriceps were burning. Sweat dampened her forehead. The not knowing was the most difficult part of this operation.

They had no clue where their UNSUB was right now. He might be doing this remotely, or he might be escalating and be on-site. He could be here or at either of the other hospitals. The possibilities were endless. And alarming.

What he might be armed with was another consideration. The man had killed in so many different ways, nothing was outside the realm of possibility.

In the few minutes since they'd left the ABI, word had come to them of more bodies. One brutally beaten with a laptop—a sure sign their guy was off the rails.

Carrie's phone buzzed, and she raised her eyebrows at Parnell.

He nodded and the silence in the hallway deepened.

"Hello?" She answered quietly, hoping and praying that it was and wasn't their guy all at the same time. She didn't want to hear that voice again, but she wanted this to be over.

"Carrie, we found Susan." Brad's voice cracked.

She released a breath and shook her head at Parnell. "Is she okay?"

"No." The other ABI agent practically growled the word. "She and her husband are both dead."

"How?" She held up a finger to the FBI agent breathing down her neck.

"We believe her car was hacked and slammed into a tree—*after* she was shot twice and placed in the driver's seat. There's a note. It says, 'my little mole.' Guess that explains how the note got in your file, and perhaps even the bug in your coat? Her case had been Wasilla, so it wouldn't have been hard for her to do it. I don't know. This guy creeps me out." Brad's voice hardened with anger. "How he got into Susan's head is beyond me. I've worked with her for three years. But in the passenger seat, we found a folder with pictures. Our guy must have sent them to Susan as blackmail. That's what led us to her husband. He was bound and gagged with a shot to the head at a remote location in the valley."

Closing her eyes against the pain of another loss, Carrie used everything within her power to hold herself in check. She'd like nothing more than to lose it right now, but what if their guy was watching?

At this point, she wouldn't put anything past him. "Thanks for letting me know, Brad."

"Please tell me you're close to catching him?"

"I—"

"Kintz!" Parnell's harsh whisper cut her off.

"We'll end this." She spat the last words and then hung up the call. Parnell made his way to her. "Well?"

She filled him in and didn't miss the emotion that passed through his unyielding gaze. "This has to end today."

His radio crackled again. "Clear at Providence."

That left their location and one other.

Parnell checked in with his team. They'd been sweeping the entire place, making sure there wouldn't be any threats to other lives if they had to storm the OR. But that took time. Especially in a large hospital.

So here they were. Crouched in the corridor outside the OR, waiting for word that it was safe. But every second that passed put her on edge.

Would they be too late?

◻ ◻ ◻

DOWN
8. Eight letters. This surgery can't help you now because I've got you.

February 11—12:47 p.m.
Alaska Bureau of Investigation

Scott sat in front of his laptops watching every bit of action on the hospitals' Wi-Fi feeds. It would help if they knew which hospital was the target. They had narrowed it down to two. And Carrie was at one of those. Knowing that made his gut churn even more.

Jason was helping from Fairbanks, so each of them had taken a hospital server, but unless their guy showed his hand in some way, they were flying blind and had to watch every little thing.

As he scanned the servers, movement caught his eye. There.

He followed the trail and signaled to Chris, the FBI agent with him. "Get on the radio. Someone just changed the destination of a heart. They're sending the heart intended for Memorial to the Surgical Center."

Chris repeated everything into the radio and listened to the response. "Surgical Center has been cleared, so it's got to be happening at Memorial."

Before everything disappeared, Scott put every bit of his skills to the test to trace the origin of the transmission. With his ears tuned in to the radio, he hoped and prayed the team would make it in time.

"They're moving." Chris stepped closer and hovered over his shoulder. "Can you trace it?"

Thanks to Jason and his Cyber Solutions team's help, his computer was working at what Mac used to call warp speed. Then it pinged.

"Gotcha." He growled.

Chris bent over and checked the screen. "We've got a location."

"Head there now." The voice over the radio was hushed. "We are about to enter the OR."

The next few seconds were filled with commands over the radio and lots of shouting.

Chris grabbed his arm. "Take only what you need. You're coming with my team."

As they raced out to their vehicles, Chris gave Scott the play-by-play. The FBI team at the hospital had successfully stopped a transplant surgery right before they removed the patient's heart. Since the correct organ had been sent to the wrong hospital, they were waiting for it to return before placing the patient on the bypass machine. Thank God the team had gotten there when they did, because once on a bypass machine, the patient had a limited time to live without the transplant.

It didn't take long for medical personnel to scramble and rectify the situation once they knew what they were dealing with.

But now they needed to get in place to see what this . . . Scott sighed. He was running out of adjectives to describe the depth of evil this man created.

The van careened into a parking lot six blocks away from the hospital. Scott glanced at Chris. "What are we doing here?"

Chris shoved a bulletproof vest at Scott then slipped his own on over his suit. "We don't know if this guy is watching our every move. There are several tunnels in this section of the city. A couple run right by the hospital. We need to check for explosives."

Explosives? Tunnels? Anchorage was Scott's hometown, and he had no clue about any underground tunnels.

Chris's voice was matter-of-fact, as if they were talking about the latest basketball scores. "Our guy should have sent you a schematic. I need you to pull it up. You're our eyes as we navigate this maze. We need to make sure that we're clear below so the team above knows they are free of every possible threat."

Scott nodded, wondering if the numbness he was experiencing would subside eventually. At what point would his brain stop processing the twists and turns of this case? He clipped the vest on and grabbed his laptop. He opened it and tapped quickly, finding the information Chris said would be there.

He needed to get a grip and focus. Right now, lives were hanging in the balance. He could sort through the complications of his emotions later. "Ok. I've got the schematic pulled up. If we enter through the sewage entrance here"—he pointed to a dot on the screen—"we go forward about twenty feet, then a sharp left. It looks like this tunnel will take us about six blocks and then it's a few quick left then right turns before we will find ourselves under the hospital."

Chris nodded and the small tactical team began their descent into underground Anchorage. Their progress was slow but thorough. Scott was not only impressed by the dedication of this team but thankful. Thankful for men and women who put their lives on the line to keep people safe every day.

As they made their way through the maze, and no explosives were found, Scott relaxed a little. He wouldn't be fully comfortable until this guy was caught. And Carrie was safe. Was she at this hospital? He couldn't remember. She was at the forefront of his mind, but he had to focus. And so did she, especially if she were in the middle of all this.

They turned another corner and Scott stopped. "We're under the hospital now. This will lead to the staircase that goes up into the hospital parking garage," he whispered. Chris nodded and signaled for his men to go past Scott and examine the next several hundred feet of tunnel.

The last forty-five minutes of his life had been the most stressful he'd ever encountered. Never in his life had Scott imagined he would be on an FBI raid. But that's where he found himself. Because he'd done his job. He was still stunned that his work had brought them to this point.

"We're clear," a voice crackled over the radio fifteen minutes later. "Visuals on parking garage staircase. Also confirmed clear."

"Roger that, will rendezvous there in ten."

Relief poured through Scott. At least no one was going to get blown up at this hospital today. "Any chance we can position ourselves inside the hospital?"

Chris shook his head. "We can't risk being seen by the UNSUB."

They raced to the staircase and Scott stationed himself at the bottom of the stairs with his computer and pulled up the tracking screen again. The dots of agents flashed on his screen. The senior agent handed him the walkie-talkie. "You're up. Guide them in, Patteson."

Scott grabbed the radio and took a deep breath. "This is Scott Patteson. From your position move ahead twenty feet. There should be a staircase on your right. Go up the staircase." He watched the dots on his screen. "At the top of that staircase, take a left. It should be directly in front of you."

He listened to the whispered directions from the agent in charge. Apparently, they had the area surrounded.

A shot rang out.

Followed by shouting and more gunfire.

From what Scott could ascertain, it sounded like they were in pursuit of the killer and he was shooting at them. *God, please don't let anyone else get hurt.*

FBI agents were well trained. They faced stuff like this all the time. He didn't need to worry. In his mind, he kept telling himself to do his job. Just that. Law enforcement wasn't his thing. Computers were. And he'd brought them all here.

More shots and shouts echoed on the radio. If only he could see what was happening. But he was blind to all that. The dots on his screen were the only visual he had.

Another shot, and then a lot of scuffling.

"You will never win! Don't you understand? We are everywhere." The voice laughed, crackling through Scott's radio. "Look at all the people that died without you knowing a single thing. You idiots needed clues to figure it out!" He laughed again. "You can't stop this. You can't stop us."

"We just did."

Another shot.

Then multiple shots echoed in response.

"Suspect is down." The agent's voice was loud and clear. "I repeat. Suspect is down."

CHAPTER TWENTY-SIX

DOWN
8. Eight letters. Stopping work, life, or what you do to a computer. Or a person . . . permanently.

February 11—5:01 p.m.
Northeast Anchorage

WALKING IN HER DOOR FROM the garage, Carrie couldn't get over the way every inch of her felt shaky, relieved, and tense all at the same time.

Once it was over and their killer was down, she'd had a brief second to see that Scott was all right before the FBI dragged him off to their offices for debriefing. She didn't envy the poor guy. But she wished they were sitting together right now, having their own debriefing. Carrie rolled her eyes at the direction of her thoughts. When had she become a romantic?

Still, they needed to finish their conversation from a few nights ago. One that didn't involve a serial killer. Or any investigation for that matter.

Carrie plopped down on her couch. She let her head fall back to the soft cushion. The intensity of their circumstances in the brief time they'd known each other was enough to fill a stress quota for the next few years. Was that any way to start a relationship?

Of course, in her mind, they were already in a relationship. Did he feel the same?

His words from their last personal conversation said yes, he did. But did he feel the same way now? After all this? Now that he knew what it was like to date someone in law enforcement, had he changed his mind? She chewed the corner of her lip. They were useless questions when he wasn't here to answer them.

Her phone vibrated in her pocket.

A reminder that it had been one of the longest days of her life, but it wasn't over. She knew that.

She pulled out her phone and answered it with a less-than-enthusiastic "Carrie Kintz."

"Great job, Ms. Kintz." The voice belonged to the Anchorage director of the FBI.

That had her sitting up straight. "Thank you, sir."

"My team commends you for the way you handled this case. I must admit, it was fascinating to read how all the clues had been solved. You've got a good team."

"Thank you." She swallowed and worked to keep her voice calm. At least she hadn't burned all her bridges with the FBI. Although, at this point, her dreams were of a certain cyber expert and hopes to stay with the ABI. To carry on Kevin's legacy with Alan and the rest of the team.

"It would be an honor to work together again in the future."

"Thank you, sir." She really should come up with a few more words to respond, but it was the best she could do.

"If you would join us for a press conference this evening, you and Mr. Patteson—along with your team, including the late Mr. Hogan—will be commended for your assistance."

That stung. It wasn't their *assistance*. It had been the ABI's case after all. But she wouldn't argue at this point. Being acknowledged was enough for now. Especially if they gave credit to Kevin. The man had made the ultimate sacrifice and lost his life serving and protecting the people of Alaska. "I'll be there, sir."

As the call ended, she glanced at the clock. No time to change. She blew out her breath and stood. Plucking her bag off a dining room chair, she headed out the door.

It was over. Finally.

◻ ◻ ◻

DOWN
8. Three letters. The one I've been waiting for.

February 14—8:30 p.m.
Glacier Brewhouse

"Sorry it's so late, but it's the only time I could snag a reservation." Scott escorted Carrie up the steps with a hand at the small of her back and their coats slung over his other arm.

Clothed in a gorgeous red dress, she took his breath away. "I don't care about the time. We're here. We're alive. That's what matters."

He couldn't agree with her more. The past two days had been the most incredible of his entire life. Nothing spectacular had happened. No more FBI raids.

Just time away from work. Two entire days to spend with her. Just her. They'd done nothing but talk, eat good food, and watch a couple of funny movies. The time together only solidified what Scott knew he'd felt from nearly the first moment he met her.

The host gave them menus and, as much as he tried to wait, he couldn't do it any longer.

"Carrie?" He set the menu down.

She looked up and did the same, a sparkle in her relaxed eyes. "Yes?"

"I know we haven't known each other long, but I know in my heart that you are the one I've been waiting for all these years." He watched as her smile stretched and filled her cheeks. "It's kinda back-ward for me to ask you to marry me—and yeah, it's cliché since it's

Valentine's Day—but I want to ask you. Ugh! I'm not good at all this romance stuff. I should probably ask you to be my valentine first. Or maybe ask you to date me for an appropriate amount of time after we've had a bit of normalcy for a—"

Her laughter mercifully cut off his rambling as she reached across the table and grabbed his hand. "Let me ask you a different question. Is this weekend good for you?"

His heart picked up pace. "For what?"

"To meet my parents." She picked up her glass and took a sip of water. "They're excited to meet you."

He stared at her as his pulse quickened. "Um . . . sure." Why did that suddenly make him nervous? What if they didn't like him? Then reality punched him in the gut. She hadn't answered his question.

Her laughter erupted again. "Man, we are really bad at this."

He couldn't help but join in. "But at least we're bad at it together."

Lifting her phone out of her little purse, she raised her eyebrows. "Mind if I show you something?"

"Not at all." He leaned forward and rested his elbows on the table.

Their server took that moment to appear, and Scott asked her to give them a few minutes.

When they were alone again, Carrie turned her phone to him. "Since our first awkward get-together, I've been texting my parents about you."

Oh boy. He wasn't expecting that. He glanced at the screen and read:

> I've met the one. At least,
> I think I have. Mom, help?

His heart sped up even faster as heat spread through him.

Carrie pulled her phone back, her cheeks a bit pinker than usual. With her eyes focused on her screen, she licked her lips. "Ever since that first text—which seems like eons ago—I've been talking with my parents about you. Their wisdom kept me grounded in reality, at least most of the time. And our growing relationship gave me something to look forward to during this awful case." She blinked. "I have definitely doubted myself a few times. Didn't think you could handle having a wife in law enforcement. Wasn't sure if I was good enough for you."

Scott waited. No need to rush anything tonight. No matter how sought-after their table might be, dinner could wait.

With an upward glance at him, she drew in her bottom lip, then blew out a breath. "My parents started praying for us immediately. And not just for the case—for *us*. Mom said she knew after that first night she and Dad prayed that you were the one and that we were about to go through the fire together. So as trying and weird and horrifying and ugly as all the last twenty-five days have been, I've had the peace of knowing that my family was praying and that you and I would be fine, no matter what we encountered. Or how caught up in my own head I got."

She looked up again with a breathless giggle. "God gave me peace when I handed it over to Him. Not that I didn't try to yank it back a few times." She widened her eyes and sent him a knowing smile.

"I'm glad to hear that." He swallowed back the urge to ask her the original question again. Instead, he reached for her hand.

Her face softened as she stared down at their hands. When she glanced up, she licked her lips. "So, to answer your question . . . Yes. I want to marry you. I want to date you. I want to be your valentine. I say we continue our weird streak and do things outside of what's considered normal. I'm ready to start a life with you."

"Me too."

"A spring wedding sounds nice."

"Right after breakup. Don't want to be caught in the middle of all the slush and melting snow." He chuckled. Come on, early spring.

"Sounds like a plan to me."

"I'd better do this properly, then." He stood up and walked around to her chair. Leaning over, he lowered his voice to a whisper. "Better be prepared for our awkward streak to continue." He got down on one knee. "For the rest of our lives?" He winked at her. Everyone else disappeared. It was just the two of them. There wasn't a sound other than his pulse pounding in his head as he waited.

Turning to face him completely, she touched his cheek. "I look forward to it."

The room erupted in applause, and people across the restaurant stood. A guy in the back shouted, "Hey, did she say yes? We couldn't hear."

Carrie lifted her chin and shouted back. "Yes!" Then she leaned toward Scott.

Laughter swelled as the clapping subsided and the regular hum of a busy restaurant became the soundtrack around them.

On his knee still, he pulled her into his arms and kissed her. It wasn't the private place he'd hoped for the kiss to seal the deal, but he didn't care. Why not add a little more awkward to their story? As much love and passion as he felt toward her in that moment, he pulled back. They had their whole futures together to share intimate kisses.

EPILOGUE

DOWN
8. Four letters. ____maker. Great when it works. But I can stop it.

Downtown Anchorage

"HE'S NOT THE GUY, SCOTT. It can't be the guy. I know it." Mac pleaded with him.

Scott shared a glance with Carrie, then looked back at his friend. His heart broke at the anguish etched into the lines on Mac's face. "This is why we asked you to meet us here."

Carrie handed each of them a pair of pale blue shoe covers and a pair of latex gloves. "Put these on." She put on her own set of protective gear. Then she lifted the crime scene tape and unlocked the door. "Don't touch anything. Even though everything has been tagged and a team is coming in an hour to bag it all, we need to make sure we don't contaminate any evidence." She led them into the room.

The apartment that belonged to the deceased suspect, Peter Chandler, was nothing more than a small studio. Every inch of wall space was covered with pictures. From every detail of the Fairbanks terrorist attack to each victim taken during the last couple weeks. It was eerie and disconcerting. And gory.

She put a hand on Mac's arm. "All the evidence is here. Routers, servers, tons of extra burner phones. Paperwork that shows all his

241

planning. How he hacked each device. How he created the crossword puzzles."

With a glance to Scott, she stepped away. "I'm sorry, Mac. I know this is difficult, but maybe now you can have some closure. We got our guy. It's over." After a nod in his direction, she went over to the door and waited.

Mac shook his head. "No. It's not him. It can't be." His mouth hung open as he surveyed the room. "It's too perfect. All tied up with a neat little bow. Don't you get it? This guy . . . no. This isn't the guy who killed my family. I've seen that man." His face began to crumple. "I saw him, Scott. I know I did. He looked just like the sketch I gave you."

Several awful seconds passed. Scott didn't know what to say. While Peter resembled the man in Mac's sketch, he wasn't an exact match. But he'd been a match for the sketch the forensic artist had created based off Carrie's description. He shared a long glance with his fiancée. Her eyes held the same anguish.

Coming back across the room, she tucked her arm around Mac's and led him out of the apartment. Scott followed, unable to fully digest the devastation he saw in his friend. Once they were in the hallway, Carrie wrapped the big guy in a hug. Her eyes closed tight as tears streaked down her cheeks. "I get it, Mac. I do. I saw him too. He taunted me. Did horrible things. Killed way too many people before we were able to stop him. But I saw his body at the morgue." She stepped back and opened her eyes. "There aren't any more what-ifs. It *is* him."

Mac just shook his head. Tears streaked his face. He rushed down the stairs and outside. Scott chased after him. They needed air, yeah. But now Mac couldn't get a breath. What was happening? The man who'd been his rock, his mentor, was falling apart in front of his eyes.

Mac's shoulders shook as sobs erupted out of him. Scott stepped up and slid his arm around the shoulders of the big man.

Mac's knees buckled and Scott had a hard time keeping his friend from tumbling onto the concrete. He dragged Mac to a bench, and they sat. "I'm here, man. We'll get through this together."

◘ ◘ ◘

DOWN
8. Four letters. Surprise.

Six weeks later—3:00 p.m.
Healy, Alaska

Mac stared through his high-powered binoculars at the man leaving the cabin a mile away. From his perch way up the mountain, he had a bird's-eye view. The hideout was off the grid, far from any common trails or highways. He'd needed the four-wheel drive on his truck to get over several large rocks on the trail up here.

How many criminals were hiding out in the vast wilderness of Alaska? It made him angry to even think about it.

It didn't matter what Scott and Carrie had found in that other man's apartment; Peter Chandler wasn't responsible for the death of Mac's wife and daughter. Sure, there were routers and paperwork and pictures in his tiny apartment. But Mac had seen the man, and he was still alive. Still plotting. Here, at this cabin.

Whatever he was up to next, Mac would stop him. He had to. There wasn't anyone else.

Unsure where his target was headed, Mac vowed to stay on his tail every step of the way. Now that he'd found the man, he wasn't about to let him out of his sight.

Something was off though. The guy slept for at least sixteen hours every night and seemed jittery and . . . *off* during the day. What had happened to him? This wasn't at all the calm, collected, grim looking man he'd seen in Anchorage in January.

Mac shook it off. Maybe it was all part of the elaborate plan to make sure no one found him.

The disheveled appearance.

The lack of any modern tech devices, internet, or even electricity.

The overall lifestyle of a squatter, a bum.

But Mac wasn't fooled. He glanced again at the sketch. It *was* him. The man who murdered his wife and daughter. He'd had a sling on his left arm for weeks.

Lifting the binoculars back up to watch, Mac studied every way the man moved. Every mannerism. He'd been journaling and recording all of it with cameras for weeks now. Everything inside him was telling him to be prepared. To watch carefully.

The hairs on his neck stood up. He held his breath and counted to thirty. Maybe he was overreacting. His intuition in the past had always been spot-on, but ever since Sarah and Beth had been taken from him, he wasn't sure he could trust his instincts anymore. Grief clouded everything. Except his anger.

Taking a long, deep breath, he rubbed his eyes and repositioned himself. And then it happened.

The jerk had the audacity to lift his face to the sun and smile. Then, with a two-finger salute in Mac's direction, he took off on foot toward the woods and disappeared.

Mac scanned the trees and couldn't see him. Looked harder, circled back to the cabin. He could see the old truck and the snowmachine still sitting outside the cabin. The guy had no other transportation.

But he was gone.

Gathering up his equipment and his bag that was always packed and ready to go, Mac climbed into his four-wheel-drive pickup and raced down the mountain.

This wasn't over.

It would never be over until that man paid for what he did. Mac wouldn't live with it any other way.

◻ ◻ ◻

DOWN
8. Six letters. Assault with a deadly yet unexpected weapon.

Undisclosed location

With one last glance at the screen, Griz hit Send with his left hand. The sling on his left arm helped the throbbing in his shoulder, but maneuvering with one arm was a pain.

It didn't matter right now. He had plenty of time to heal and plan his next actions. Oh, he was going to have fun with this.

He glanced back at the screen and read his words. The communication was simple. They'd know who sent it.

To the esteemed Members:
Since you decided to turn against me, this is your only warning.
Do not say a word about me. Not. One. Word. For all you know, I never existed. Got it?
Do not try to find me. If I want to speak with you, I'll be in touch.
I am no longer interested in your plans, your manifesto, or the puppets you put into play. Feel free to continue on however you please. Without me. I won't stand in your way. I won't harass you or blackmail you.
But do not forget. I know who you are. I know everything about you and every single member of your family. I won't hesitate to kill anyone who gets in my way.
Let me restate that: I *will kill* anyone who gets in my way. That's a promise.
Understood?

ACKNOWLEDGMENTS

AFTER THIRTY-PLUS BOOKS, YOU MIGHT be tired of reading that it takes a tribe of people to bring a book into your hands. But I would be ashamed of myself if I didn't tell you again.

First and foremost, I have to thank my Lord and Savior. He is the one who gave me the gift of story and to be honest, He *is* the story.

Next, I have to thank my husband of thirty-two-plus years (how are we that old?). Jeremy, you are quite simply the best. I love you more and more each day.

My mom, who has become one of my biggest cheerleaders, went through a horrible loss. But she's never stopped encouraging and telling me to "get to writing the next book." Thanks, Mom.

To my siblings, Mary and Ray, I'm so thankful for both of you.

My kiddos, Josh and Kayla (and Ruth and Steven), thanks for always putting up with your crazy mom and alllllllllll the deadlines.

Steven gets an extra line of credit because he has been foundational to each of these stories. Thanks for being one of the best brainstorming partners ever. ☺

To all my Alaska friends, I love you guys. An extra big shout-out to Eryn and Leah.

To Carrie Kintz—dear friend, prayer partner, and project manager. This book literally wouldn't be here without you. THANK YOU. From the depths of my heart.

To my contacts at the FBI and ABI. Thank you for sharing your insight with me.

Jeane Burgess—wow, you are amazing. Thank you for all you did to help *26 Below* get out there.

The team at Kregel—Janyre, Rachel, Katherine, Catherine, Kayliani, and all the rest of you brilliant people. It is such a joy to work with you. One of these days, I'm hoping to write a book for you guys with a little more . . . normal life. But thanks for sticking with me through the craziness and grief.

Last but not least, I need to express my deepest gratitude to all my readers and friends. Really everyone in my life who reached out and gave me so much grace and support through the loss of my sweet dad. You all helped to get the word out about *26 Below*'s release mere weeks after he passed, and it meant so much to me. Thank you.

Love to you all.

NOTE FROM THE AUTHOR

As we race toward the end of this series, I hope you are looking forward to *70 North* as much as I am. These have seriously been some of my favorite books to write, and I love hearing from all of you about how much you've loved *26 Below*.

If you have been a reader of mine for a while, you know that I lost my father during the writing and editing of this story. The entire time I was writing the first draft, he was declining rapidly and it was difficult for me at times. But it was the cheering of my readers— the encouragement and support—that kept me going in my creative journey. (And that was even before they'd read the first book in the series!) All that to say, I really appreciate all of you.

It would be a huge blessing to me if you would do a shout-out on social media or talk to your friends about *26 Below* and *8 Down*. I'm not too proud to say that it's because of readers that I am privileged to do what I do. When my first book came out, I used the phrase "buy a book, save an author." And now we use it as a hashtag.

Even though these are thrillers and high-action suspense, I pray that the Lord has shown you His goodness and graciousness through the stories.

As always, I love to hear from my readers. You can find me at kimberleywoodhouse.com.

Below is a list of books that helped me in my research for this book.

Signature Killers by Robert D. Keppel, PhD, with William J. Birnes
Inside the Criminal Mind by Stanton E. Samernow, PhD
The Sociopath Next Door by Martha Stout, PhD
The Riverman by Robert D. Keppel, PhD, with William J. Birnes
Criminal Profiling: An Introductory Guide by David Webb
Casebook of a Crime Psychiatrist by James A. Brussel, MD (SUPER COOL!!!)

Until next time,
Kimberley Woodhouse
James 1:2–4

DID YOU FIGURE OUT THE CLUES?

IN *26 BELOW*, THE TICKING clock was the temperature and then the time since the blackout. In *8 Down*, the ticking clock was the crossword clues. For all you crossword enthusiasts—here are the answers.

Prologue
DOWN
8. Six letters. Number 6 on the periodic table—**Carbon.**

Chapter 1
DOWN
8. Five letters. Related to metrical stress—**Ictus.**
8. Nine letters. Creates a multitude of rubberneckers—**Collision.**

Chapter 2
DOWN
8. Six letters. A different way to get where you're going—**Detour.**
8. Eleven letters. Lawsuit due to negligence—**Malpractice.**

Chapter 3
DOWN
8. Nine letters. A metronome for your ticker—**Pacemaker.**
8. Eleven letters. What claustrophobia can inspire—**Panic attack.**

Chapter 4
DOWN
8. Four letters. Penicillin source—**Mold**.
8. Seven letters. Sweet sugar high for your body—**Insulin**.
8. Seven letters. It cuts like a knife—**Scalpel**.

Chapter 5
DOWN
8. Seven letters. A pilot's home away from home—**Cockpit**.
8. Six letters. Snowed under—**Buried**.
8. Eleven letters. Irregular heartbeat—**Tachycardia**.

Chapter 6
DOWN
8. Four letters. It's breath taking—**Lung**.
8. Eight letters. Silent killer—**Monoxide**.

Chapter 7
DOWN
8. Eight letters. Mishap and mayhem—**Accident**.
8. Five letters. Isolated—**Alone**.
8. Seven letters. Misdemeanor or felony battery—**Assault**.
8. Eight letters. A violent, shaking attack, can be brought on by flashing lights—**Paroxysm**.

Chapter 8
DOWN
8. Eight letters. A breakdown in communication—**No signal**.
8. Seven letters. Reaction with aversion—**Allergy**.
8. Fourteen letters. The heart's pacemaker—**Sinoatrial node**.

Chapter 9
DOWN
8. Five Letters. Breaks. Pounds. Thumps—**Heart**.

8. Five letters. Bloop. Bloop. Bloop—**Radar.**

8. Ten letters. Where glucose likes to live—**Bloodstream.**

Chapter 10
DOWN

8. Ten letters. Counts your steps, measures your sleep, tracks your heartbeat—**Smartwatch.**

8. Five letters. Panic attack—**Spasm.**

Chapter 11
DOWN

8. Eleven letters. Independent source of warmth; unrelated to your furnace—**Space heater.**

8. Six letters. Destroying the flow of traffic—**Pileup.**

8. Five letters. Welts that appear whenever I come near, but it's not because you hold me dear—**Hives.**

Chapter 12
DOWN

8. Nine letters. Like diabetes and the flu. Oh, but not this time—**Treatable.**

8. Eight letters. Once it's broken, your body can't fix it—**Pancreas.**

8. Seven letters. A taking or attack—**Seizure.**

Chapter 13
DOWN

8. Seven letters. Leave stranded—**Abandon.**

8. Seven letters. Bone to break if you want to get to the heart of the matter—**Sternum.**

8. Five letters. Perforation kills—**Bowel.**

8. Seven letters. Used to blow the snow—**Propane.**

Chapter 14
DOWN

8. Nine letters. Used to measure conductivity—**Electrode.**

8. Six letters. To accuse, put on trial for; or TNT—**Charge.**

Chapter 15
DOWN
8. Four letters. TV show featuring a plane crash—**Lost.**
8. Eight letters. Club—**Bludgeon.**

Chapter 16
DOWN
8. Nine letters. An old drug used to treat irregular heartbeat—**Practolol.**

Chapter 17
DOWN
8. Five letters. Last, strangled breath—**Agony.**
8. Twelve letters. The opposite of a natural avalanche—**Planned slide.**

Chapter 18
DOWN
8. Five letters. Smartwatch stat—**Steps.**
8. Three letters. Carbon monoxide—**Gas.**
8. Three letters. The diagnostic test used to diagnose epilepsy—**EEG.**

Chapter 19
DOWN
8. Two letters. Overdose abbr.—**OD.**
8. Seven letters. Gridlock—**Snarled.**
8. Eight letters. Falling sickness—**Epilepsy.**

Chapter 20
DOWN
8. Ten letters. Brain bleed, can be caused by a smash to the skull (or so I've heard)—**Hemorrhage.**
8. Four letters. All alone in the middle of nowhere—**Lost.**

Chapter 21
DOWN

8. Six letters. Pulled a switcheroo on—**Fooled.**

8. Eight letters. Surgery. Too bad you won't make it—**Excision.**

8. Six letters. Create havoc, punnily enough—**Wrecks.**

8. Four letters. Chest flexors—**Pecs.**

Chapter 22
DOWN

8. Six letters. Too much of this gave you hyperglycemia and the stroke that took you too soon—**Glucose.**

8. Eleven letters. Blood and belly accessory that makes you feel safe (but you're not)—**Insulin pump.**

Chapter 23
DOWN

8. Five letters. Inhaler output that can't save you this time—**Vapor.**

8. Seven letters. Private health data now in my possession—**Records.**

Chapter 24
DOWN

8. Five letters. I watch you when you're sleeping, I know when you'll awake—**Alarm.**

8. Seven letters. North, south, east, or west, you can't escape me—**Compass.**

Chapter 25
DOWN

8. Three letters. Anaphylaxis treatment that you don't have—**Epi.**

8. Six letters. I know where you are in your car—**Satnav.**

8. Six letters. The poison in your blood, creating a silent death. I did that—**Sepsis.**

8. Eight letters. This surgery can't help you now because I've got you—**Thoracic.**

Chapter 26
DOWN
8. Eight letters. Stopping work, life, or what you do to a computer. Or a person . . . permanently—**Shutdown.**
8. Three letters. The one I've been waiting for—**You.**

Epilogue
DOWN
8. Four letters. ____maker. Great when it works. But I can stop it—**Pace.**
8. Four letters. Surprise—**Stun.**
8. Six letters. Assault with a deadly yet unexpected weapon—**Attack.**

ABOUT THE AUTHOR

KIMBERLEY WOODHOUSE IS AN AWARD-WINNING and best-selling author of more than forty books. A lover of suspense, history, and research, she often gets sucked into the past, and then her husband has to lure her out with chocolate and the promise of eighteen holes on the golf course. Married to the love of her life for three-plus decades, she lives and writes in Colorado, where she's traded in her hat of "Craziest Mom" for "Nana the Great." To find out more about Kim's books, follow her on social media. To sign up for her newsletter and blog, go to kimberleywoodhouse.com.

SNEAK PEEK OF
70 NORTH

PROLOGUE

Latitude: 70.25955° N, Longitude 148.44526° W
Flow Station 1—Deadhorse, Alaska

TWO YEARS, TWENTY-ONE DAYS, THREE hours, and seven minutes had passed since that monster—that crazed lunatic—had murdered his family.

Mac winced and shook his head as he leaned over the sink in the tiny restroom of the flow station and splashed frigid water onto his face. When he looked into the mirror, he hardly recognized himself. Long gone was David McPherson, husband, father, friend.

His faith lay in tatters. His relationships cut off. He didn't know who he was anymore.

Other than the man chasing the monster . . . and failing to find him.

Almost two years ago, he'd lost the murderer in the wilds of Alaska.

No one else believed the creep was still alive. Even Mac's closest friends thought he was crazy for chasing after a ghost. But he didn't care what anyone thought.

He didn't care about anything anymore. Except for justice.

For Sarah. For Beth.

Just because the police, state troopers, ABI, and FBI all said the culprit behind the 26 Below attack and the serial killer had been taken down didn't mean that he had to believe it. He knew better.

The man had taunted him afterward. Showed he was still alive.

Mac could never let that go. Now all the authorities thought *he* was the crazy one. Even though he'd once been their ally and cyber-security specialist. He'd been tossed aside as a grieving man. An obsessed man.

An untrustworthy man.

Well . . . that wouldn't continue. He'd prove to everyone that he'd been right all along. Not to be ugly or to receive accolades. No.

He simply wanted the monster caught. Stopped. For good.

It had been more than a year since he halted communication with anyone who knew him because everyone tried to convince him to let it go. To cling to God. To grieve and heal.

But he couldn't do that.

He *wouldn't* do that.

Sarah and Beth deserved better.

Every family member of everyone the monster had killed deserved better.

Once Mac found him and it was over? Then he would rest. He would mend his broken relationships. Somehow find a way to live again. Crawl his way back to God and pick up the pieces of his shattered faith. If he could.

At least he would have peace and justice would be served.

He exited the building and climbed back into his SUV. The anonymous email he'd received saying that what he sought was in Deadhorse had raised all kinds of alarms in his mind. But no matter what he tried, he couldn't find out who the sender was . . . or how they knew what he was looking for . . . or *why* they would help him.

Still, he followed the tip. What choice did he have?

The rough eleven-hour drive from Fairbanks up to the North Slope was grueling, but the closer he came, the more his gut churned.

The monster *was* here. In the middle of nowhere at the top of the world. Hiding amongst the oil fields and workers. Mac could feel it.

He'd find him and—

Crack!

Mac was flung back against the seat by the force of the bullet. His eyes darted to his window but all he could see was the splintered hole in the glass. Everything else blurred as spots danced before his eyes. Fire shot through him, and he struggled for breath.

He blinked away the fog as time seemed to stand still. So . . . hard . . . to breathe.

His chest burned. While his arms and legs chilled in the frozen air.

A man in all white tundra gear walked around the front of the vehicle. He stopped and pushed the hood back from his face.

Mac swallowed against the pain, forcing his eyes to focus as blood seeped out of the right side of his chest.

The man smiled, saluted, and walked away.

The monster had shown himself.

But no one would know . . . because Mac would die here. Alone.

The riveting debut of the Alaskan Cyber Hunters trilogy

"An action-packed page-turner that . . . blew me away. If you like stories of intrigue, action, romance, and biblical hope, this is the story for you."
—**Tracie Peterson**, ECPA and *USA Today* best-selling author